Llyfrgell Sir POWYS County Library
Llandrindod Wells LD1 5LD

www.powys.gov.uk/libraries

HAMER, Malcolm
Patriotic Games

This book must be returned by the last date stamped above.
Rhaid dychwelyd y llyfr hwn erbyn y dyddiad diwethaf a stampiwyd uchod.

A charge will be made for any lost, damaged or overdue books.
Codir tâl os bydd llyfr wedi ei golli neu ei ni weidio neu heb ei ddychwelyd
mewn pryd.

Malcolm Hamer

ISBN 978-1-909121-18-8

www.acornindependentpress.com

Malcolm Hamer has written six other novels, which are now
available as e-books:

The Chris Ludlow golf mysteries

Sudden Death
A Deadly Lie
Death Trap
Shadows On The Green
Dead On Line

Predator – a novel set in the world of international sport.

His non-fiction includes:

The Ryder Cup – the Players
The Guinness Continental Europe Golf Course Guide.

MALCOLM HAMER has been associated with sport in many forms:

Among the 30-plus books he has had published are five crime novels (the 'Chris Ludlow' series) and a blockbuster ('Predator'), all of which have sporting backgrounds, as well as the Guinness Guide to European Golf Courses and a history of the Ryder Cup.

His agency represents sportsmen and his past and present clients include Gareth Edwards, Phil Bennett and Gerald Davies; Johnny Miller; Denis Law and Trevor Brooking; John Snow and Barry Richards; Jonah Barrington; and Muhammad Ali.

He played football for Shrewsbury Amateurs, Cambridge University and Corinthian-Casuals.

To Jill

With love and thanks

1

It is only a few hundred yards from Horse Guards to the Foreign Office, where James Clifton worked, but on this day it took him a great deal longer than the usual few minutes. Most of the muscles in his body were complaining and his legs were trembling. As he limped along Whitehall he reflected that, when he'd agreed to do a bit of part-time spying for his country, no one had mentioned the 'special training' that was in store for him. He was strong and athletic, but he had been unprepared for the battering his body had just received at the hands of his instructor, the formidable Staff Corporal Cowie.

It was the month of July, 1914, and James had been persuaded, by his father of all people, to assist a relatively new organisation called the Secret Service Bureau.

As part of his training for this new role he had been sent for some 'basic instruction in self-defence techniques'. His instructor's view of self-defence was, however, a far cry from what James had learned on the playing fields of Winchester College.

When he had presented himself at the headquarters of the Household Cavalry, he had been met by the Staff Corporal. Cowie was a tall man, strongly-built and with luxuriant whiskers decorating his florid face; he had bustled James along a colonnade, down some stairs and into a large room with some thick matting on the floor. The basic gym equipment included a couple of vaulting horses, wall bars and some ropes dangling from the ceiling in one corner.

'Right, sir,' said Cowie briskly, 'off with your jacket and shirt, and your shoes.' He rummaged in a tin trunk next to the wall and handed James a dingy white vest and some thick woollen socks.

'Now, sir, I'm going to try and teach you a few basic moves which'll keep you out of trouble. Forget yer boxin'. Them Queensberry Rules is suspended if you're in a spot of bother. You've gotta know how to thump the shit out of the other bastard before he thumps you. OK?'

Cowie crouched in front of James. 'Protect yerself the best you can with yer elbows and yer forearms – and remember they're the best form of attack as well, along with yer knees and yer feet. Not yer fists, you'll only hurt 'em, 'specially if you catch 'im on the top of the 'ead. So, you've gotta get in close and get in fast, and then you've a chance of taking the bugger by surprise. A bloody good start is to smash the bastard in the face with your forearm.'

Cowie picked up an oblong leather bag from the floor and handed it to James. 'OK, sir, hold that in front of you and I'll show you how it's done.'

The Staff Corporal suddenly shifted his weight and smashed his right forearm into the stuffed bag. James staggered back several feet under the power of the blow.

'Right, sir, your turn.'

James tried to emulate his instructor, who stood firm and roared at him, 'Come on, sir, yer not dancing with yer lady friend. Make it count. You've got to put this bastard out of the fight, smash his nose in, break his jaw. You want rid of 'im.'

During the next thirty minutes, James learned how to use not only his forearm to disable an opponent, but also the heel of his hand, his elbows, his knees and his feet; he was also shown how to gouge and how to chop someone's windpipe. All of this was accompanied by Staff Corporal Cowie's bloodthirsty demands that he 'made it count' and that his blows were powerful enough 'to make the claret flow'. Cowie also instructed him in the basic technique of disarming a man who was attacking him with a knife.

James was streaming with sweat when Cowie called a halt, handed him a grey scrap of towel from the trunk and some tepid water in a rusty tin mug.

'Of course, sir,' Cowie said, as James got back his breath, 'the best defence of all is to leg it. A fight is a last resort for someone in your situation. I know that you're a sportsman and that you're fitter than most of the men who come here, so leg it if you can and live to fight another day. The sort of scum who might be after you won't catch up with you, sir. I've seen you play football for the Corinthians, down at the Chelsea last year, so I know you're quick on your feet.'

'You like football, Staff Corporal?'

'Yes, sir, played a bit meself. That Wooster who plays for you, now he's a handful, isn't he?'

'Woosnam. Max Woosnam.'

'That's him. He'd always be in my team, sir.'

Next Cowie took him down another flight of stairs into a cellar, which had been converted to a firing range. The instructor unlocked a stout wooden cabinet, looked at a variety of pistols on their hooks and selected two of them.

'The Webley mark four, sir, British Army issue. It's reliable and it's got enough fire-power to stop some fuzzy-topped nigger who's off his head on jungle juice and charging at you with murder in 'is 'eart and a bloody great spear in his mitt. It's quite heavy to handle, though.' He picked up another slightly smaller gun. 'This 'ere's the Luger, just as reliable, but not quite so much biff in it. A good weapon, though.'

James hesitated as he tried to grasp the implications of carrying a gun around London. When he had first met Captain Vernon Kell, who was in charge of the Secret Service Bureau, Kell had described his part-time spying as a little non-confrontational eavesdropping. But now, apparently, he was to be sent out armed to the teeth. If his mother ever found out, heaven help him. Heaven help his father, too, for putting her beloved son in danger. 'Staff Corporal,' he said diffidently, 'I was told to get some instruction in self-defence. Guns are a rather different matter, aren't they?'

'Guns can be very effective, sir,' he said drily. 'I know that you're just doing a bit of nosing around, not startin' a war, but I was told to set you up, just in case. Anyway, the way things is goin', you'll be firing in earnest at them soddin' Krauts before you're much older. Me too, I 'spect.'

Cowie peered again into the cupboard and pulled out another gun. 'Beretta, sir. It's a lady's gun, really, not very reliable. A bit like those Eye-talians who make it, eh?' He smiled broadly.

That's the likes of Julius Caesar, da Vinci, Michelangelo, Galileo, Dante and Verdi put in their place, James thought, as he smiled back at the Staff Corporal.

After some more tuition about the mechanisms of the pistols, and how to aim and shoot them, James fired the Webley and the Luger at the targets, which were about twenty yards away. The noise was loud in the confined space. He was disappointed to miss the mark several times, although he hit the outer rings and managed one hit on the inner.

'That's not so bad, sir,' Cowie said. 'Remember, these pistols are for close work, so as long as you get a bullet into your target...'

After some deliberation James chose the Luger since it was less bulky, and Cowie told him that it was a good choice.

As the soldier led him to the front of the Horse Guards building he said, 'One other thing, Mister Clifton, when you collect the pistol you'll also get a clasp-knife. In the short run it may be more use to you. As well as the blade, there's a screwdriver that fits into the handle. Good luck, sir, and remember, make that first blow count. Put the bastard out of the game and make sure he's out of it for good.'

That summed it up very succinctly, James thought, as he walked stiffly away along Whitehall. He also thought how he'd like to have Cowie at his back if the need for violent action ever arose. That made him consider the commitments he was about to make. It was one thing to agree to a bit of fraternising with Germans, who might or might not wish harm to his country, and to report their views to Vernon Kell and his colleagues; but the matter suddenly seemed much more serious after the redoubtable Staff Corporal Cowie had shown him how to disable a man with his bare hands – or with his feet, elbows, knees and any other part of his anatomy for that matter.

However, the fact that he was about to be equipped with a pistol and a knife took the whole business to yet another level of potential danger. He realised that, if these Germans really were spies, they would be dangerous men, men like Cowie, who would know that their exposure meant only one thing: death by firing squad. They would fight for their lives.

* * *

Less than three weeks ago James had been leading the settled life that a man with his education and upbringing would have expected. Apart from his interesting, if undemanding, job at the Foreign Office, he led a full social life and had numerous opportunities to indulge his love of sport during the seemingly endless sunny days that marked that summer of 1914.

The Huntercombe House cricket week, presided over by its patron, Lord Fitzsimon, was one of James's favourite occasions. It was now drawing to its close and the final match was subsiding gently into an easy victory for the home side. The fall of the final wicket was the signal for some languid applause from the few dozen spectators, who then moved with restrained eagerness towards the terrace in front of the pavilion where bottles of champagne and jugs of lemonade were lined up.

Huntercombe House itself towered above, a pseudo-Gothic extravaganza which would have looked spectacular perched on a bluff above the Danube or the Loire, but was unsuited to the placid eastern edge of Dorset. The cricket ground sat on a ledge below the terrace and beyond lay a stretch of undulating parkland which meandered towards the scattered houses of the village, and then the sea.

James Clifton, who had been left stranded on a score of 48 when the final MCC wicket fell, was greeted by his team-mate and friend, Richard Hildreth, at the pavilion door.

'Bad luck, James, you deserved your fifty.'

'Thanks, but that fellow Price is the very devil to play.'

'Of course he is. He's Fitzsimon's professional. After all, he used to play for Derbyshire.'

'And should've played for England, so they say. Mind you, I'm sure the wicket's prepared specially for him. There are some bumpy patches just short of a length.'

Hildreth laughed. '"A bumping pitch and a blinding light, an hour to play and the last man in".'

'Not quite that dramatic,' James replied, 'come on, let's have some fizz. I'll change later.'

They strolled towards the terrace where the tables, covered with white linen cloths, were laden with plates of game pie, legs of chicken, tiny lamb cutlets, smoked salmon sandwiches, heavy slabs of fruit cake and festoons of chocolate éclairs.

As the two men approached the first table, they were intercepted by Lord Fitzsimon himself, a tall and grey-haired man whose long and fleshy face was notable for its flattened nose. The story, neither confirmed nor contradicted by the noble lord, was that it had been broken in his youth during a brawl with a pimp outside a house of ill repute in San Francisco. He was now immensely wealthy; as well as being the chairman of a prestigious bank, he was known to have interests in mining and agriculture in many parts of the world.

Fitzsimon shook James by the hand. 'A capital innings, Clifton. Well played.'

'Thank you, sir. It was a treat to play on such a superb wicket. As always.'

'You're very kind.' Fitzsimon waved a meaty hand towards the tables and at once a servant appeared at his side with glasses of champagne for James and Richard. 'Enjoy yourselves. Drinks in the drawing room at eight, dinner at nine. Now, if you'll excuse me.' He swept off to join another group of guests.

The two men took several sips of champagne and, seconds later, a servant glided up to them and topped up their glasses. 'This is damned good stuff,' said Richard.

'The noble lord can afford the best.'

'He certainly can. I wonder how he accumulated his riches?'

'It's a mystery,' James replied. 'Who said that behind every great fortune there lies a great crime?'

'I can't remember, but that's a bit cynical, James, isn't it?'

'Yes. And anyway, he enjoys the good things in life and that's a great virtue. Talking of good things, where's your lovely sister?' Richard's sister had rarely shown the slightest interest in sport, but James was nevertheless disappointed that he had not managed to reach his fifty while she was watching.

'Oh, Emily's probably lecturing some poor devil about votes for women. It's all she thinks of these days.'

'Or the rights of the poor and down-trodden working man.'

Richard, who was an inch or two above six feet in height, craned his neck and peered over the crowd. 'Over there, James, shall we rescue the poor souls she's trying to convert?'

In his more reflective moments James thought that he probably did adore Emily. She was beautiful, but not distant; she was elegant, but not fussy; and she had interesting views, which she was determined to express, rather than settling for the platitudes that masqueraded as conversation in the circles in which they both moved. Emily was formidable and that probably explained why, in her mid-twenties, she was unmarried and had not, to James's knowledge, ever had a serious suitor. Even he, who had known her since they were children, sometimes felt intimidated by her; that was perhaps why he had never seriously considered trying to initiate a courtship. Or was it because he thought of her almost as a sister?

As he and Richard approached, Emily was talking animatedly to three other guests. James eyed her slim frame, enclosed in a light blue dress overlaid with lace; her dark blue shoes peeped out from beneath her skirt.

Handshakes and half-bows were exchanged and Emily said, 'Jeremy was asking me if I would be at Lord's for the Gentlemen versus Players match and I was explaining that, much as I like the rituals of cricket, one game watched a month is more than enough excitement for any woman.'

Emily's gentle sarcasm escaped Jeremy and he asked her eagerly, 'What about Glorious Goodwood? Surely you'll be there?'

Jeremy Lascelles had been at Eton with Richard and, like Lord Fitzsimon, was a banker in the City of London. However, his many social obligations had a much higher priority in his life than his career in finance.

Richard tried to head him off. 'My sister isn't very sporting, Jeremy. She's more interested in books and the arts, aren't you, Emily.'

'Good Lord, novels and plays and things like that?' Lascelles blurted out.

James saw Emily's eyes turn upwards; he could not decide whether in despair or in supplication to some higher and more charitable power. 'Shaw and James Joyce and Eliot and Wyndham Lewis have some interesting things to say,' she stated patiently.

'Odd, that Shaw feller, isn't he? A socialist, eh? Doesn't eat meat. I like musicals myself.'

'We're going to see *Hullo Ragtime* soon,' Richard said quickly. 'Looking forward to it.'

'Ah, I need to talk to you both about the arrangements,' said Emily. She smiled at Jeremy Lascelles and his two companions. 'Please excuse us.' She led Richard and James to a corner of the terrace and murmured, 'Dear God, has that man ever said anything interesting in his whole life?'

'Oh, he's not that bad,' her brother replied. 'And he is very rich.'

'Not bad,' Emily said sarcastically. 'He's like virtually every other man I've met in London during the last three years. I shall ignore your remark about how rich he is.'

'Perhaps your standards are too high,' James suggested with a laugh.

'Impossibly high,' said her brother.

'You may be right,' his sister replied and James detected a hint of sadness in her voice.

He decided to change the subject. 'Richard, are you going on this trip to Brazil? It sounds fun, but the boat leaves on the first day of August, which isn't far away, so the chairman has been on to me to make a decision.'

'Football in Brazil,' Richard sighed. 'It sounds wonderful and I did of course miss the Corinthians' trip four years ago. How nice of the Brazilians to name a football club after us.'

'Yes. The Corinthians of Sao Paulo. It certainly has a ring to it.'

They all paused as a waiter re-filled their glasses with champagne and Richard continued. 'But it may be difficult for me. It's Mother. We've got some business problems to resolve, nothing serious...'

'Mama needs our support,' Emily interrupted. 'But more than that, how can you two talk about gadding off to Brazil with this country and the rest of Europe in such a state. Even here in Britain we're on the brink of civil war in Ireland, Carson and his gangsters are arming themselves for conflict...'

'The northern Irish would never fire on British soldiers,' James said, 'and somehow Asquith and the government will force through home rule.'

'Damned Irish', said Richard bitterly. 'Nothing but trouble.'

James braced himself for another wrangle between brother and sister about the rights and wrongs of their family owning nearly a hundred thousand acres of prime agricultural land in Ireland; their brother, Adam, ran the estates and did it very well.

'Our family has earned lots of money from Ireland and still does. You call that trouble, Richard? I suppose the Irish should be like women and children, seen and not heard,' Emily said forcefully.

'Please don't lecture me, Emily. Anyway, if you and your suffragettes made a little less noise, you might make more progress.'

'We will keep on until we get the vote. However, it may become a minor issue,' she said gravely. 'Europe is in chaos. The Germans are re-arming and so are the Russians.'

'So what,' her brother responded. 'Let them get on with it. Why should we get involved?'

'Because the Germans want a dominant position in northern Europe. Their real target is France and they'll trample on the Belgians to get there,' James said.

'So we'll be dragged into it,' Emily said triumphantly, 'because for one thing we have a treaty with Belgium and honour will demand that we defend an ally.'

'You are all looking far too serious.' The deep tones announced the arrival of Rupert Wavell at Emily's side. He seized her hand and kissed it with mock-reverence, and then brushed his dark hair back into place as he straightened. He was wearing the vividly-coloured blazer of the I Zingari Cricket Club and a cravat to match. James noticed his glance flicker briefly, almost dismissively, over Emily and then Wavell turned to her brother.

'Why so solemn on such a lovely day?' Wavell asked. 'Oh, and well played, James, such a straight and steady bat. In the true Corinthian spirit.'

'Thanks, Rupert. We were talking about the trip to Brazil. I'm told you're going.' James knew that Wavell had few constraints on his time, though his nominal occupation was as a director of one of his father's trading companies, which imported raw materials such as cotton, sugar and timber from the colonies and turned them into products that were sold back to the world's eager markets. His good looks and charm made him a great favourite among the many predatory mothers, who during the 'season' were on the hunt for rich and well-connected husbands for their daughters.

'Yes, I wouldn't miss such an expedition. Brazil sounds fascinating and my father has business interests there.'

'Oh, really,' said Richard. 'For instance?'

'Coffee, of course, rubber, sugar, cattle, that sort of thing,' Wavell said vaguely.

He's really got his finger firmly on the pulse of the family business, James thought nastily.

'And what will you do if a European war breaks out while you're in Brazil?' Emily asked tartly.

'We'll get back to England and help to knock the enemy for six,' laughed Wavell. 'Anyway, Emily, you shouldn't worry your lovely self about such matters. They're for the men to sort out, and sort them out we will.'

'Perhaps it's a pity that you men don't apply the sort of commonsense that women would bring to such matters. War is not a game of cricket, played to strict rules in a jolly sporting atmosphere, with tea and cakes during the interval and three cheers for the winners at the end.'

'Emily, please...' said her brother.

'Let me finish, Richard. I just want to point out that war is about fear and despair, torture and death. It's about children losing their fathers, women losing their husbands and their sons and their brothers. It's certainly not a game.' The fierce sadness in her voice reduced those around her to silence.

Emily paused and her brother said, 'This is neither the time nor the place for another lecture.'

'Where is the place for it? Do you think I want to wave you off to war and wonder if I'll ever see you again? The way I waved off Papa when we were children.'

Richard took his sister gently by the arm as the tears filmed her eyes. 'Come on, we'll go inside out of the sun. It's been a long day.' They walked away towards the house.

'Oh dear, what brought that on?' asked Wavell.

'Her father was killed during the Boer War,' James replied, 'and like many women and many men for that matter she can't bear the thought of another conflict.'

The two men chatted about the cricket and the forthcoming football trip to Brazil and after a few minutes Richard rejoined them. Soon afterwards Wavell strolled off to talk to a gaggle of other guests.

'Rupert isn't the cleverest of men, is he?' Richard stated.

'He was considered clever at Repton.' James replied.

'Quite. I rest my case.'

'Really, Richard, how effortlessly you convey the intellectual superiority of an Old Etonian.'

'Thank you,' he said smugly. 'Anyway, what does it matter? Rupert is rich and rather dashing. It's said that the ladies like him.'

'The ladies?'

'Yes, you're not suggesting...'

'Certainly not. And he's a superb footballer,' James said swiftly.
'A great asset to the Corinthians. Quick, elusive.'

'Elusive. Yes, that's a very good description of Rupert Wavell,' James said with a quiet smile.

* * *

While the cricket match was taking place at Huntercombe House, the Archduke Franz Ferdinand, heir to the throne of the Austro-Hungarian empire, and his wife were assassinated in Sarajevo by a Bosnian extremist called Gavrillo Princip.

Within eight days the Kaiser of Germany, Wilhelm II, had declared his support for Austria. The seeds of the First World War had been sown and were to have a rapid growth.

2

On reaching the Foreign Office on the Tuesday after the cricket match, James found a pile of letters awaiting his attention. He shuffled through them and recognised the broad and decisive strokes of his father's handwriting on one of the envelopes. As he had done since his boyhood, when letters had arrived at his boarding school from the great cities of Europe, he smiled with pleasurable anticipation. His father always managed to be interesting. He remembered when it had been a few comments about Jack Hobbs's batting technique and how James should study his wonderful balance when he next watched him at the Oval; or he might mention a new novel he was reading, or some paintings he had seen in Paris or Berlin. Sometimes his father wrote about some of the remarkable people he had met in the course of his work.

This time the short note inside invited him to lunch at his father's club on Tuesday of the following week and he immediately scribbled his acceptance.

Henry Maurice Clifton's career as a diplomat had been cut short by ill- health just before he was eligible to become one of His Majesty's ambassadors. He had retired a couple of years short of his fiftieth birthday, having served in several European countries, but primarily in Russia and Germany; he had spent some time in St Petersburg and his final years in Berlin. As a young boy, James had little understanding of what his father did, although he liked the gracious houses in which they lived in such interesting cities. Those experiences, added to his fluency in foreign languages, gave him a patina of glamour and, thereby, an advantage over many of his fellow-pupils at school in England.

Later, he gained some insight into the complex and usually inconclusive negotiations in which his father was involved on behalf of the British government. These diplomatic manoeuvres were particularly labrynthine when conducted in Russia's capital city, where a brutal regime grabbed all the benefits of industrialisation without wishing to concede anything in the way of social and political reform.

James thumbed through the other papers on his desk and found a memorandum from his head of department about the murder of the Archduke on the previous Sunday. His superior's opinion, outlined on one neatly-typed page, was that the death of the heir to the throne of the Austro-Hungarian Empire at the hands of an unbalanced fanatic was just a ripple on the surface of Balkan politics. In short, the Austrians would make a fuss for a time and then the matter would fade into the background.

He wondered how realistic that view would seem in a month or two. Emily Hildreth had of course expressed a more apocalyptic vision of the future and James respected her intelligence just as much as that of his head of department. As he flicked through various reports, many of them relating to German armaments production, he thought about the forthcoming trip to Brazil. The Corinthians were due to leave on the SS *Asturias* from Southampton on the first of August. Admittedly the first-class fare was thirty pounds, but with his father's permission he would dip into a small legacy left to him a couple of years ago by his Aunt May. He was in his early twenties and he wanted to see an exotic country like Brazil before he settled into marriage, fatherhood and a career at the Foreign Office. There was also the lure of playing football in a team of such distinction. Richard was a muscular and acrobatic goalkeeper; Anthony Loxley and Max Woosnam were strong and sure-footed defenders; and Guy Willett and Herbert Grosvenor were elegant and speedy forwards. They had all played for their countries and James aspired to do the same.

Carpe Diem was one of his father's mottoes and, although James possessed a young man's natural optimism, the future seemed to him to be uncertain, even bleak. There was talk of war in Europe and even of revolution in Britain, as the Irish question grew more and more entangled. To make matters worse, the Trades Unions were threatening all-out strikes, and many young women like Emily, marshalled by the rhetoric of Emmeline Pankhurst, were demanding their right to vote and to participate in the government of their country.

James was holding a sheet of paper with estimates of the size and constituents of the German navy, but the figures were meaningless to him as he pondered the rights and wrongs of the suffragettes' cause. He thought of Emily, without a vote, and then of the hapless Jeremy Lascelles, the object of her scorn at Lord Fitzsimon's cricket match on the previous Sunday. He knew whom he would prefer to have a vote.

His reverie was interrupted by a knock on the door and Sarah, one of the department's secretaries, entered and asked him if he would like some tea. She was about his own age and soberly dressed in a plain grey dress, its drabness relieved only by the collar of a white blouse. Although Sarah was not conventionally pretty, James found her attractive; perhaps it was her regular features and wide-spaced, intelligent eyes. He knew little about her, only that she lived in the rapidly expanding suburb of Ealing with her parents and that her father was a local solicitor. He would have liked to know more about her and her opinions, for example what she thought of 'votes for women', but fraternisation, however innocent, between the different layers of the Foreign Office hierarchy was frowned upon. Perhaps she went to suffragette meetings in her spare time, or threw stones at the windows of cabinet ministers' houses, or dug up the greens of golf courses during the night. Somehow, he doubted it; Sarah looked too sensible. But, he reflected, when a lot of people espoused a single evocative cause, common-sense was the first victim.

3

There was a noticeable air of excitement as James Clifton, his mother, and Emily and Richard Hildreth took their seats in the stalls just before the curtain rose on the popular show from America called *Hullo Ragtime*. It had been running at the Hippodrome for a year and a half and nearly every performance had been sold out.

Richard craned his neck to look around the audience; the stalls, the boxes, and, as far as he could see, the gallery and the upper circle were crammed with expectant theatre-goers. He had heard that extra trains had been laid on from outlying parts of the home counties to cope with the demand to see the show.

The audience stilled and went quiet as the orchestra hit the first loud and brassy notes of the overture and the curtain began to rise. Spontaneous applause rang out as Shirley Kellogg led two dozen chorus girls, dressed in elaborate pseudo-military costumes, across the front of the stage. They pranced and pirouetted as the star of the show, Ethel Levey, belted out the first of Louis Hersch's songs. Most of the men in the audience had their eyes glued to the chorus girls, since their skirts finished at knee level and exposed their legs and ankles. The young and inexperienced among them had never seen more than a glimpse of a woman's ankle and later, when they did, many of them would be disappointed to discover that they were not necessarily as elegant as those of a chorus girl.

The applause at the interval was prolonged and almost ecstatic; very few people had seen a show with such vitality, had watched singers and dancers with such energy, or heard songs that were such uninhibited fun.

As the Cliftons and the Hildreths sipped their glasses of champagne in one of the bars, there was a joyful buzz to the conversations around them.

'It makes me want to get up and dance,' Richard said.

'Steady, brother dear, your dancing damages floors, not to mention ladies' toes,' Emily said drily. 'What did you think of it, Mrs Clifton?'

'Remarkable. It makes me long to visit New York and see and hear the real thing.'

'Do you think Father would like that?' asked James.

'Who knows? But perhaps I'll take my three sons when the other two are a little older.'

'Brazil one year, New York the next,' Richard said, 'you'll be quite the transatlantic traveller, James, won't you?'

'That's a beguiling thought.'

'Unfortunately, I won't be going with you to Brazil,' Richard said. 'I've told the Corinthians' chairman. He didn't take it well, I'm afraid.'

'Well, I can't say I'm surprised, Richard. How can he be happy at losing the club's best goalkeeper? But what a trip to miss. What made you change your mind?'

Before Richard could answer, the interval bell rang to summon them back to their seats. As they manoeuvred their way into the auditorium, Emily touched James on the arm. 'Look, there's Mrs Kitson-Clark. Goodness, isn't she glamorous? And that dress, so, er, chic.'

James looked past Emily at Beatrice Kitson-Clark and hoped that she hadn't noticed his face redden slightly at the mention of her. Beatrice had recently married an eminent lawyer, a widower who was consulted occasionally by the Foreign Office. James had met her on several occasions at receptions and, a few months before, had received an invitation to tea. He had accepted it and went to her house in Belgrave Square on the following Thursday. He had been surprised to find that he was the only guest and, after Mrs Kitson-Clark had dismissed the butler, was even more surprised to be led upstairs to her bedroom. Since then, he had waited eagerly for her summons and they 'had tea' together two or three times a month. James had become very fond of Beatrice, but was irritated that she kept her emotional distance from him. Her occasional gifts, cufflinks from Garrard's, champagne from Berry Brothers and, most recently, a copy of James Joyce's *Dubliners*, did not compensate for her studied coolness. Very much aware that he was wrong to commit adultery, he also knew that such trysts were the common currency of the lives of women like Beatrice.

It seemed hardly possible, but in the second half the cast managed to outdo the vim and vigour of their previous efforts. Shirley Kellogg led the chorus in some more rousing routines such as the 'Ragtime Soldier Man' and Ethel Levey held the audience in thrall with 'The Man I Love' and 'You're My Baby'. She even did a burlesque of Anna Pavlova.

At the end the curtain calls went on and on, and rightly so.

As they left the theatre, Richard pointed out one of the many posters featuring Ethel Levey; she was pictured looking seductively over her shoulder with much of her back exposed.

'Stop licking your lips, brother dear,' Emily said, 'It's embarrassing.'

'Actually, I was admiring her lovely skin tones,' Richard replied.

'Her bone structure is superb, too,' said James.

'Yes, she's a very enticing young woman,' said Mrs Clifton. 'Though whether she should bare quite so much to the vulgar gaze is another question.'

'Surely she has every right to show off her body to the best advantage,' argued Emily. 'You move in artistic circles, Mrs Clifton, where inhibitions are frowned upon, I imagine.'

'You're right, Emily. The human body can be a beautiful thing and we shouldn't be puritanical about it.'

James looked at Emily with even more interest, especially when she gave him an almost imperceptible wink and a quick grin.

They had reserved a table at Romano's in the Strand and decided to walk. It was hard progress along the packed pavements, where the smells of a crowded city lay heavy in the humid air. Both the men scanned the passing crowds for any sign of pickpockets, who were all too skilled in the dark art of distracting a pedestrian, snatching a wallet or a purse and then racing away into the confusion of streets off the main thoroughfares.

There was the usual gaggle of beggars on the fringes of Trafalgar Square, drawn there by the charity offered at the church of St Martin-in-the-Field. Two ragged and pathetic children of an indeterminate age somewhere between ten and fourteen caught Mrs Clifton's attention and she stopped to speak to them.

'Where do you live, child?'

'Off St Giles, mum,' one of them whispered.

'Are you hungry?' They both nodded and Mrs Clifton produced a sixpenny piece from her handbag. She handed it to the smaller of the two children and, as she began to admonish him to spend it on food, the other child snatched it away and ran hard towards St Martin's Lane.

'You feckin' bastard,' shouted the smaller child as he set off in pursuit.

'There you see capitalism in action, Mrs Clifton,' said Richard.

'No,' said his sister, 'there you see wretchedness and despair, you horrible man.' She punched him lightly on the arm and he smiled affectionately at her.

Eventually they reached the safe haven of Romano's restaurant, its entrance crowned with a display of cavorting nymphs. The long room, decorated in gilt and deep colours, was almost full. A waiter ushered them to their table halfway along the one wall and Mrs Clifton and Emily sank into the plush seats with relief.

The waiters at Romano's knew the importance of putting some wine and bread on the table and within minutes the Cliftons and the Hildreths were drinking their glasses of white burgundy and picking at chunky pieces of bread.

Just as their first courses arrived at the table, there was a flurry of activity at the doorway as a burly man made his entrance. He was only about five and a half feet tall and his well-cut dark suit couldn't disguise his great bulk. His hair was combed straight back from a broad and fleshy face, and his expansive grin emphasised a noticeably long upper lip.

Horatio Bottomley was greeted effusively by Romano himself, who led the party of a dozen or so people towards the tables at the back of the restaurant. As they went down the long room Bottomley waved his large cigar in greeting to some of the diners and stopped for a word with others; it was noticeable how they reacted, with pleasure, with delight almost, at being acknowledged by a man who played several roles in his business life, not least as a promoter of a variety of companies and the proprietor of the popular magazine, *John Bull*.

'The famous Horatio Bottomley,' said Richard.

'Indeed,' said Mrs Clifton, 'with his usual retinue of Gaiety girls, a brace or two of financiers...'

'And that's Wells, the boxer,' finished James.

Billy Wells, the British heavyweight champion, was wearing a tweed suit which seemed to exaggerate his formidable size and build.

'What a handsome man,' said Emily.

'Perhaps not as handsome as Georges Carpentier, nor as good a prize-fighter,' commented James.

'Oh?'

'The Frog knocked out our champion in just over a minute last year at the National Sporting Club.'

'That's why they call him the horizontal heavyweight,' said Richard. 'He can certainly deliver a punch, but not take one. By the way, I'm told that he also plays football.'

'Good heavens. He's a big man for football. A goalkeeper like you, Richard?'

'No, a defender. He's played occasionally for Fulham.'

'Oh well, anyone can play for Fulham.'

The two men laughed companionably and were admonished by Mrs Clifton. 'Really, you boys are so superior about your football. Now, my father thought rugger was the game for a gentleman.'

'Er, we do play cricket against the Barbarians rugby men. They're jolly good company, Mrs Clifton, I must say,' said Richard tactfully.

There was a sudden concerted popping of champagne corks from Bottomley's table, some cheers from the men and shrill laughter from the Gaiety girls.

'It must be Pommery,' Bottomley said loudly, as their glasses were filled. 'It's the only fizz worth drinking.'

'I like a man with a sense of style,' Emily said, 'even if he is a little over the top.'

'Any man can show style with other people's money,' her brother said quietly.

'Wasn't he bankrupted a couple of years ago?' James asked.

'That's right. He's been in Carey Street on many occasions. He's floated more companies than the Royal Navy has battleships.'

'My husband once told me that he became extremely rich by trading Australian mining shares in the nineties,' Mrs Clifton said.

'So, where did all the money go?' asked Emily. 'Why was he bankrupted? It can't all have gone on champagne.'

'No, it's a mystery,' said James. 'Is he a gambler?'

'Oh yes,' Richard replied, 'he makes huge bets and he also owns racehorses and that's a quick way to lose fortunes. Then there are his lady friends. He has a string of mistresses in flats dotted around the West End, and they're nearly as costly as racehorses.'

'More fun, though,' James laughed.

'Now then, you two, let's keep the conversation seemly,' Emily said with mock severity.

'And he also has a substantial country house with a couple of dozen servants,' Richard continued.

'So he probably needed all the money he made from the sweepstake on last year's Derby race,' said Mrs Clifton. 'The one he ran through *John Bull*.'

'So he's one of those rogues who gets away with his misdemeanours by sheer charm and bravado,' Emily summed up. 'He's the sort of man who might've popped up in one of Charles Dickens' novels.'

'He was said to be a good Parliamentarian,' James said. 'I remember when he had to apply for the Chiltern Hundreds because he'd been made bankrupt. F E Smith, of all people, said that his absence from the Commons would impoverish it.'

'He is a very fine speaker,' Mrs Clifton agreed, 'on the other hand Ramsay MacDonald referred to him as a man of doubtful parentage who has lived all his life on the threshold of jail.'

'So, he's obviously had a life any other man would envy,' said James, 'a non-stop enjoyment of wine, women, song and sport, and he's clever at making lots of money. Though I can see from the expression on Richard's face that he doesn't approve of our Horatio.'

'I don't disapprove of making money, but I do object if someone makes it dishonestly, at the expense of others.'

'Are you saying that Bottomley's a swindler?'

'Let's say that whenever one of his companies crashes, he never suffers and no one is able to find out where the money has gone.'

'You sound bitter.'

'He is,' said Emily, 'because our mother has invested a lot of money in one of his schemes.'

'Emily, that's a private matter. I don't think that Mother would like it to be discussed, even with our friends.'

'Well, our friends, especially James, should know, because that's why Richard won't be going to Brazil, because Mama has got herself into financial difficulties and Richard must help her to resolve them.'

'Ah, now I understand,' James said. 'But didn't she talk to you before she made the investment?'

'Oh, only vaguely. I think she was bowled over by Bottomley's charm, as so many people are.'

'Is it being naïve,' Mrs Clifton interrupted, 'to suggest that your mother asks Bottomley to give her money back?'

'I did write to him, but the answer we got, and it came as no surprise, is that the money is a long term investment and cannot be returned until the dividends are realised for all the investors.'

'Perhaps a personal approach would be more effective?'

'No, I don't want my mother to go near the man again. I was talking to a fellow in my club the other day and he told me that his father had put a lot of money into one of Bottomley's schemes, but had thought better of it and demanded it back. He was granted a meeting with the great man and by the time Bottomley had told him a lot of grandiose nonsense about his companies and filled him up with champagne, the old boy put another five thousand pounds into the scoundrel's pocket.'

As they all contemplated Richard's story in silence, a waiter bearing a magnum of Pommery champagne appeared at their table and said that Mr Bottomley invited them to 'partake of a glass of fizz with him'.

'We might as well,' said Richard, 'it's people like Mother who are paying.'

A minute or two later, after the waiters had poured champagne for everyone in the room who wanted it, Horatio Bottomley rose to his feet at the end of the room, tapped a glass and called for silence.

'Ladies and gentlemen,' he said in a resonant and commanding voice, 'I will not interrupt your evening for more than a moment or two. But I would ask you to raise your glasses and drink a toast to our great country, whose courage and resolve may soon be tested once again.' He paused and held his glass aloft. 'I give you Great Britain and her loyal and courageous people.'

Everyone rose and repeated the toast and then the babble of conversation resumed.

'Quite the demagogue,' James said thoughtfully.

'Yes,' said his mother. 'Such people can of course be very valuable in a crisis.'

'And very dangerous,' Emily countered.

* * *

The Cliftons and the Hildreths went their separate ways from Romano's. One taxi was bound for James's flat in Sloane Street, from where it would take his mother to stay with her sister, Olivia. She lived in a rambling house in Flood Street, Chelsea, with her artist husband and their five children. The other taxi took Richard and Emily to their family home in Portman Square.

As they travelled west along Piccadilly, Mrs Clifton asked her son a question which had been in her mind for some time: why didn't he take Emily Hildreth more seriously?

'But I do,' he replied. 'She's a lovely-looking girl and jolly intelligent, but...'

They rattled into Hyde Park Corner. 'But what, James? You're nearly twenty-five now and you should be thinking of marriage and children. Why not Emily?'

'Match-making doesn't suit you, Mama. Anyway, I'm not sure I'm the man she's seeking. I'm not sure what she actually wants from her life. Maybe she has wider horizons than marriage and children. All this talk of women's rights, pacifism, it can be quite... oh, I don't know.'

'Demanding?'

'Possibly.'

'A man like you needs a woman who can think, who has a strong mind.'

'Is that why Father married you?'

'I hope so, yes.'

James, a dutiful son, offered to accompany his mother to Flood Street, but she told him it wasn't necessary. As the taxi stopped outside his building, which was halfway down Sloane Street and close to the Cadogan Hotel, he kissed his mother on the cheek and opened the door of the taxi. His mother clutched his arm. 'If the worst happens and a war begins, you don't have to fight, you know that, don't you, James?'

He got out of the taxi, held the door open and said, 'You've been listening too much to your friend, Bertie Russell.'

'I've always been a pacifist.'

'Yes, and I respect your views, Mama, as you well know. But how could I desert my friends? I have to do what I know they will do.'

'He who fights with monsters should be careful lest he becomes a monster because of it.'

'I'm surprised to hear you quoting Nietzsche, Mama.'

She smiled resignedly at her son and bade him goodnight. Despite such an enjoyable evening, James suddenly lapsed into a sombre mood, though it did not last when he thought about his forthcoming lunch with his father. If he'd known what his father had in mind for him, he would not have been so light-hearted.

4

Settled comfortably in a corner of the bar in the Oxford and Cambridge Club in Pall Mall, Henry Clifton had a large whisky in front of him and a copy of *The Times* in his lap. With great despair he had read the gloomy reports of impending chaos in Europe and he now stared at the letters page for a while without taking anything in. He was wondering whether he had done the right thing in recommending his beloved eldest son to Vernon Kell, even though he knew the latter to be both intelligent and reputable. Clifton believed whole-heartedly in the great tradition of serving one's country and had himself tried his best to do so. Nevertheless, his doubts about Kell's shadowy world would not go away. During his career as a diplomat Henry Clifton had often used rumour and subterfuge, but, he assured himself, only within certain strict limits. To lie or cheat, even in his country's interests, would have seemed a betrayal of his own and his country's values.

He had great confidence in his son's intelligence and in his common-sense. He knew that James was able to assess other people quickly and accurately and Kell had, after all, assured him that his new recruit would be limited to occasional forays to 'look and listen', that he would not be exposed to any danger. Nevertheless, the elder Clifton knew that the world of secret intelligence could be a dangerous place, especially when the shadows of war were falling across Europe.

He sighed and turned over the pages of his newspaper until he found an account of the Oxford versus Cambridge cricket match at Lord's.

* * *

James left his office at just after midday, in plenty of time for his lunch with his father at the Oxford and Cambridge Club. He would have preferred Rules or the Café Royal, but his father liked the rituals of a traditional men's club.

As he strolled along Whitehall he noticed anew how the sunshine exacerbated the smells of the city; horse dung lay rotting on the road and was overlaid with the stench of petrol fumes from the cars which competed for space with the carriages and carts. It didn't spoil his cheerful mood; to mitigate the problem, he breathed through his mouth.

He decided to walk up Haymarket in order to buy some cigarettes for his father, who had developed a taste for Abdullah Turkish, a brand which was always available at Fribourg and Taylor.

The newspaper sellers were shouting their headlines on the street corners; the big story was that, following the assassination of the Archduke Franz Ferdinand a week ago, the Kaiser had predictably declared his support for Austria against Serbia.

James glanced at the front page of the *Daily Mail*, which prophesied war within a couple of weeks. The young man selling the paper, who looked as though he had not eaten a solid meal in months, pressed a copy into his hand and James did not have the heart to deny him his halfpenny. His father would be mortified that he'd put money into the hands of Northcliffe, however indirectly, since he despised the man. 'He has all views and no views' was his father's oft-repeated opinion of him and he had been apoplectic when Northcliffe had acquired *The Times* and reduced its price to one penny. He was even more incensed when the result was a three-fold increase in the newspaper's circulation.

James loved this part of London and he ambled along Jermyn Street, glancing into various shop windows. As he went past the Cavendish Hotel, he just avoided bumping into the formidable form of Rosa Lewis; she was leaving her hotel while still issuing orders over her shoulder to one of her employees. She had been a great favourite of Edward VII, and on his death she had locked his private cellar in the hotel and given instructions that it was not to be opened until after her death. Given Rosa's excellent health, James wondered when someone would pick the lock and arrange a premature release of the many superb vintage wines and brandies.

He turned down St James's Street and paused to look into the windows of Lock's, the hat maker, whose clients included royalty, writers, politicians and many another famous person, including one of his favourite poets, Lord Byron. A century before, when the first two cantos of 'Childe Harold' had been published, Byron had been living in that same street and had 'woken up to find himself famous'.

James went through the imposing entrance of the Oxford and Cambridge Club and nodded a greeting to the doorman, who drew himself up and, in a hoarse old soldier's voice more used to barking commands on parade grounds than mouthing greetings in the hushed confines of a gentleman's club, said, 'Good morning, Mister James. Your father's at his usual table, sir.'

James strode up the broad staircase and turned right into the dining room. His father's usual table was beneath a portrait of George Canning, who had been the Prime Minister in the 1830s, and by the tall windows which overlooked the street.

Henry Clifton still had the tall and spare frame of the sportsman he had once been; at Cambridge he had achieved the difficult feat of winning his blues at both cricket and golf, while also attaining a first class degree in the classics. He rose halfway to his feet to greet his son, who noticed that the effort induced a slight wheeze in his father's throat. 'James, it's good to see you.'

James thought that his father's face was now looking gaunt rather than lean, that his cheekbones were more prominent and his nose more pinched than a few months before.

Although his father refused to discuss his illness, James knew that it was some form of tuberculosis, since its presence was marked by a loss of weight and a persistent cough. He recalled that his father had gone to Ventnor on the Isle of Wight to attend a sanatorium noted for its treatment of the complaint. However, after ten days, he had discharged himself and returned to the family home near Godalming; he had cited severe boredom and the lack of a decent golf course on the island as his reasons.

As they sat down, his father asked him if he'd scored any runs at the weekend and James replied, 'A few in the Fitzsimon match on Sunday. I was left stranded on forty-odd.'

'That old rogue Fitzsimon, eh. It's odd how nobody has ever worked out how he made all that money.' He stubbed out his cigarette, poured some of Berry Brothers' claret into his son's glass and said, 'I've ordered for us both. Potted shrimps, followed by steak and kidney pie. Is that to your taste?'

'Of course. How are you, Papa? And Mama? She was in good form at the theatre last week.'

'I'm fine. A bit of a cough, that's all. As for your mother, she's steamed up about Home Rule for the Irish. She supports Asquith, of course. Also steamed up about votes for women. And convinced we should stay out of the war when it comes.'

'That seems a full programme even for Mama,' James laughed.

'And she's trying to make me eat vegetables and fruit only. That bloody man Shaw has a lot to answer for.'

Henry Clifton coughed deeply and instinctively reached for another cigarette, lit it and drew hard on it. His son handed him the tin of cigarettes which he'd bought for him. His father nodded appreciatively and put them in the pocket of his suit. 'Very soothing, a Turkish ciggie. They seem to help my throat.'

The potted shrimps were served by a deferential waiter who had worked at the club since the end of the Boer War, and their glasses were topped up with wine.

'Do you really think we'll have to go to war?' James asked.

'I'm afraid I do. The murder of the Archduke was just the excuse the Austrians wanted so that they can hammer the Serbs. You see, they've been causing no end of trouble in other parts of the Balkans, encouraged of course by the Russians.'

'I've read about the Serbs and their Black Hand extremists,' James replied. 'But why should we get involved in a conflict in the Balkans, which means nothing to us? The ordinary Englishman wouldn't know where Sarajevo is, and wouldn't care either.'

'The short answer is that Germany, as predicted, has waded in to support the Austrians and that the Russkies will back Serbia. And there you have the ingredients for a very nasty and probably very protracted European war.'

It was obvious to James that the perils his father was anticipating had put him in a melancholy mood, so he turned the conversation to less taxing matters and they spent some time speculating about the likely winners of cricket's County Championship.

But when the main course arrived, portions of steak and kidney pie which filled each plate and a large bowl of vegetables, Henry Clifton returned to the matter that was uppermost in his mind. 'I used to know the only man in England who really understood the Balkans problem,' he mused. 'An historian at Cambridge, well, he was at Trinity, like us. Unfortunately, he died last year. Simpson, I think his name was.'

'But surely Britain should remain neutral,' James persisted. '*Realpolitik* dictates that we should protect our trading interests around the world, since they're vital to our prosperity. We could even benefit from the chaos in Europe and extend our commercial interests.'

'That's a good point, James. Foreign Secretary Grey would probably agree with you. I'm told that he hates the idea of a war so much that he would even consider aligning us with Germany.'

'Against France?'

'Quite. That's a major difficulty. But the real problem, though it's perhaps a technical one in the real world of politics, is that we have a treaty with Belgium. If Germany invades her, we must go to her aid.'

'Which we would do anyway because Ostend and Zeebrugge are vital gateways for our trade with Europe.'

'Exactly, and the Germans covet those ports. But it's we British who make them sick with envy and rage. They hate our influence and trading power and want to challenge it. When I was last in Berlin I sensed an almost tangible madness in the nation. They were still wallowing in their last victory over France. It was in

1871, for heaven's sake. And that militaristic fool, Kaiser Wilhelm, is encouraging his nation in a lust for expansion. It's a frightening prospect.'

Henry Clifton lit another cigarette and ordered a glass of whisky, while James was content with a cup of coffee. With a smile his father said, 'Anyway, I'm glad to see from your grasp of current politics that your history degree wasn't wasted. A pity you missed your First.'

'Oh well, Papa, that leaves you as the family's academic top dog, doesn't it.'

Henry Clifton grunted. 'Harry and John are very promising. They may put both of us in the shade.'

'I hope so, and if the worst happens, they're young enough to escape going to war.'

'Please God. Anyway, your mother's doing her best to turn them into pacifists. She took them to lunch with Bertrand Russell the other day and no doubt he filled their minds with his peculiar ideas.'

'He's probably a genius, and a Trinity man to boot.' James smiled.

'I admire his intellect, but not necessarily his opinions.'

'His pacifism?'

'Yes, that's a problem for me. A year ago, such views were of little importance. We had some difficulties, of course. The suffragettes, strikes by organised labour and that damnable Irish question, which my friends in Whitehall tell me brought us to the brink of civil war. Nevertheless, the other portents were good. New and exciting developments like the telephone, motor cars, and travel by aeroplane seemed to promise a bright future. There'd even been some social progress, help for the unemployed, better wages for the working man and so on. Now it may all turn to dust.'

James glimpsed a shadow of despair, or even fear, touch his father's gaunt face, and his voice was low and sombre. 'I fear for us all, my boy, and especially for your generation.' He drew strongly on his cigarette and chased the smoke down his throat with a gulp of whisky. 'We could all be embroiled in war on a scale none of us could ever have imagined.'

'Some of the chaps in the Turf Club say that it'll all be over by Christmas. We'll be doing our shopping in Berlin.'

'You and I know better, James. After all, our army hasn't had to fight a war in Europe for nearly a hundred years. Our troops are used to putting down local uprisings, to gunning down savages with nothing to offer bar their naked courage.'

'And we didn't cover ourselves with glory in South Africa, did we?'

'Certainly not. But we will have to do our duty, one way or the other. Which brings me to you, James. I have something to ask you.'

The older man leaned back in his chair and gazed up at the ornate ceiling as if for guidance. 'As you know, although I had to retire from the Foreign Office, I keep in touch. They ask my advice occasionally and I met a fellow called Kell the other day. Vernon Kell. He used to be a soldier. I first came across him in Berlin and then in St Petersburg. He's head of some secret department now. I think he called it the Secret Service Bureau.'

'He sounds like someone in one of G A Henty's adventure stories.'

'Yes, that's about it. He's a sound fellow and a brilliant linguist, speaks half a dozen languages apparently.' He lowered his voice. 'Anyway, he's tracking a gang of Germans in and around London. He needs someone to make contact with these people, to infiltrate them and find out whatever he can.'

'And you thought of me.'

'I did because your German is fluent, and you are reasonably intelligent...'

'Thank you, Father.'

'And you are young and fit. This is just a suggestion, not a command. After all, you have an important job in Whitehall.'

'I'm also supposed to be leaving for Brazil with the Corinthians in less than four weeks' time.'

'Heavens above, I'd forgotten. Well, James, that's a trip that you shouldn't miss. However...'

James knew what his father's 'however' really meant, and what was expected of him. The eagerly awaited visit to Brazil, a land unknown to him and therefore the more exotic, would have to wait. He thought briefly of all the fun to be had in the company of his friends, and of his chance to play the game he loved in front of new and enthusiastic spectators. Above all, those memorable occasions when a group of individuals transforms itself into an entity with a single purpose, when it grows into a team and somehow gathers a strength beyond itself.

James smiled a little ruefully and said, 'However, there is a national emergency and everyone must do his duty.'

'I wouldn't dream of putting it to you in that way, my boy. You're old enough to make such decisions yourself.'

'There'll be other tours, I'm sure, and if a war starts, I don't want to be thousands of miles away.' His father began to speak, but James interrupted him. 'It's all right, Father, I'll tell old Dickson, the chairman, that work precludes my going. There are plenty of other fine players clamouring to go.'

'You're sure?'

'I am, Father. When do I meet Mister Kell?'

'Today week, in the afternoon and I hope you don't mind but I've already spoken to your head of department. Oh, and for heaven's sake, don't breathe a word about this to your mother, will you.'

'That her eldest son has become a part-time amateur spy? No, but I'd better talk to Erskine Childers and find out how it's done.'

'This is rather less romantic and much more mundane than anything in *The Riddle of the Sands*, my boy. You'll probably be sitting in cafés in rather squalid parts of London and trying to pick up bits and pieces of conversations. Vernon Kell and his fellows already have a long list of suspects. They will direct you to the right places.'

'I don't think Trinity College has any tradition of spying, has it?'

'No, James, so you can lay the foundations.'

5

A week later James made his way in the late afternoon to Watergate House, which sat at the bottom of York Buildings, just off the Strand. It was a solid-looking building dating from the end of the last century and a part of it overlooked the gardens of the Embankment. It was there that he was to meet Vernon Kell, the director of the Home Section of the Secret Service Bureau.

As a boy James had loved tales of intrigue and adventure and had devoured books written by G A Henty, Herbert Strang and Percy F Westerman, as well as the yarns of derring-do in the pages of magazines like *The Boys' Own Paper*. Now it seemed that he was about to take his own first faltering steps into this glamorous world; he was both excited by the prospect and apprehensive about his ability to perform the unfamiliar tasks that would be demanded of him.

In the care of a silent, uniformed policeman, he walked up three flights of stairs, whose walls were painted a dreary battleship grey. It brought him back to earth; after all, he was a civil servant and, as his father had told him, he was about to be asked merely to take on a few extra and no doubt routine duties.

Eventually, the policeman knocked on a door, opened it and took James into a large and unremarkable office. Its walls were mostly hidden by filing cabinets and there were six desks, four of which were occupied. The one woman who was present looked up and nodded a greeting; the three men remained intent on the papers littering their desks.

The policeman led him to the back of the room, where a door to another office had Vernon Kell's name painted on it. The policeman knocked, and after Kell, in clipped tones, had told him to enter, he announced: 'Mister James Clifton to see you, sir.' So, he can speak, James thought as he thanked him.

Kell rose to his feet, a smartly-dressed man, whose upright posture clearly proclaimed a military past. His thinning hair was brushed neatly across his scalp, his moustache suited his regular features and he wore a pair of rimless spectacles. Through Kell's windows James could see the gardens of the Embankment and the Thames beyond.

Kell greeted him in fluent and colloquial German as he invited him to sit down and make himself comfortable. They continued in the same language while Kell checked various details about his background and career.

'Your German is faultless, Clifton,' Kell eventually said in English. 'I think I could even detect a slight Berlin accent. Would that be fair?'

'Yes, sir, I spent several years there in my youth, when my father worked at the embassy.'

'I know your father, of course. A very fine man. It's a shame he had to retire young. He has a good opinion of your talents, by the way, but then he would, I suppose.'

Back-handed though the compliment was, James nodded his appreciation and sat back to listen as Kell outlined what he wanted him to do.

He explained that his department, which only numbered a dozen people, including two investigators and several clerks, had set out to monitor 'subversives' who were thought to be active in Britain. Over the past few years they had built up a card index system, which summarised information on over ten thousand suspects. They also intercepted letters between Germans, read them, re-sealed them and then sent them on their way again.

'All of this work is time-consuming and gives us only limited information of any real value,' Kell said. 'And we also have to keep a watchful eye on the other extremists. As well as Irish revolutionaries and some of the more radical suffragettes, there are quite a few Russian anarchists in London, as you will know. I believe you speak Russian as well.'

'Yes, sir, but it's not as good as my German.'

They chatted in Russian for a few minutes and Kell announced that James would be able to mingle without any difficulty in Russian émigré circles. 'But we're mainly concerned with these enclaves of German spies. We need to dig deeper and that's where you might be useful to us. We want you to visit one or two places, cafés and public houses where these people meet. That's all you need to do.'

'That doesn't sound too testing, sir.'

'Perhaps not, but I would emphasise one thing. We don't need heroes, Clifton. If you want glory, the army will welcome you with open arms. Our kind of work. . . intelligence work. . . is mostly dark, lonely and unsavoury.'

Though he was slightly taken aback, James said, 'I understand, sir, and where in London will I be doing this, er, lonely work?'

'Mostly in the Clerkenwell area, one place in particular initially. It's called the Old Vienna restaurant. Take it slowly. It's a bit like a courtship. Let them get to know your face, and then try to infiltrate the group. But don't try too hard, because they will be suspicious and I gave your father my word that you wouldn't get yourself into any dangerous situations.' Kell gave him a quick and rather chilly smile and continued. 'Above all, you must have a plausible story. Why are you there? Why do you want to make friends? Think about that and we can discuss it in a week or so. Now come and meet the others.'

Kell led him into the outer office and introduced him to two of the men and the woman, Jane Elkins, who was in charge of the filing system and also acted as Kell's secretary.

Finally, he turned to the man sitting slightly apart from the others at a desk in one of the corners of the room.

'This is Gregory, Maundy Gregory. He's been instrumental in compiling the dossiers on all these rather questionable people. He knows a lot about a lot of people, don't you, Gregory?'

James noticed a cutting edge to the last remark and wondered what lay behind it. Gregory had a fleshy face, with a wide, turned-down mouth that made him look sulky or dissatisfied. His mud-brown eyes were expressionless as he half-rose from his seat and shook hands perfunctorily with James. His age could have been anywhere between thirty-odd and fifty.

'When the time comes, Gregory will provide you with all the information you need about the various people in whom we have an interest.'

Kell guided him towards and through the door and, as they walked downstairs to the front door, said, 'One more thing, Clifton. You look fit and I know that you're a sportsman, but do you know how to defend yourself?'

'Well, I boxed at school.'

'Every little helps, I suppose. But I'm going to arrange for you to have an hour or two with one of our close combat instructors. Staff Corporal Cowie. He's with the Household Cavalry. What about firearms? Have you had any training?'

'At school, sir, a bit. I did the usual course with a rifle when I was in the cadet force.'

Kell grunted and said that he ought to have some training with a handgun.

'I thought I was just being asked to do a little eavesdropping,' James said, trying to keep any nervousness out of his voice.

'You are, but better to be safe than sorry.' As he said this, Kell's accompanying smile was even more glacial than before.

6

Arthur Dickson, the chairman of the Corinthian Football Club, was a firm believer in team spirit. He had played both cricket and football with Charles Burgess Fry, who had a remarkable talent for both games, and Dickson's own unswerving faith in the concept had been reinforced by his discussions with the great 'CB'. He was also a passionate advocate of the principles of the scouting movement, as laid down by its founder, Lieutenant-General Robert Baden-Powell: do your duty to God and the King, help other people at all times, and be loyal and honourable. In Dickson's opinion, life was very much like sport; it was a team game and all the better for it.

The impetus for the formation of the Corinthian Football Club had come thirty years before, when the England team had suffered a series of defeats at the hands of the Scots, who played regularly together and as a result were better-organised and apparently more skilful. In order to compete with them some of the leading English footballers were gathered together as the Corinthians. Invitations to join the club were in general limited to those from the main public schools and from Oxford and Cambridge, where the best players were to be found in those days before the expansion of the professional game.

There was a further and very important aspect to being a Corinthian: the highest standards of behaviour were expected of a member.

Such an obligation ensured that Arthur Dickson was the ideal man to be the figurehead of such a club, since his ideals were perfectly in tune with those of the Corinthians. He even adhered to the principle of 'fair play' in his business life. He had followed his father into the estates agency business and would proudly boast that he and his father had, between them, sold many large estates in southern England many times over. The landed gentry had come to trust Dickson for good advice and fair dealing.

He was looking forward to the expedition to Brazil, as he looked forward to all the tours which the Corinthians undertook. Despite his innate distrust of foreigners, he rarely failed to make friends amongst them and was convinced that the fellowship that sport induced and fostered could be used to resolve disputes between nations. He held to this view in spite of history's conclusive evidence to the contrary.

On this Thursday night, the chairman was taking some of the Corinthians to a boxing match at Olympia, followed by dinner at a private dining club in Kensington's Brompton Road. He loved such sporting occasions and this promised to be a rousing one, since the great French fighter, Georges Carpentier, was challenging Gunboat Smith of the USA for the white heavyweight championship of the world.

The American negro, Jack Johnson, had been the heavyweight champion of the world since 1908 when he stopped the Canadian, Tommy Burns, in Australia. Johnson was acknowledged to be a great boxer; some said he was invincible, but his arrogant and abusive behaviour had alienated his public, especially in his homeland. His countrymen could not stomach a negro living in such an extravagant way; wine, women and song were all very well, but not when the man was black and the women were white. In 1912, Johnson had to flee the USA when he was convicted of taking a white woman, Lucille Cameron, across state lines 'for immoral purposes'. Less than three weeks before Carpentier was due to fight Smith, Johnson had retained his world championship by beating Frank Moran in Paris.

Some time before, the search had begun for a 'Great White Hope' to tumble the negro from his pedestal. A part of this had been the initiation of a heavyweight championship open only to white fighters and, earlier that year, Gunboat Smith became its first holder when he knocked out the Canadian, Arthur Pelkey, an honest but limited mauler, in Daly City, California.

Since Arthur Dickson lived in a house overlooking the river just to the west of the Hammersmith Bridge, the half a dozen Corinthians gathered to meet him in a pleasant Thames-side pub called The Dove: James and Richard, Rupert Wavell, Hugh Pryce-Morgan, Guy Willett and Henry Corbett. Dickson ordered some jugs of ale and, when they had lowered them, they strode towards Olympia down the Hammersmith Road. The crowds thickened as they approached Brook Green.

Since the chairman had many influential friends in sporting circles, the seven Corinthians entered the famous exhibition hall through a side-door and were shown to their ringside seats. Temporary seating spread outwards and upwards around them under the span of the glass roof. As the spectators began to take their places there was a growing surge of conversation, with many bets being laid both between individuals and with the touts who were working the crowd.

Everyone was caught up in the excitement, in the anticipation of two accomplished and dangerous boxers confronting each other for a world championship.

'Who's your money on, Hugh?' Dickson asked. Before Pryce-Morgan could answer, the chairman had turned to wave at someone who was sitting two rows away. 'Johnny, good to see you. You're the expert, so who should I back?'

'I always back the bigger man, Mister Dickson. So, my money's on Smith.'

'That's Johnny Douglas,' said Dickson. 'He won the middleweight gold at the '08 Olympics. Fine cricketer, as you know.'

'There's that fellow Bottomley again,' James said quietly to Richard. He pointed to his left. 'With Bombardier Billy Wells.'

'Who's lost to both of tonight's fighters.'

There was a sudden commotion from the opposite side of the arena and loud cheers and shouts of 'good old Marie' signalled the arrival of Britain's most popular music hall star, Marie Lloyd, with her third husband, the Irish jockey, Bernard Dillon, in close attendance. The crowd struck up a ragged chorus of 'My Old Man Said Follow the Van' as she began to make her way to her ringside seat. She stopped in the aisle, turned her buxom figure to the crowd and conducted the impromptu choir, a delighted grin on her chubby features. Her huge flower-bedecked hat wobbled dangerously as she beat time with great enthusiasm.

The Marie Lloyd show was, however, swamped by the huge cheer which greeted the French challenger, Georges Carpentier, as he walked slowly down the aisle towards the ring. He looked very calm as he waved to the crowd, his black hair slicked back, a dressing gown thrown casually across his broad shoulders. As he clambered into the ring, followed by his trainer, a group of his supporters began to sing *La Marseillaise*. Carpentier bowed low in their direction.

Then the American champion, Gunboat Smith, made his entrance. Brisk and business-like he stalked down the aisle towards the ring, thumping his gloves together menacingly. The American flag was painted on the bag carried by his trainer.

'He must be two or three inches taller than the Froggie,' Richard said.

'And a stone heavier,' Guy Willett chipped in.

'He looks like a heavyweight, doesn't he, whereas Carpentier looks what he is, a light-heavy,' said James.

'But Carpentier more than punches his weight,' Richard replied.

As the announcements were made, Richard backed Carpentier for one guinea even with Rupert Wavell, and then the two boxers were squaring up in the centre of the ring. They circled each other warily for a while, probing with straight left leads, then moving out of range, and then closing in again as they looked for openings.

Both men moved quickly and athletically and the round seemed to be evenly fought as it drew to its close. Then there was a sudden explosive movement from Carpentier as he trapped the American in a neutral corner. James thought he saw four blows, two to the body and two to the head, but Carpentier's hands were so quick that there might have been more. The result, however, was clear; Gunboat Smith was on his backside in the corner, his right arm draped over the ring's middle rope and his left hand scrabbling for purchase on the floor.

Most of the crowd was on its feet and Richard was shouting 'It's over, Smith's gone' as the referee counted up to seven. Then the bell rang for the end of the round, Smith's trainer rushed into the ring with a wet sponge and some smelling salts and hauled his man over to his stool.

'Well, Richard, you said he had a punch.' James struggled to make himself heard in the hubbub.

The bell for the second round tolled and Carpentier leapt across the ring in his eagerness to put his opponent away; but Smith was an experienced and cagey boxer, well able to get in close and cling on to the Frenchman's arms and stifle his blows. By the end of round two Smith had recovered his strength.

The next three rounds were evenly fought and it seemed possible that the bout would last the full distance. If Carpentier looked the more dangerous puncher, Smith had a rugged determination and strength that was clearly frustrating for his opponent.

The sixth round, however, proved to be decisive. Smith trapped Carpentier on the ropes and hit him with the classic combination of a left hook to the body and, as the Frenchman tried to cover up, a right cross to the side of the head. Carpentier sprawled on to the floor, but to everyone's surprise rose to his feet on the count of three. He wobbled slightly and dropped on one knee in order to gather his wits, at which moment Gunboat Smith closed in eagerly and, in his excitement, unleashed another right-hander to his jaw.

Once again every spectator was on his feet and each seemed to have an opinion to share with his neighbour. The referee jumped between the two boxers and pushed Smith towards his corner, while Carpentier's trainer helped his man over to his stool, where the Frenchman's manager, Francois Deschamps, was waving his arms wildly and screaming at the referee.

His protests ceased immediately, however, when the referee walked over to Carpentier and, without any hesitation, raised his hand in the air. The Frenchman was the new white heavyweight champion of the world.

While supporters of Carpentier clambered into the ring and lifted him triumphantly on to their shoulders, *La Marseillaise* again rang out from the back of the hall. Eventually, the new champion was allowed to get his feet back on solid ground and he pushed his way through to Gunboat Smith's corner. The vanquished American could just be seen, his head bowed, while his trainer tried to console him. Carpentier patted him on the back, said a few words to him and then pulled him to his feet, grabbed his right fist and raised it in salute to the crowd.

Despite the disappointing finale to the fight, the crowd gave both boxers a round of applause, which rang out for several minutes.

'My word,' said Rupert Wavell, 'the Frenchman is quite the gentleman, is he not?' He reached into his pocket and tried to hand a guinea to Hildreth.

'No, Rupert, I can't take the money. Not on a disqualification, it's hardly right.'

'That's very decent of you.'

'Not at all, we'll have double or quits on another wager sometime.'

* * *

The dinner at Gladwin's Dining Rooms was lavish, noisy and bibulous, as the Corinthians ate their way through potted pheasant, smoked salmon with scrambled eggs, ribs of beef, treacle pudding with cream and an assortment of English cheeses; it was accompanied by some fine French wines. Arthur Dickson was a munificent host and liked nothing more than to entertain his footballing friends.

As they passed the port around the table, the chairman proposed a toast to the Corinthian Football Club and then spoke quietly to James and Richard. 'I'm only sorry that you two won't be in Brazil. We'll miss you. I know you have your reasons, but let's hope you get another chance to make such a trip. At present, the world is too much at the mercy of fools and knaves like the Kaiser and all those pusillanimous politicians who kow-tow to him and other rulers. At times I despair.'

'*Plus ça change,*' said Richard.

Dickson took a strong pull at his port. 'Enough of that, however, tonight is a night for enjoyment and good fellowship.' He waved an empty bottle of port at one of the waiters. 'Two more bottles, please.'

7

In the Cabinet Room of 10 Downing Street five men sat at a table which was littered with tea and coffee cups and plates of biscuits. They had formed a semi-circle at one end of the table and were facing the windows. They all looked troubled, none more so than the Prime Minister; the cares of high office were marked clearly on Herbert Henry Asquith's solid features. In his six years as Prime Minister and leader of the Liberal Party he had battled to change Britain for the better, but his attempts to introduce a degree of social justice had earned him the contempt of the moneyed classes, who refused to understand that it was equitable and just that higher taxes on unearned income should pay for pensions for the aged. His attempts to bring Home Rule to Ireland had Britain teetering on the edge of civil war, while the increasingly spectacular antics of the suffragettes and the militancy of the Trades Unions had added unstable and highly volatile elements to Britain in the early part of a century that had once seemed so full of promise. Now he and his countrymen faced the prospect of a European war.

Asquith turned to the man seated on his left. 'Foreign Secretary, what is the state of play vis-à-vis Serbia and Austria?'

Sir Edward Grey clasped his hands above his notepad and looked towards the windows, as if hoping they would shed some light on the problem. A frown disfigured his well-turned features and he spoke softly. 'I believe that the Austrians are preparing some sort of ultimatum, which they will present to the Serbs.'

'Who will undoubtedly reject it.' The interruption came from the First Lord of the Admiralty, who occupied the chair next to

Grey. A thin ribbon of sunlight enlivened the copper sheen of Winston Churchill's hair. Irritably, he tapped some ash from his cigar into an elaborate bronze ashtray.

'We don't know that, Winston,' said David Lloyd George. As the Chancellor of the Exchequer he sat, appropriately, at the Prime Minister's right hand. In general, he disliked formality and, with the exception of Asquith, tended to address his colleagues by their first names. 'Surely, no one wants a conflict in Europe. The Austrians will wield their big stick, perhaps with support from the Germans, the Serbs will take the hint and that will be that.'

Lloyd George's quick, light voice, overlaid with a pleasant Welsh inflection, contrasted with Churchill's more sonorous tones.

'I agree with the Chancellor,' Grey said quickly. 'This is not a European problem, it's a local problem, with which the Austrians and the Serbs can grapple.'

'Your good sense may not, unfortunately, find echoes in Berlin and St Petersburg,' said Churchill. 'The Kaiser will welcome this crisis. My view is that he wants a war with Britain, since he has made it plain that he resents British power and will do whatever he must to reduce it.'

'We can and will exert all our diplomatic influence to keep the peace,' Grey replied quietly.

'I hope you've emphasised to the Germans that, if they invade Belgium, we are bound by treaty to help protect that nation,' Churchill said forcefully. 'Reasoned diplomacy is all very well, but the Germans thrive on other nations' weaknesses, and we must present our sternest face to their provocations. So, Sir Edward, I ask again if the Germans have been made aware of our position.'

'As I have already said, we are making our most strenuous efforts to stabilise the situation,' Grey replied. Everyone in the room heard Churchill's growl of dissatisfaction.

Lloyd George began to speak, but Asquith interrupted and asked for the opinion of the fifth person in the room. He was Lord Kitchener, Britain's most distinguished soldier, and regarded by many as its greatest military leader since the Duke of Wellington.

Kitchener was silent for a moment, as if marshalling his thoughts into a precise military formation. 'Thank you, Prime Minister, for inviting me to this meeting in an informal capacity. I am just a simple soldier and I am not privy to the facts that you gentlemen no doubt have. However, like the First Sea Lord, I am apprehensive of Germany's ambitions. I fear that the little Balkan skirmish may put a tinder to the fire, so to speak.'

'Great heavens, Kitchener,' said Lloyd George forcefully, 'Sir Edward is surely right to say that the diplomatic efforts of us and the French, and even the Russians, can stave off disaster.'

'I am probably being naïf, but the Kaiser is, after all, related to our own royal family,' Asquith said, ' and I know that the King is making strenuous efforts to maintain a friendly relationship.'

Churchill grunted loudly and spoke through a haze of cigar smoke. 'What if the worst happens, Prime Minister? What is our state of preparedness? As you know, I have fought long and hard, with the invaluable assistance of Admiral Lord Fisher, to build up our fleet of dreadnoughts. Soon we will have nineteen ready for action, with their powerful guns and greatly enhanced speeds. So, the navy is prepared. But what of the army?'

Asquith hesitated and fiddled with the cup, long empty of tea, that lay before him. 'The figures I have suggest that we may have two hundred thousand serving men, but most of them are scattered around the empire. Lord Kitchener, if there should be war, what would be our requirements?'

'The first point to make is that we are in a parlous state compared to the Boche. Their army is nearly two million strong, with many more trained men in reserve. So, first we must secure the return of many of our troops from foreign parts, while leaving sufficient men in place to defend our possessions. Then there is an immediate need for at least five hundred thousand men.'

'And if the war is prolonged?' asked Lloyd George.

'Who knows, but we must at least equal the strength of the German foe.'

'Another two million men,' Churchill said quietly. 'A very tall order.'

'And they must be trained and equipped,' Kitchener emphasised. 'It will of course be a different war this time.' He spoke with the authority of the renowned military leader that he was acknowledged to be. 'The Germans are very well-equipped and well-disciplined. Our men won't be in a quick fight with a few natives armed with spears and protected by shields made from sticks and animal skins.'

'Will our soldiers be equal to the task?' Asquith asked. 'They are already seen as the dregs of society, thieves and beggars who have no desire to do a good day's work for a fair reward.'

'Our rapacious and licentious soldiery,' muttered Grey.

'Nevertheless, they're the ruffians who helped to seize an empire for us,' said Churchill sharply.

'Along with our far-sighted and enterprising traders. The gentlemen of the East India Company, for example,' Asquith said judiciously.

Lloyd George rapped the table urgently. His Welsh accent was more pronounced as his words tumbled out. 'I must make the point that many of the men who've volunteered to fight our battles had no option. They were destitute, their wives and children were starving and they had little hope of finding work. That's the other side of the story, Prime Minister.'

'Yes, Chancellor, and this government has tried valiantly to improve the lot of the working man,' Asquith said soothingly. 'But we are here to discuss the diplomatic crisis, which some of us think will worsen and turn into a full-scale war. In that event, we will need all the expertise we can muster, especially yours, Lord Kitchener. In essence, we need great numbers of fighting men, but we also need to ensure that as many as possible are fit young men, since they will face a momentous task.

'I would encourage you all to consider how we achieve such an objective,' the Prime Minister concluded. He then rose to his feet and thanked the other four men for attending the meeting. As they headed for the door, he asked Kitchener to remain for a moment or two longer.

8

A second meeting had swiftly been arranged at the offices of the Secret Service Bureau and, to James's disappointment, it had to take precedence over an invitation to 'take tea' with Mrs Kitson-Clark. He sent her a letter by the mid-morning post and her reply was waiting for him when he arrived at his flat in the early evening. 'Dear James,' it read, 'I am so sorry that you are unable to keep our engagement, one which was arranged several days ago. I have a husband who also seems to value his business affairs above all else, and I hope that our friendship will not be afflicted by a similar indifference.'

It was signed as usual with a flourish and in full: Beatrice Kitson-Clark. James was disconcerted by her attitude and wondered if he should write to her to assure her of his continuing devotion. Perhaps not; actions would speak louder than words, that is, if the chance again presented itself.

* * *

When James returned to Watergate House he was met by the same uniformed policeman. As he followed him towards Vernon Kell's offices, James could see the sheen of sweat which had gathered on his neck in the summer heat.

Kell was sitting with Maundy Gregory and a rather gaunt, grey-faced man, who had the look of a recently retired army officer. 'This is Assistant-Commissioner Basil Thomson,' Kell said. 'We work under his direction and I thought you should meet him before you begin to help us.'

James shook Thomson's outstretched hand and then took the only available seat next to a large wooden filing cabinet.

Without any preamble, Gregory began to speak in his expressionless voice. 'If you're to achieve anything for us, we need to agree on your cover story. We of course have some ideas, but we wanted to hear any suggestions you might have. Perhaps you've got a background story that suits you?'

James hadn't given it any close consideration and replied hesitantly. 'I think I ought to have a German family.' He felt even less sure of his ground, as he surveyed the three men with their set faces. 'Perhaps my mother should be German. Married to an Englishman and, like me, they lived for several years in Berlin.'

'What was your father doing there?' asked Thomson.

'He was a minor official in the British Embassy and he deserted my imaginary mother when I was five years of age.'

'No, no,' Gregory said sharply, 'they might take it into their heads to check the name.'

'Not if I make it clear that I decided to use my mother's name when I later found out he'd deserted us.'

There was a short silence and Kell said, 'And your story is that you deeply resent your father's treatment of you both.'

'Yes, and I regard myself as German not English, and I want to do whatever I can to further the cause of Germany.'

'Why are you in London?' asked Kell.

James paused. 'Well, perhaps I work for a cousin of my mother's who imports German products. Sausages, beer, that kind of thing.'

'No, no. That won't do at all,' Gregory's tone was even more impatient than before. 'A lot of the people we have under surveillance work in hotels and restaurants and they might ask awkward questions.'

'I think, Gregory, that we should use that shipping company again,' Kell said. He then turned towards James. 'We have an arrangement with a firm in the City, they will provide a cover story for you. The story is that you're employed partly because of your facility in foreign languages. When you tell these Germans that you move around the docks and the City, you'll be seen as a potential source of intelligence.'

'Yes,' Thomson agreed, 'that should work and we will provide you in due course with some harmless pieces of information about the movement of both merchant and Royal Navy ships. This will gain you a measure of acceptance.'

James noticed Thomson looking closely at him, assessing him perhaps, and he felt rather uncomfortable under the man's scrutiny.

'You look far too smart, Clifton, to be a shipping clerk. Where did you get that suit? Savile Row?'

'Nearby, sir, a tailor in Clifford Street.'

'Well, get some cheap clothes from somewhere. Where do you suggest, Gregory? Pimlico, somewhere like that?'

Gregory nodded and Thomson went on to question James about where he lived. He told him not to reveal his address to any of what he called his 'new German friends'. 'It's best to be vague, say that you move around, that you share a room with some friends near Victoria Station perhaps, and sometimes with friends who live off the Shepherd's Bush Road. Fortunately for us, these people are not particularly professional, so they're unlikely to follow you home in order to check your story. However, make damned sure that they don't ever do so.'

The Assistant-Commissioner rose to his feet and the other men showed their respect for their superior by at once doing the same. Thomson said, 'Gregory will tell you where to go and who to look out for. Find out what you can, but do so with great caution. Remember that it will take time for you to be accepted and we don't want the work we've done so far and so well to be nullified.' He nodded at his two colleagues and left.

Maundy Gregory took James through to the other room, delved in a drawer in his desk and gave him a sheaf of papers. 'These are some notes on the background of three of the men we're interested in. Ralf Weber is a baker in Clerkenwell, Axel Fischer is a waiter and the other, Kurt Neumann, is a chef at the Old Vienna. That's also in Clerkenwell. They call it a restaurant, but it's a glorified alehouse, really. That's where they usually meet two or three times a week and always on a Saturday night when they finish work.'

James scanned the papers, found pencil sketches of the three men and held them up questioningly.

'Those likenesses are the best we could do,' Gregory said. 'We didn't think it was wise to ask them to pose for a studio photograph.' James hoped that he didn't show how startled he was by Gregory's rare moment of levity. Then he decided that it was just cheap sarcasm.

'You'll easily spot Neumann,' he continued, 'because he's well over six feet tall.' He leaned back in his chair and put his hands behind his head. 'These people, and others like them, work for a man called Gustav Steinhauer. He's their spymaster, to use a rather romantic term.' He grimaced. 'He's based in Germany, though he's made regular trips to England. Neumann and his associates don't worry us because we know most of the addresses in Germany where they send their information. With the help of the Post Office and Special Branch, we intercept the letters, copy down the contents and send them on their way. In the last three years or so, we've seen at least one letter every day.'

'Very impressive,' James said.

'Steinhauer pays some of them about one pound a month, which is not a lot of money when you consider they could be shot for what they're doing.' He smiled grimly.

'So, if they're under control, so to speak, what am I trying to achieve?'

'We need to know more about the sources of their information. Of course we have some names. For instance, we know about some clerks in a Royal Navy office in Portsmouth, and some ratings, who seem willing to betray their country. But they're just low-level trash and we need to know where the important leaks are, and those leaks are obviously much higher up the chain of command. When the war starts with Germany, and it's only a matter of weeks away, we might want to arrest these spies and the traitors who are helping them.'

'Or feed them false information, perhaps?'

Gregory looked sharply at James. 'Yes, that's also a part of our plans.' He got up from his desk to signal the end of the meeting.

'So what happens now?' James asked.

'Miss Elkins over there has a few shillings for you, so go and buy yourself some cheap clothes. Cheap but clean, as befits your station as a clerk in a shipping office. And buy them immediately because you're making your first sortie to the Old Vienna tomorrow night. Make contact if you can, but even if they just register you, see your face, that's a start. Don't be too eager because they're not stupid, they'll spot anything suspicious.'

James nodded and Miss Elkins handed him a few coins. As he reached the door, Maundy Gregory said, 'By the way, there's a message for you from Staff Corporal Cowie. He's got a package for you and will you please go and pick it up.'

James opened the door and was halfway through it when Gregory called out, 'Be careful with those toys Cowie has for you, won't you, Mister Clifton. We don't want you to hurt yourself.' The sneer in his voice was plain to hear. James hoped he wouldn't have too close dealings with such an odious man; even better, perhaps he could contrive to meet him in a dark alley and knock some of the bile out of him.

As the door shut and James's footsteps receded down the corridor, Gregory muttered, 'I don't understand why we're being saddled with someone like him. What's the point?'

'The point is that he's had the courage to volunteer, isn't it, Mister Gregory? And he might lead us to the Germans we really want to find. He seems clever enough to do that.'

'If you fancy your chances with him, Miss Elkins, forget it. He's far too posh for you.'

Jane Elkins flushed with annoyance, but said nothing, since she knew how sharp his tongue could be.

Gregory grunted. 'I might get somebody from Special Branch to shadow him. Just in case.'

9

On Saturday James joined three friends at Sunningdale for a round of golf, but, conscious of his new responsibilities as a British spy, turned down their invitation to have some drinks and then dinner at Rosa Lewis's Cavendish Hotel. He gave the excuse that he was dining with his family, but his intention was to spend an hour or two in his rooms in order to prepare himself for his first foray on Vernon Kell's behalf. He was apprehensive about what lay ahead and knew that he must keep his wits about him; despite his attempts to remain light-hearted about his 'part-time job', the seriousness of his task seemed to have increased markedly since his father had proposed it with such a casual air.

In the evening, he had some bread and cheese and a glass of claret and then settled down in an armchair to read some of the stories in 'Dubliners'. Inevitably, his thoughts turned to the woman who had given him the book, Beatrice Kitson-Clark, and he wondered wistfully if he would ever see her again; he missed his tea-time romps with her.

Deliberately, he delayed his departure for the Old Vienna until the light began to fade. He then dressed in an old flannel shirt that he'd found in the bottom of a drawer, some scuffed shoes from the back of his wardrobe, and the nondescript and ill-fitting suit that he'd bought that morning from a shop in Queensway. He grinned at his reflection in the mirror; what a dreadful mess he looked. His own mother probably wouldn't recognise him. Just as he was about to leave, he tucked the clasp-knife that Cowie had provided into his pocket. Just a precaution, he told himself.

In order to avoid being recognised in such unusual clothing, he left his rooms by the back stairs. Having emerged into the mews behind the building he walked swiftly towards the Brompton Road. He was also wearing an old cloth cap and he kept his head down. After a couple of changes of omnibus, he arrived near Clerkenwell Green at just after ten o'clock.

As he walked into the Green, James tried to make himself as inconspicuous as possible; his normal gait was brisk, and he held his head up and his upper body balanced over his hips as befitted a sportsman in the prime of his health. But now, as he passed the elaborate classical façade of the Old Sessions House, he walked with a shuffle, his shoulders stooped and his eyes cast down; he looked at least ten years older. The Green was busy, with drinkers clustered outside the Northumberland Arms, many of them sitting on the pavements as they let alcohol, mostly in the form of gin and beer, take them to the brink of insensibility. It was what the people of London had been doing for centuries, especially those who lived such desperate lives. As he registered the way people lived in this poverty-stricken part of London, his shoulders drooped even more in sympathy.

Clerkenwell Green was where Oliver Twist had been taught how to pick pockets by the Artful Dodger and James saw a few of his real-life descendants lurking on the edges of the groups of drinkers. They would have easy pickings in an hour or two. As he strolled around the Green he glanced down the various side-streets and alleys where other ale-houses were doing a thriving trade. So were the shilling-a-go whores who would see to their customers' needs in the hallways of the nearby tenements, against the doors of the many neighbouring warehouses, and even in the graveyard of St James's Church. He saw one of them, a painfully thin girl in a tattered dress, stagger off towards Turnmill Street with a man even drunker than she was. He guessed that she might well have a male accomplice waiting nearby to cosh the man into unconsciousness before stealing his money, his coat and even his boots, if they were worth taking.

James headed down Britton Street past a variety of small shops, which took up the ground floors of the two- and three-storey houses: a clockmaker, a silversmith, a printer and a pawnbroker. He paused by the open door of the Jerusalem Tavern. It was another warm night and he felt the need not only to quench his thirst but also to settle his nerves before his visit to the Old Vienna. The tavern was not as crowded as those on the Green and he eased himself through the open doors and past a knot of drinkers in the first small room and found a position for himself at the far end of the tiny bar in the inner room. Behind him, four men were talking animatedly in Russian and, while he waited to be served, he listened to them. He had hoped to hear wild talk of anarchy and revolution. Clerkenwell had after all been a centre of radicalism and religious dissent for centuries, from the time of the Lollards, through to the Chartists of the middle of the 19th century; and James was aware that Lenin had, a dozen years before, edited an underground revolutionary paper called *The Spark* from premises in Clerkenwell Green. He was, therefore, disappointed to hear only boasts from the Russians about their prowess as lovers and drinkers.

After ordering a pint of strong ale and drinking deeply, James looked unobtrusively at the other customers, who seemed to comprise a typical cross-section of London's varied population, the workers who kept the wheels of industry and commerce churning, for very little reward. They were the men who laboured in the local breweries and distilleries; the printers and watchmakers who thronged Clerkenwell; the shop workers, warehousemen and street traders; and, above all, the clerks from the thousands of offices around the city. Many of them were dressed like James, in worn-out clothing bought from second-hand shops or handed down from a brother or a father, and he was pleased that his shabby clothes fitted in so well. In the light of the gas lamps everything looked drab, just shades of grey and brown, occasionally relieved by a shirt that had once been white.

The group of men next to him at the bar were celebrating a birthday and were ordering glasses of gin with beer chasers.

By the time he had finished his beer the volume of noise had increased considerably and, with careful nods of apology as he squeezed past the various knots of drinkers, he left the tavern and walked towards the Old Vienna restaurant.

James registered its grubby windows and then went through the double doors into an unprepossessing interior. On the left there was a long wooden counter which displayed a few unappetising pastries, some stale chunks of bread, some shrivelled pieces of sausage and a hot water urn. An emaciated man wearing spectacles sat on a stool behind the counter and did not look up from the tattered book he was reading. Clifton glanced at the cover. It was a popular novel by Paul Heyse, called *Kinder der Welt*. Children of the World. Behind and above the man, a few bottles of schnapps and German beers sat on a rickety wooden shelf. Straight ahead, its presence confirmed by the smell of grease and cabbage, James could see a small kitchen. There were only a few tables, each of which could seat about six people. Five men occupied one of the tables at the back of the room.

Speaking in German, James asked the dedicated reader behind the counter for a glass of schnapps and, without a word, the man reached above and behind him and poured it.

'And a jug of water, please,' James added.

He sat down near the counter and facing the five men. It wasn't difficult to identify Kurt Neumann, because, as Maundy Gregory had stated, he was a big man; he looked as heavy and as muscular as Gunboat Smith and, with his flattened nose and a scar above his right eye, might well have been a pugilist in his time.

James did not have to strain to hear the men's conversation, which centred on the forthcoming wedding of one of their daughters. He heard the names Ralf and Axel mentioned, so Weber and Fischer were present, too. So far, so good, he thought, but remembered Kell's repeated warnings not to foist himself on their company, so he didn't linger. On this first visit he merely wanted his face to register with Neumann and his associates, so he made short work of his schnapps, stood up and nodded to the barman on his way to the door.

He repeated his visit on the Monday evening and when he asked for his schnapps James exaggerated his Berlin accent a little, by softening his 'g' and hardening his 'ch'.

His accent had the desired effect. Soon after he had sat down, the man from behind the counter appeared at his elbow and said in German, 'You're from Berlin?'

James kept any eagerness out of his voice as he agreed that he was and the two men then swapped platitudes about the beauties of the city and how much they missed it. The man introduced himself as Martin Schmidt and James gave his assumed name to Schmidt, who then reached over to the bar, poured himself a slug of schnapps and re-filled James's glass. They drank a toast to Berlin and Schmidt called out, 'Kurt, you must meet Herr Pieter Westermann.'

As well as assuming this name as part of his disguise James had been told by Kell that he should claim to work for a shipping and transport company called Josiah Morris and Sons, based in Farringdon Road.

'If your new German friends check up on you,' Kell had assured him, 'the office manager will confirm that you work there. We pay him a small stipend to help us out from time to time.'

Nevertheless, James had arranged to visit their offices and the manager, a dapper man in his fifties called Tom Belmont, had given him a concise and interesting account of the workings of the company.

Kurt Neumann paused in his conversation and with a meaty hand waved them both over. James judged him to be in his early forties and his close-cropped grey hair emphasised the squareness of his large head; his florid cheeks suggested a man who, like most cooks, was fond of his tipple.

'So what brings you here, Herr Westermann?' he asked.

He's straight to the point, James thought, as he explained that he'd seen the restaurant a few days before and hoped to find some German speakers there.

'Do you work around here?' Neumann then asked.

'Yes, in the Farringdon Road.'

'What work do you do there, Herr Westermann?'

'I work for a small shipping firm.'

'Lots of those around here,' Neumann said. 'Which one? My brother works for one near here.'

James gave the name of the firm, but he had already noticed a quickening of interest in Neumann and his associates at the mention of a shipping company. He hoped that he hadn't revealed too much too soon.

After a few more exchanges, he glanced at his watch, a cheap one provided by Maundy Gregory, and said that he must get home before the last buses stopped running. Neumann walked to the door with him and said, 'You're welcome here any time, Pieter Westermann. We're here on most evenings, and especially on Saturday and Wednesday, so come along. Do you have far to go?'

'No, not far. At the moment I'm in a room off the Tottenham Court Road,' he said. They shook hands and James walked south along Britton Street towards Charterhouse Street and Holborn.

Neumann had paused in the doorway to watch him walk down the street. He looked thoughtful as he rejoined his companions and sat down. 'What do you think of him?'

'He speaks better German than I do,' said Axel Fischer, 'and you can hear that Berlin accent loud and clear.'

'He seems intelligent,' Weber said.

'Check that he really works at that shipping firm,' Neumann said. 'If he does, he could be useful to us.'

* * *

On the following Monday James made a brief visit to the Old Vienna, which was deserted except for Schmidt, the barman, and two days later found only Ralf Weber and Axel Fischer there. He bought himself a beer, chatted to them in German for a few minutes and then left, telling them that he hoped to return on the following Saturday. At the very least he was making sure that they were noticing him.

When he arrived at the restaurant on the Saturday evening, Neumann was sitting in his accustomed position at the head of the same table, his associates grouped around him.

To James's surprise, he greeted him in English and there was hardly a trace of a German accent. 'So, Pieter, you're back. It's good to see you. You're obviously in need of some good German beer. Get yourself a glass.'

There were several bottles of beer on the table and Schmidt, who could have been the owner of the restaurant, or merely the barman, brought him a glass.

'Sit down, Herr Westermann, and tell us a little more about yourself. What brought you back to England?'

James was on his guard, because he calculated that a conversation in English must have a purpose; possibly so that Neumann could assess his accent. Was it too genteel and therefore not in keeping with his lowly status as a shipping clerk? Fortunately, James was a good mimic, a natural skill that lay behind his ability to speak other languages. He knew that his normal middle-class English accent would arouse suspicions in Neumann's mind and he flattened his vowels slightly to produce a mild London accent.

'My father was a teacher in Berlin, well, he taught people to speak English, mostly rich children, I think. That's where he met my mother and they got married. We all came back to London a few years ago and then he ups and leaves mum, for another woman, of course.'

'Where's your mother now?'

'Back in Berlin, but I use my mother's name and its German spelling.'

'You're a brave man,' Neumann said. 'We Germans aren't exactly popular in London these days.'

'I'll take that risk,' James replied and, after a few more questions from Neumann, went on to tell them more about his work as a clerk for the shipping company, work which took him to the London docks and occasionally to Portsmouth. At this stage, Neumann became quite animated and called for another round of drinks. The group had reverted to speaking in German and the conversation became lively as toasts were drunk in both beer and schnapps. James noticed that Neumann slipped occasional questions into the conversation. They were clearly designed to test his knowledge of Berlin and of German customs, so he remained very much on his guard.

At just after midnight James looked ostentatiously at his watch and said he must get home. Once again Neumann accompanied him to the door, shook hands with him and, just as James went through the door, said quietly, 'Pieter, keep in touch. Maybe you could help us. You've told us that your sympathies lie with your mother's country, with our country. Is that correct?' James nodded. 'So, if you come across any useful information, would you be prepared to pass it on, for Germany's sake?'

'What sort of information?'

'Anything that you think might be useful to our cause.'

James paused as if giving the question proper consideration. 'Yes, I would. My loyalties lie with my mother and therefore with Germany.' Neumann's shovel of a hand grasped his again and wrung it painfully.

As James was halfway through the door Neumann said, 'By the way, what's your father called?'

'Joyce, like that Irish writer. Arthur Joyce.'

* * *

Later on the following day, 26 July, Erskine Childers landed 900 obsolete Mauser rifles and 29,000 rounds of ammunition at Howth Harbour, just north of Dublin, and put them in the hands of the Irish Volunteers.

The author of the celebrated spy novel, 'The Riddle of the Sands', had at last become the real-life man of action that he had always wanted to be.

With his wife, Molly, and a sympathiser called Mary Spring-Rice, he had sailed his 28-ton yacht, *Asgard*, from Cowes to the mouth of the River Scheldt in order to take delivery of the armaments from a German supplier. On the way back he had negotiated one of the worst storms for decades and had then contrived to sail through the British Fleet, which was being reviewed by King George V off Spithead.

Childers, though a pillar of the Establishment, was a staunch supporter of the idea of a free and united Ireland. His gun-running was a largely symbolic gesture of support in the face of the chilling intransigence of the Ulster Volunteer Force. That body, in contrast, had imported 25,000 rifles and three million rounds of ammunition just a few months previously.

10

Towards the end of July, the deteriorating diplomatic situation prompted another meeting in the Cabinet Room at 10 Downing Street. The same five men, who had recently discussed Britain's military requirements if a war with Germany began, were present, and their demeanours were even more sombre than on the previous occasion.

Prime Minister Asquith spoke quietly, 'I think that we can predict that a state of war will soon exist between Austria and Serbia, and we have had reports from our ambassador in St Petersburg that the Russians are beginning to mobilise their army.'

'And the Russian foreign minister, Sazanov, has made it clear that he thinks a European war is inevitable,' added Lloyd George.

'We can still avoid that by vigorous diplomatic pressure,' Sir Edward Grey insisted.

'I fear that I don't have Sir Edward's profound faith in diplomacy,' said Churchill, who was prowling about the room, an unlit cigar in his hand.

'Like Sazanov, I think a war involving all the great European powers is only a matter of days away. We must gather what forces we have and set about raising a huge army of recruits to fight the German foe wherever we might find him.'

There was silence for a few moments and then Grey said, 'Nevertheless, we must continue our efforts to prevent a minor blaze being fanned into an all-consuming conflagration.'

The Prime Minister grunted. 'To quote Baden-Powell, we must be prepared, and at present we are not. I recall that Lord Kitchener, at our meeting just a couple of weeks ago, estimated that we need at least half a million men now and another two million within a few months. Is that right, Kitchener?'

The renowned soldier nodded. 'And, as we agreed at that meeting, we need men who are fit and strong, not the sweepings of the gutters of London and Manchester.'

'We should make the young men who play sport one of our main targets,' Lloyd George said. 'In general they are fit and strong. And football is easily our most popular game, there are hundreds of thousands of footballers throughout Britain, so we must set about recruiting them.'

'How?' Asquith asked. 'Who can help us to accomplish that?'

'The Football Association is supposed to be in charge of the game,' Lloyd George replied. 'Whoever runs that body can confirm the numbers we are dealing with, and, perhaps, how to obtain their support.'

'To whom do we address our questions?' The Prime Minister asked impatiently.

'Is it Kinnaird?' Grey said hesitantly.

'Yes, that's the man,' said Churchill, waving his cigar, which was now alight. 'Crusty fellow, a fine footballer in his time, he would help us.'

'Charles Fry?' Asquith said. 'Would he be useful?'

'Yes,' Lloyd George replied, 'he has his feet in many sporting camps. Cricket, football, athletics…'

'But how do we persuade as many of these footballers as possible to volunteer?' Asquith persisted.

'Perhaps Northcliffe would be of value,' Churchill suggested. 'After all, he owns *The Times* and *The Daily Mail* and he certainly understands how publicity can be used to great effect.'

'He's a mountebank, he's not to be trusted,' Lloyd George said angrily. 'What was his nickname at school? Dodger, I think he was called. I could think of many more appropriate names for him.'

Churchill was well aware of the ill-feeling that existed between the two men. Northcliffe had once referred to Lloyd George as 'oblique, evasive and Welsh' and the comment had, as intended, travelled back quickly to the Welshman. 'That may be so,'

Churchill said, 'but in time of war we have to use all the talents we have at our disposal. Would you not agree, Prime Minister?'

'I would, and in view of the Chancellor's antipathy towards Northcliffe, perhaps you would make the initial approach, both to him and Lord Kinnaird.'

'With pleasure, Prime Minister.'

* * *

At about the same time that Prime Minister Asquith was concluding his meeting, James Clifton left the Foreign Office. It was shortly before one o'clock and he was surprised to hear a commotion coming from Downing Street, normally sedate amid the comings and goings of government ministers and civil servants.

Curious about the cause of the disturbance, James went into the famous street and saw a crowd of people milling about in front of Number 10; they seemed to him to be just short of erupting into violence. On the one hand there was a formation of about twenty policeman, who were there to protect the Prime Minister's house; and on the other there was a gathering of at least a hundred women, many of them brandishing 'votes for women' banners, and all of them chanting suffragette slogans. At their head James could see the frail but indomitable figure of Emmeline Pankhurst.

He noticed that the demonstrators were well-dressed and their voices, as they shouted 'Asquith the coward' and 'Where are our votes?' were clear and refined. The suffragettes came predominantly from the middle classes, as personified by Mrs Pankhurst and her daughters, one of whom had earned a first class degree at Oxford University. Although there was plenty of support for the cause among working women, their menfolk, many of whom were also disenfranchised, did not share their enthusiasm.

James paused to see how this confrontation would develop. The British did not usually go in for demonstrations and riots; that sort of nonsense was for the Frogs and other foreigners. But the shrill shouts of the suffragettes grew louder as the door to Number 10 opened inwards; perhaps they thought that Mr Asquith was about to appear and would address them from the steps of his official home. But it was another policeman. The profusion of braid on his uniform and hat proclaimed a senior officer. The women's cries turned into genteel jeers of disappointment.

As he scanned the crowd, James recognised a familiar profile. Emily Hildreth was brandishing a banner vigorously and was ten yards away from him, but nearer to the entrance to Number 10. Just as James tried to push his way through the crowd towards her, the senior police officer gave an order to his men and they marched suddenly and with great determination into the suffragettes' ranks to force them away from the Prime Minister's door. Their tactics were simple: to use their superior strength to herd the women out of Downing Street. If the suffragettes were trampled on, so much the better, but their most potent weapons were their rolled-up capes. James heard their resounding thuds as they met tender female bodies, and the resultant screams of pain.

Anxiously he looked around for Emily and just glimpsed her head as it disappeared when she and several of her nearest companions yielded to the charge of two sturdy policemen. As he saw their capes rise and fall, he yelled Emily's name and then thrust himself into the crowd towards her. Emily was on all fours and struggling to rise to her feet as one of the men, his sweating face contorted with effort, brought his rolled-up cape down on to her back with a sickening thwack. James did not hesitate, but raced past Emily and put his shoulder hard into the man's chest. It was his first tackle of the approaching football season and, later, he thought it would remain one of his fiercest, even if it was an illegal one according to the rules of Association Football. The policeman landed on his back several feet away and lay there, bemused, as James grabbed Emily around the waist and hauled her to her feet.

'Come on,' he shouted in her ear, 'time to go.'

They pushed their way through the melée and to her credit Emily lifted up her skirts and made a creditable effort at a sprint towards Whitehall. As they rounded the corner, James slowed them both to a walk. 'Are you all right?' he asked. 'No broken bones?'

'No, thank you, James.'

'Shall I take you to a hospital? That miserable bully must've hurt you.'

'Don't be ridiculous. I'm a young woman, not a china doll.' He noticed, however, that she was wincing as she walked. He questioned her again.

'Don't fuss, it's just a bruise. A hot bath and I'll be as good as new.'

He was far from convinced, but suggested that they had lunch together and they agreed to go to the Lyons Corner House in Coventry Street. Emily insisted on walking, arguing that it would do her good.

They were soon seated at a corner table in the second-floor restaurant and a neatly dressed waitress took their order almost immediately: chicken and barley soup for Emily and lamb chops with all the trimmings for James. In the far corner a small orchestra was playing tunes from *Hullo Ragtime.*

Emily was shifting uncomfortably in her seat and, when the food arrived, James asked the waitress for a cushion. She was back with one within seconds and, in a motherly fashion, tucked it behind Emily's back. 'There, that's better, love,' she said with a smile.

Emily thought she was about to burst into tears at this little act of kindness and covered her confusion by retrieving her handkerchief from the sleeve of her dress and dabbing at her nose and eyes.

James saw her hands tremble and the tears start in her eyes. He looked away and thought how even Emily, who appeared to be so strong, could be affected by unanticipated violence. 'A little delayed shock,' he suggested.

'It's nothing.'

'Should you expose yourself like this? I saw the look on that policeman's face, he was really enjoying himself.'

'No doubt he was. But we mustn't give up our right to demonstrate peacefully for our cause.'

'I know, Emily, but the extremists haven't helped your cause. Setting fire to letter-boxes, breaking windows, heavens above, some lunatic put a bomb in Lloyd George's house. What if he and his family had been there?'

'Perhaps the lunatic, as you call her, knew that he and his family would not be there, James.'

'It's still lunacy. And the woman who slashed the Rokeby Venus. It's sacrilege to damage a great work of art like that.'

'It's sacrilege to prevent women from taking part in the government of their country, isn't it?'

'Yes, you are undoubtedly right, but it will change. Now we have other bigger problems.'

'That's what Asquith's been saying since 1906.'

'Well, this time he's right. We'll probably be at war within a week or two.'

'And are you prepared to die for your country, James?'

'If I must.'

'Well, if you must be a hero, I want you to marry me before you go to war.'

James experienced a few moments when everything around him went still and his mind seemed mercifully clear of all extraneous thoughts. He came to, gulped and said, 'Am *I* not supposed to propose to *you*? Preferably on bended knee, in the moonlight.'

He became aware that the middle-aged couple at the adjacent table were staring at them and unashamedly listening to every word.

'So what is your answer, James?' Emily's gaze, her expression and soft smile made it very clear that her question was serious.

11

At 6pm on 28 July, 1914, the Austrians declared war on Serbia. On the following evening, Arthur Dickson had convened a meeting of just a few of the Corinthians who were to sail for Brazil in two days' time. His purpose was to go over some of the final details of the trip and four of the players had gathered at Dickson's Chiswick house. They sat in his large and ornately furnished sitting-room, whose wide windows gave agreeable views of the Thames. His butler was in attendance to keep their glasses of wine and beer well-charged.

The chairman began by brandishing a letter at his guests. 'I've had this letter, bloody odd, not to say presumptuous, from Winston Churchill of all people. He wants the Corinthians to play a special game against one of the professional sides. Blackburn Rovers, he suggests, since they're the First Division champions.'

'I didn't know that Churchill had any interest in football,' Rupert Wavell said, in his languid voice. 'So why has he suggested this?'

'He thinks it will help to recruit people for the army. What a bizarre idea. He says that a major conflict with Germany is imminent and that we need millions of men to volunteer.'

'Excitable bugger, Churchill,' Wavell murmured. 'Half-American, of course.'

'Quite. Anyway he wants fit young men for the cause. He says that Lord Kinnaird, chairman of the Football Association, has recommended that we participate.' Dickson paused and drank deeply from his glass. 'Kinnaird's a decent fellow, but I don't give two damns for his so-called recommendations, and that's that.'

'We've played many professional sides in the past,' objected Anthony Loxley. 'So what's the problem? I would be delighted to play against Blackburn.'

'The problem, Anthony, is that we represent the Corinthian Football Club and it is a completely independent amateur body. We and we alone decide where, when and against whom we'll play. And we already have quite a full fixture list, apart from our jaunt to Brazil.'

'But can we reject an approach from a minister of the crown?' asked Wavell. 'Churchill is an important man.'

'Self-important, like most of these damned politicians. He talks about involving Northcliffe and his newspapers in this game. Ridiculous. Oh, by the way, it might be two games, one in London and one up there. In my view, it's a lot of nonsense and, if you agree, I'll pour cold water on the idea.' With hardly a pause, he continued. 'Fine, that's settled then. Now, let's get on with more important matters, details of our games in Brazil.'

* * *

Two hundred miles away and a day later, the reaction of the chairman of Blackburn Rovers Football Club to Winston Churchill's letter was rather different. When Ken Bradshaw opened the letter with its House of Commons crest, he assumed that Blackburn's Member of Parliament was on the scrounge yet again for some complimentary tickets for the forthcoming season. He was taken aback when he saw Churchill's signature at the foot of the letter. He greatly admired the man and, when the Liberal Party had won the election of 1906, he had been one of the huge crowd which had acclaimed Churchill as he spoke from the first floor balcony of the Reform Club in the centre of Manchester.

Ken Bradshaw had started a bakery thirty years before and it had become the dominant supplier of bread, cakes, and meat and potato pies in the Blackburn area. He had always loved the game of football and it had been his proudest moment when he was offered some shares in his local club and been asked to join its board of directors. Eventually, his ultimate ambition was realised when he became chairman of his beloved Rovers; he had to admit that it was good for business, too. Above all, when Blackburn won the First Division Championship twice in the three years from 1911 to 1914, he felt vindicated for the time, energy and, not least, the money he had poured into the club.

Bradshaw was well aware of the Corinthians' reputation. They were the aristocrats of the game and played flowing, attacking football. Even if the club had lost a little of its lustre in the past decade, owing to a dispute with the Football Association, that quarrel had now been resolved, and Bradshaw knew that the amateur club was still a great attraction. They brought the crowds into the football grounds and that meant revenue for whichever professional club was opposing them. In addition, the two matches proposed by Churchill would be useful practice games for Blackburn before the new season began in earnest in the first week of September.

He knew that the extra gate money would persuade the board of directors to approve the games. He was also aware that the players would not raise any objections; they were the club's employees, just like the men who worked in the local industries, the difference being that a footballer earned a good deal more than the pittances paid to factory hands. However, there was one member of the team to whom Bradshaw had to speak.

Bob Crompton was not only Blackburn's finest player, but was regarded as one of England's most accomplished footballers. A tall, strong and mobile full-back, Crompton was scrupulously fair on the field of play and was a model for every footballer in the land. Such was his reputation that he had been the first professional to captain England.

Bradshaw understood that both good manners and commonsense decreed that he should consult Crompton about Churchill's proposal. His captain lived with his growing family on the northern edge of the town and Bradshaw knew that it was his habit to have a quiet pint of ale in the early evening. At six o'clock, he took one of the delivery vans from the bakery yard and arrived at the Oddfellows Arms at Mellor half an hour later.

As he went through the narrow doorway into the low-ceilinged public house, he saw the celebrated footballer sitting at a corner of the bar. As always, Crompton was smartly dressed; he was wearing a dark, tweed suit, and had a pint of beer on the counter before him and an unlit pipe clenched in his hand.

Crompton stood up as he saw his chairman approaching and Bradshaw registered anew the man's height and size; it seemed remarkable that such a man could move so quickly on the field, and with such balance and control.

'Mister Chairman, a pleasure to see you in these parts. You'll take a drink?'

'Aye, a pint, thanks, same as yours, Bob.'

Crompton nodded to the landlord, who pulled up a pint of Thwaites's best ale.

'You're looking right fit, Bob.'

'Aye, I feel good and strong. Lots of walking with the dogs and a bit of cricket with the village team. They're a grand bunch of lads.'

Bradshaw supped hard at his glass and pointed to a table in a quiet corner of the bar. 'I need to talk to you in confidence, Bob. Let's sit down.'

'Nothing amiss, I hope, Mister Chairman.'

'Not at all.'

When they were seated, Bradshaw gave the letter to Crompton, who read it quickly and then read it again, more slowly. 'I didn't think this bit of bother in Serbia, or wherever it is, was anything to do with us. If the politicians are that worried, well...'

'We'll have to wait and see, as Mister Asquith is fond of saying, but what d'you think of Churchill's idea?'

'All in favour. The Corinthians can put out a fine team. Just the job to give us some practice before September. And the lads'll love a trip to London. We can have a night out, maybe see Marie Lloyd or George Robey.'

'Aye, good, but keep it under your hat, Bob. I'll reply in the affirmative to Mister Churchill.' Bradshaw felt rather pleased with his last phrase and smiled broadly.

Bob Crompton grinned in his turn, finished his pint and said, 'That's my quota, Mister Chairman. I'm for home now.'

They bade goodnight to the landlord and strolled outside. Bradshaw gestured towards his van and offered Crompton a lift home. But Crompton pointed at a small and obviously new saloon car, which was parked on the other side of the road. 'I've bought myself a car. Two weeks ago. Paid cash, you know me, I won't be beholden to anybody.'

Bradshaw knew that his captain was careful with his money and that in addition to his wages, he earned significant sums of money to attend certain dinners on behalf of local manufacturers, or to be seen at the openings of shops and offices. He was also a partner in a thriving plumbing business in the locality.

Nevertheless, he paused for a moment in surprise and then touched Crompton briefly on the arm. 'Good on you, lad, you deserve it.'

'It's a Ford. I picked it up from the dealer and talked to the lads in the workshop, so they gave me a nice discount.'

'And so they should've. I'd be prepared to have a very big bet, Bob, that you're the first professional footballer to own a car.'

* * *

When James arrived at his rooms that evening he found several letters waiting for him and he recognised Emily's firm and rounded hand on one of the envelopes. He was still both confused and elated by what she had said to him at the end of their lunch together, but was almost glad that the looming crisis meant that he didn't have time to dwell on her spontaneous proposal of marriage. On the other hand, although he had managed to avoid giving her an answer, he knew what that answer ought to be.

He walked quickly into his living room, deposited the other letters on a table and tore open Emily's letter.

'My dear James,' it read. 'First of all, I want to thank you for rescuing me from danger today. Some benevolent higher power must have glanced my way and ensured that you were there to be my knight in shining armour. Thank you, also, for letting me recover my wits over luncheon with you. Well, almost recover my wits, since I am keenly aware that I embarrassed you dreadfully with my outlandish proposal at the end of our meal together. I can only assume that I was still in a state of shock. Please forgive me. Needless to say, my proposal was not to be taken seriously and please, James, let it remain a secret between us and us alone. Yours sincerely and with great affection, Emily.'

James sat in his chair without moving for some minutes. The mild state of euphoria, which had affected him for the last few hours, had suddenly left him. He rarely drank alcohol alone, but now he went to a corner cabinet, poured a generous measure of whisky into a glass and quaffed at least half of it in one gulp. He was the base Indian, he thought melodramatically, who threw a pearl away, richer than all his tribe.

12

The Corinthians' party was due to leave for Brazil on Saturday, 1 August. Fifteen players, the chairman, Arthur Dickson, and two other members of the committee were booked on the boat train to Southampton and from there on the SS *Asturias* to Rio de Janeiro, with various stops along the way, the first being at Lisbon.

By six o'clock on the previous evening Rupert Wavell had done all his packing. He was looking forward to the trip, even if the long sea voyage would tax his patience. He was easily bored, but the agreeable company would be a consolation. His one regret, as with some of the other Corinthians, was that he would miss the racing at Glorious Goodwood.

Wavell had agreed to have dinner with his parents on his final evening in London. They had a house in Berkeley Square and he lived nearby in Mount Street, so the Ritz Hotel was an obvious choice. The food and service were exceptional as always and Wavell was able to bask in his mother's admiration and his father's clear if more guarded approval.

Rupert had been a late and unexpected addition to Frances Wavell's family; she thought she had more than done her duty to her husband by giving birth to two sons and two daughters, and another child in her mid-thirties was not entirely welcome. However, her qualms during pregnancy had soon been replaced by pride in producing such a beautiful baby, who became a charming and handsome youth and then a dashing young man. His winning ways ensured he was deluged with invitations to all manner of social occasions. In addition, he was a fine sportsman and, by courtesy of his father's financial acumen, he was rich. Showered with all these gifts, he was indulged by almost everyone he met and outlandishly spoiled by his mother, who considered that he could do no wrong.

Frances Wavell's faith in her son had never wavered. When he had been accused of stealing some money from another pupil during his final year at school, she had rushed to his side. Even though Rupert's headmaster had failed to be impressed by Mrs Wavell's arrival in a chauffeur-driven Rolls-Royce, he had succumbed to her stately beauty, her dignity and eventually to her impassioned defence of her son's reputation. A donation of one hundred pounds to the school's Appeal Fund had also helped.

A couple of years later, Mrs Wavell had again flown to her son's defence when a chambermaid at their Sussex estate had complained of being forced to do certain unspecified sexual acts with Rupert. The girl had bruises on her face and body, but the housekeeper had reported to Mrs Wavell that the wench's father was a notoriously violent man, especially after a Saturday evening spent in the village pub, where he could be counted upon to down a dozen pints of Harvey's Sussex Ale. Mrs Wavell knew that the girl was lying and sent her packing, though with five pounds tucked away in her pocket.

At around eleven o'clock Rupert Wavell made his excuses to his parents and left the Ritz, ostensibly to go home to bed. He strode across Piccadilly, down Berkeley Street, hailed a taxi on the corner of Hay Hill, and directed the cabbie to drive him to Farringdon Road. Over the years Rupert had become interested in a variety of sexual activities which would have dismayed his adoring mother. Most of all he liked to inflict pain and, if sexual sadism was his main preoccupation, he didn't mind an occasional dalliance with a deformed woman; a whore with a limp or a withered arm was interesting, but one with a leg-iron or a missing limb was even better.

The West End prostitutes rarely offered him what he really desired and, with the prospect of a tedious sea voyage ahead of him, Wavell wanted something special on his final evening in London. Clerkenwell was one of his hunting grounds and he knew of a brothel in a tenement building on the corner of Shoe Lane and Plum Tree Court. He had visited it once before with one of his cousins, who was in the wine business in Bordeaux and had been on a sales trip to London. Several of the girls had offered 'correctional training' and Wavell had experienced a modestly stimulating evening with one of them.

Having been admitted to the brothel by the scraggy, grey-haired woman who was its 'madam', he found four women available for business in the dingy sitting-room. He picked a rangy, full-busted woman with long black hair; she was dressed in a tight-fitting blue dress and, after he had paid his money to the madam, she led him to a room at the back of the flat. In the light of the wavering gas lantern Wavell could just see a bed with a sheet and a grey blanket and a table with a cane, a set of handcuffs and some ropes on it. Submissive sex had never appealed to Wavell. He liked to be the aggressor and he didn't need any artificial aids in order to inflict pain; his own hands were more than adequate to the task.

He spent a pleasurable forty minutes or so with the girl, who turned out to be strong and willing, even if he had to muffle her squeals once or twice. If pressed, he would have admitted to being over-enthusiastic at times, but he left a generous tip on the bed, where the girl, curled up in a foetal position, was groaning and sobbing.

After midnight Wavell left the tenement in a hurry and scuttled along Farringdon Street towards Ludgate Circus, where he found a taxi to take him home to Mount Street. He could smell his own sweat and the whore's cheap scent on his body. He felt a great depression settle over him. But he knew that it would soon pass, and he also knew that he would visit the same brothel on his return from Brazil.

* * *

On the following day, by the time that the SS *Asturias* had set sail for Brazil, Germany had declared war on Russia.

13

During the next three days the rulers, politicians and diplomats of the major European nations contrived to totter towards the brink of an all-out war and, without too much reflection, drag each other into the abyss of the most destructive conflict in history.

On Sunday, 2 August, while Britain was promising naval protection to France if she were attacked by the German fleet, an anti-war demonstration took place in Trafalgar Square and was attended by thousands of people. Several Socialist luminaries addressed the crowd, including Keir Hardie, Arthur Henderson, Ben Tillett and Cunningham Grahame. A casual spectator might have thought that some much-needed caution about the dangers of a European war was at last being shown; Emily Hildreth and Mrs Clifton certainly thought so and were there with a number of other suffragettes. However, there were plenty of people in the crowd who were not only opposed to Socialism, but were also in favour of a war against Germany. As *The Times* reported: 'The singing of the *Red Flag* was answered with the strains of *God Save the King* and *Rule Britannia*… The next incident was the hoisting of a red flag in the crowd. The rejoinder came at once. A Union Jack was waved and the cheering and singing of patriotic songs grew louder than ever.'

* * *

The following day was the Summer Bank Holiday and Belgium had refused to allow the Germans to tramp across their territory in order to invade France. Germany declared war on France anyway, and the British government delivered an ultimatum to Germany. It would expire at midnight.

Throughout the Bank Holiday, in anticipation of a declaration of war against Germany, great crowds had gathered during the afternoon and evening in Trafalgar Square, Whitehall, Parliament Square and outside Buckingham Palace, on whose balcony the King and Queen, together with the Prince of Wales and Princess Mary, appeared on several occasions to great acclaim. *The Times* commented that 'the cheering and singing which had marked the earlier hours of the evening died away as the hour approached at which the British demand must be answered by Germany. A profound silence fell upon the crowd just before midnight. Then as the first strokes rang out from the Clock Tower, a vast cheer burst out and echoed and re-echoed for nearly 20 minutes. The National Anthem was then sung with an emotion and solemnity which manifested the gravity and sense of responsibility with which the people regard the great issues before them.'

* * *

At the Oval, Jack Hobbs scored 226 runs for Surrey in his benefit match against Kent and, on the following day, the Army commandeered the Oval and the game was transferred to Lord's.

* * *

Many people did not share the enthusiasm for war shown by the crowds in London. For instance, Sir Edward Grey stared out of his window in the Foreign Office as the long summer day turned to dusk. J A Spender of the *Westminster Gazette* stood by his side as Grey said despondently, 'The lamps are going out all over Europe. We shall not see them lit again in our time.'

* * *

En route to Brazil, the SS *Asturias* had reached Lisbon on the very day that the war began. Most of the Corinthian party had left the ship to stretch their legs and explore the city. When they returned, the captain read out the contents of a telegraph received from his company in London. Since a state of war existed with Germany, the ship was to return to Southampton 'with all despatch'.

* * *

Prime Minister Asquith had been acting as the Minister for War and he persuaded Lord Kitchener to undertake that onerous task. The machinery of war began slowly to grind into motion.

By the weekend the SS *Asturias* had returned, unharmed, to Britain and the Corinthians of military age were making plans to volunteer for various branches of the army and navy; most of them had long-standing family connections with specific regiments. However, their plans to enter the fray as quickly as possible were to be frustrated.

14

Amid the frenzied activity which overtook the nation as it prepared for a major war against a powerful foe, there was one overwhelming imperative. Fighting men. As Kitchener had emphasised time and time again to Asquith and his colleagues in the Cabinet, there was an immediate need for half a million men to fight in France and a long-term requirement of four times that number.

As well as producing a snowstorm of posters to urge the men of Britain to volunteer, Kitchener seized enthusiastically on the idea of making special targets of sports clubs, and he had not forgotten the idea of staging two great matches between the English champions, Blackburn Rovers, and the celebrated amateurs, the Corinthians.

In one of their many meetings, the War Minister had asked Winston Churchill what had been the responses of the respective chairmen to the idea.

'Whole-hearted support from Blackburn and a very unsatisfactory reaction from the Corinthian fellow. Some pompous stuff about the amateur spirit, their independence and so on.'

'We're at war now, Winston,' Lloyd George said, 'so we can compel the Corinthians to turn out. We simply play the patriotism card.'

'Nevertheless, we need their genuine co-operation,' said Kitchener.

'And I'm sure we'll get it,' Churchill replied, 'if we present the idea to them in the right way. After all, they're some of our finest young men, who will no doubt be among the first to volunteer.'

'But we don't want that,' Lloyd George said quickly. 'We don't want them scattered among various army regiments. We want them available as part of our recruiting campaign. They'll do more good here in England than getting their heads blown off in France.'

'Perhaps we won't put it quite like that,' Kitchener said drily. 'We'll tell them that they're being held in reserve for important war work.'

'They won't like it,' Churchill said.

'They'll have time a-plenty to be heroes,' Kitchener said grimly. 'Let's get that chairman of theirs in here, at the War Office, as soon as possible and ask him to nominate the best possible Corinthian team.'

'When should we aim to hold these games and where?' asked Lloyd George.

'Let's ask this fellow Dickson,' Churchill said. 'But certainly within the next week or two. We'll ask Lord Kinnaird along, since he's the Football Association chairman. And we need plenty of publicity, that is the key.'

'I know what you're going to say, Winston,' Lloyd George said resignedly.

Churchill smiled. 'So, say it for me.'

'I suppose you'll want that bloody man, Northcliffe, to be involved.'

'Yes, of course. He has a powerful drum to beat. He can advance our cause, both through *The Times* and even more so through *The Daily Mail*.'

'So, he'll bring the crowds along,' Kitchener summed up. 'What about Bottomley? He has his magazine, *John Bull*, and he also has the common touch.'

'Yes, the man certainly has the latter,' Churchill agreed. 'There's something in him that appeals to people. He's a confidence trickster, a demagogue, but he has talents that the country can and must use.'

'They're a pretty pair of villains,' Lloyd George said with a grimace. 'One unprincipled newspaper proprietor and one fraudster.'

'It takes all sorts to win a war,' Churchill said, 'and win it we must. We can only hope and pray that the British nation will surge forward yet again with its traditional valour.'

'Let's hope enough of them turn up,' Kitchener said grimly.

* * *

Arthur Dickson was pleased to be summoned to the War Office in Parliament Street, even if the letter stressed that his presence was 'a matter of national importance pertaining to the participation of the Corinthian Football Club in matches to facilitate the recruitment of men to the armed services'.

The letter was signed by Lord Kitchener, but when Dickson arrived in Westminster he found that the meeting was chaired, not by the great warrior, but by an under-secretary, whatever that meant, called John Tippett. He was slightly reassured when Tippett, who appeared to be in his middle-forties, revealed that his uncle had played for the Wanderers in the 1880s. The celebrated amateur club had won the F A Cup six times in the first nine years of its existence.

Lord Kinnaird, a bulky man with a luxuriant beard, made his entrance a few minutes after Dickson, who knew him well and did not entirely trust him. When a pot of tea and a plate of biscuits had been delivered, Tippett explained how three of Britain's most eminent men, Lord Kitchener, David Lloyd George and Winston Churchill had, with the approval of the Prime Minister, arrived at the idea of using sport and especially football as a means of recruitment.

Tippett emphasised Kitchener's opinion that the army was woefully short of men and said, 'As you are both aware, football is by far our most popular sport nowadays and we must put our message across to its enthusiasts. Strongly. As Mister Lloyd George put it, a more important game has kicked off and we need the support of all footballers and those who support the game.'

'You need have no doubts about the members of our club,' Dickson said frostily. 'Most of them have already volunteered.'

Not to be outdone, Lord Kinnaird stressed that the same applied to the Old Etonians.

'That's highly commendable,' Tippett replied. 'However, we must hold the Corinthians back from active service for the moment.'

'I'm not sure that's advisable,' Dickson said, 'I know that some of them have already arranged to join their regiments. They have brothers and friends who await their arrival and they won't take kindly to being prevented from doing their duty.'

Tippett spoke soothingly, 'They will be doing a much greater service for their country if they help Lord Kitchener by playing a crucial role in the recruitment campaign. These two games with Blackburn are very important in our efforts to recruit soldiers.'

'Surely most able-bodied men will flock to the colours,' said Kinnaird.

'Not necessarily. Remember that our army has always been a volunteer army and the wars it's been called upon to fight have been on a relatively small scale. We've never had to put two, three, or even four million men into the field.'

The two men looked in amazement at the under-secretary. 'Four million men,' Kinnaird said. 'God help us. What sort of a war are we envisaging? I thought this would be a quick skirmish, that we'd teach the Hun a short, sharp lesson and that would be that.'

'Lord Kitchener thinks that we face a long and attritional war. The fire-power on both sides is formidable. A modern division can fire well over a hundred thousand rounds a minute as well as a thousand shells. There are two hundred divisions of troops in Europe at the moment.'

'Carnage,' Dickson said quietly.

'Yes, unless we and the French break through the German lines quickly and force them back to their borders.'

Tippett's two visitors sat in silence and the civil servant seized his chance. 'Mister Dickson, if you will give me the names and addresses of those Corinthians whom you wish to play in these games, eleven of them plus some reserves in case of injury, we will track them down.'

'I'll give you a letter from the club for each of them.'

'Excellent, we'll deliver them by messenger.'

Dickson nodded. 'When do you intend to play the games?'

'Soon, though we need some time to ensure that as many people as possible know about them.'

'I can send out a special newsletter to all our members,' Dickson offered.

Tippett suppressed a smile. 'That would be helpful, but we will have the invaluable help of Lord Northcliffe and he will publicise the matches through his newspapers. With his support we can fill both grounds. As for dates, let's see.' He consulted a calendar on his desk. 'The first game here in London on the last Saturday in August perhaps. The twenty-ninth. And the second on the following Saturday.'

Kinnaird interrupted. 'I think that we should have the first match in Blackburn, not here. In my view, and without being patronising, the really important match will be down here in London. Would you agree, Dickson?'

'Yes, wholeheartedly. And at least we've got a little time, so that our chaps can prepare properly,' Dickson said. 'They can do some long walks and kick a ball about. I just hope they won't be accused of shirking their duty.'

'On the contrary, Lord Northcliffe's papers will present them as heroes,' Tippett assured him.

Kinnaird grunted. 'I don't suppose they'll want too much of that nonsense, will they, Dickson? Time enough to talk of heroes when the guns are firing. Now, where shall we stage these matches? The Oval? Chelsea?'

'We thought at Crystal Palace, since it can cope with over a hundred thousand spectators.'

'And at the Rovers' ground?' Dickson asked.

'No, at Manchester United's new ground. It holds more people than Ewood Park.'

Dickson made the point that the Blackburn players would, like the Corinthians, have to be prevented from volunteering for the army, but Kinnaird told him that professional footballers were under contract to their clubs and were bound to play through the season which was about to begin.

'I can foresee a lot of criticism coming your way, Lord Kinnaird, when the casualties begin to mount up in France. Can you imagine how a family will react when they lose a father, a son or a brother and they see a fit young footballer, one who lives down the street perhaps, and he doesn't have to volunteer?'

'That's a problem we'll face when we have to,' Kinnaird responded brusquely.

15

The Corinthians selected to play in the matches against Blackburn Rovers reacted in their different ways; some with mild irritation that their initial military training was to be interrupted and some with relief. James was elated that he was to be a member of such a strong team and he looked forward with relish to playing at two famous grounds in front of huge crowds. He arranged a celebratory meal with his parents at Rules in Maiden Lane.

To both his and his father's discomfiture, his mother questioned him closely about his Foreign Office work and whether it would preclude him from volunteering for army service. She obviously hoped so and he made some vague remarks about acting as a liaison official with the War Office.

She seemed happy that he wasn't going to be on the next troop ship bound for France and when she went off to the ladies' cloakroom his father asked him if his work for Vernon Kell was going well.

Very quietly James described some of the work he had done so far in making contact with the Germans who were under suspicion and trying to gain their confidence. He concluded: 'No scrapes yet, Father. It's gone quite well, even if it's pretty low level stuff. However, I'll be giving the targets some bits and pieces about shipping movements tomorrow evening.'

'Kell and his merry men are watching over you, I hope?' James nodded. 'Nevertheless, be careful, my boy.'

'Be careful about what?' asked Mrs Clifton as she approached the table.

'With his training for these football games. Don't overdo it, James, you've had quite a break from strenuous exercise.'

'Oh, I'll be fine, we've got time to do some training in the park. And we're going to have a couple of practice games at Queen's Club.'

As they left Rules, his mother said, 'I had lunch with Emily the other day. She says you saved her skin outside Downing Street. It sounded rather dramatic.'

'Just a storm in a teacup, Mama.'

'And she assured me that the suffragettes were demonstrating quite peacefully.'

'They were indeed. The police were out for some sadistic fun.'

'All that suffragette stuff will have to cease now,' said Mr Clifton.

'Yes, as always the women of Britain will turn to and offer their support and succour to our men. 'Twas ever thus.' Her husband grunted audibly and she looked sharply at him before continuing. 'Emily's very fond of you, James, I can tell.'

'So you keep telling me, and, as you well know, I've always liked her.'

'Well, James, *carpe diem*,' his father said predictably.

'Now you're both match-making,' James said with a laugh. But he wondered what Emily had really told his mother, since he had a well-founded suspicion that women were much more open with each other than were men.

* * *

James arrived in Clerkenwell at just after 10 o'clock on Saturday night and the Green was inundated with revellers. Since the declaration of war, Londoners seemed to have been gripped by a mild form of hysteria. The urge to get drunker than usual was more apparent, undoubtedly to mask uneasy thoughts about their uncertain futures. The Northumberland Arms was jammed with drinkers and they had spilled out on to the area in front of the pub and the surrounding pavements. Many of them were already semi-comatose and would later make easy targets for pick-pockets and other more violent thieves. The customers from the pub around the corner, opposite St James's Church, added their weight to the chaos.

Careful to avoid the bodies sprawled on the ground and the occasional pools of vomit, James headed for the Jerusalem Tavern. Earlier he had noticed a small, thin man, who, despite the sultriness of the evening, was wearing a grey raincoat. He had been on the bus and as James turned into Britton Street, he noticed him again. The man was about twenty yards behind, so James ducked into an alley just before the tavern and waited. The man hurried by and James watched as he broke into a half-run and then stopped to peer down the next street on the left. He decided to tease him a little and, as the man looked back, James walked out of the alley and into the Jerusalem Tavern.

It was even more crowded than on his last visit and the noise was deafening. After buying a pint of ale, he managed with difficulty to wedge himself into a corner between the bar and the back room, which was full to capacity. James kept his eyes on the pub doors, but his pursuer did not appear and he wondered if his imagination was overtaking his common-sense. A few large gulps saw his glass empty and he edged his way through the mob to the entrance, looked briefly at the doorways on the other side of the road and turned back the way he had come. Where Britton Street met Clerkenwell Road, he crossed over and returned down Britton Street on the opposite side, in the hope of again spotting his mysterious pursuer. If someone were watching him, he assumed it could only be one of Kurt Neumann's associates who had been sent to check him out. One of them had already enquired about him at the offices of Josiah Morris and the manager, Tom Belmont, had confirmed that he employed a Pieter Westermann, but that he was usually out and about dealing with customers, rather than in the office.

James walked on and saw no one resembling the man, but he decided to have a story ready if Neumann later asked him what he'd been doing in the vicinity of Sloane Street earlier that evening.

On entering the Old Vienna restaurant, he saw the same five men sitting in the same seats at the same table, but another man had joined them. Neumann waved him over, grabbed another chair and made room for him. The table was littered with beer bottles and there were also two half-empty bottles of schnapps. Martin Schmidt, who may or may not have been the owner, was in his accustomed position behind the makeshift bar.

'Pieter, sit here with me.' Neumann nodded towards the man at the other end of the table. 'Meet Herr Lody. Carl Lody. Like you, he works in the export business.' Neumann smiled briefly, pushed a bottle of beer towards James and poured him a glass of schnapps. James raised his glass in salute to Lody, who was a wiry man, with a thin and intelligent face. He was probably in his thirties.

Neumann looked expectantly at James. 'Have you anything of interest to tell us, Pieter?'

Maundy Gregory had given him several snippets about the movement of supply ships between London and Southampton and ports in northern France, such as Calais and Le Havre. As planned, it was low-grade information, any of which could be verified by a reasonably efficient group of spies.

James spoke quietly as he gave some of the details, and the little band of Germans huddled together around the table to hear him. It would have made an excellent tableau: ruthless foreign spies plotting against gallant Britain. His remarks about the supply ships were received without much comment, but when he mentioned the preparations being made to despatch three of the navy's super-dreadnoughts to the North Sea, Neumann and Lody questioned him in more detail. They wanted to know the date of their departure, their route and their ultimate destination; James had to assure them that he would do his best to uncover more details. He noticed that Lody led the questioning, rather than Neumann. The others deferred to him; he was clearly acknowledged to be their leader. He knew that Vernon Kell would want to know as much as possible about Lody.

As the meeting drew to its close amid some mildly social conversation, James asked Lody, as casually as he could, where he lived and offered to pass on any information he gathered directly to him.

'You don't need to talk to me, Pieter,' Lody said sharply. 'Just communicate with Kurt as usual, here at the restaurant.'

James nodded and they were all having one final glass of schnapps when the first brick crashed through the front window.

Like many big men, Neumann could move fast and decisively. He grabbed a bottle from the table and raced towards the door, shouting, 'Fischer, get Lody out of here.'

Fischer pulled Lody by the arm towards the back of the restaurant where Martin Schmidt already had the heavy door open; no doubt an escape route had been mapped out through the alleys at the rear of the building.

James stood shoulder to shoulder with Neumann at the front door, with the other three men behind them, just as some more bricks smashed through the windows. He felt something strike his cheek, brushed at it and saw that his fingers were coated with blood. There were about a dozen men outside, some carrying stones and others armed with lumps of wood and iron bars.

'Fuckin' German bastards,' shouted a squat, broad-shouldered man in the middle of the group. Neumann responded by hurling his bottle at him and scoring a glancing blow on his arm.

'Too many of them,' Neumann shouted, as he slammed the door shut and threw the bolt. 'Through the back, let's go.'

The first boots at once went into the door and the flimsy frame began to splinter. Two of the attackers were busy smashing their way through a window and one of them thrust his shoulders through the gap, fell into the room and lurched after them as they sped towards their escape route at the back of the restaurant.

James was the last of the fleeing men and he half-tripped on a chair as he followed Neumann. One of the men who had broken through the window was just behind him, swinging a wooden stave towards his head, but James stepped under and inside the blow, shoved the fingers of his left hand into the man's eyes and, as he dropped his weapon and staggered back, he crashed his forearm into the man's nose. He 'made it count', just as Staff Corporal Cowie had taught him. He felt the nose give way and his adversary screamed with pain and fell into the path of the man behind him. Neumann thrust James aside and hit the second man a crushing blow in the ribs and then kicked him in the groin.

'Come,' Neumann shouted and James needed no urging, as they leapt through the heavy door and Fischer slammed it behind them and locked it. He then led them into a tenement building and out at the other side; after some twists and turns along alleyways and through another building, they arrived in Cowcross Street.

'You look as if you've been in a war,' Neumann said to James. 'There's blood all over your face.'

As James reached for his handkerchief, he realised that much of the blood had probably spouted from his assailant's nose.

'OK, we split up. We'll meet somewhere else next week. I'll let you know.' Neumann clapped James on the shoulder. 'Where did you learn to fight, Pieter?'

'Where I grew up, you had to learn to fight,' he replied.

James decided to avoid any of the main streets and, keeping to the shadows as much as possible, shuffled warily towards Holborn. He had no wish to run into any more mobs on the look-out for trouble. On one corner a young boy, clad in ragged clothing, asked him for money. He was about to hurry by and then noticed how wretchedly thin the boy was; he stopped, scrabbled in his pocket and handed the waif some change. His feeling that he was being followed was now very marked, but he attributed it to the tensions of the preceding hour or so. He decided to ignore it and picked up his pace.

The young boy, unable to believe his luck, scampered around a corner and into the far-from-fond embrace of the man who had been shadowing James. The man dragged him a few yards along the street and into an alley. 'Don't be scared, son,' he said. 'Come with me and you can earn yourself a bit more money.'

James was now intent on leaving the neighbourhood and, as he hurried around another corner, he couldn't help but blunder into someone coming the other way at a similar speed.

'For God's sake, man, look what you're doing.' He knew the voice and that he himself had no chance of remaining unrecognised.

'What are you doing in this neck of the woods, Rupert?'

Rupert Wavell jumped back and instinctively raised his arms as if making ready to defend himself. He was still in a state of panic after another visit to his favoured Clerkenwell brothel, where he had paid for the same tall prostitute as before. All had gone well until he hit her with a particularly savage blow to the stomach and she had spat in his face and, screaming with rage, raked his neck with her nails.

He had lost his head and the details of what followed were hazy. He knew that he had beaten the woman senseless and, as recompense, had tucked a half-sovereign into her discarded dress. After thrusting some money into the madam's grimy hands, he told her to look after 'that strumpet', and rushed out of the brothel into the darkening street.

'Good Lord, it's you, Clifton,' he said with some relief. 'I might ask you the same question, and what on earth are you wearing? Are you running a market stall on the quiet?'

'The questions can wait. Let's pick up a taxi in Holborn. I need a stiff drink.'

James accepted Wavell's invitation to stop at his rooms in Mount Street and, as soon as they arrived, Wavell poured them large glasses of Armagnac.

'Before you settle down, James, why don't you wash that blood off your face. You look as though you've done ten rounds with Carpentier. And that lovely suit of yours will never be the same again, there's blood all over it.'

When James returned from the rather ornate bathroom, all marble and mirrors, he told Wavell that he'd been sent to make the first unofficial contact with some German emigrés, who claimed to have some valuable information for the British government. The matter was urgent and secret and he'd been chosen since his

German was fluent. 'That's all I'm allowed to tell you, Rupert, and it's strictly confidential.'

Wavell gestured at James's clothing. 'So, who advised you to dress up like a stock-jobber's runner?'

'Well, I could hardly go along to a place like Clerkenwell in a dark suit and a stiff collar, could I?'

'No, but what happened? It all went wrong, obviously.'

'We were attacked by a bunch of thugs. I ran for it, but I was hit by some flying glass,' James said truthfully as he took a long mouthful of Armagnac. 'What are your interests in Clerkenwell, Rupert? I thought you were more of a West End man.'

'Oh, I have a lady friend, who lives in Hatton Garden. I have to be discreet, you understand.'

That sounded like a rather spurious explanation to James and he looked questioningly at Wavell, whose shrug seemed to say 'I don't care whether you believe me or not'. As he leaned over the table to pour more Armagnac into their glasses, James noticed the livid marks on the left side of his neck and on his jaw; he could also see that Wavell's hand was puffy and bruised around the knuckles.

'You also look as though you've been in a scrap, Rupert. What are those marks on your face?'

'Well, strictly between you and me, James, my lady friend can get a little frisky.'

'And judging by the state of your right fist you fight back.'

Wavell made a great show of settling back in his armchair and smoothing his immaculate trousers before replying. 'Actually, James, that was when we were fooling about on board ship, trying to keep fit, trials of strength and so on, and I fell badly, that's all.'

James did not bother to ask any more questions, but finished his Armagnac and prepared to leave. As he stood up, Wavell looked at him closely and said, 'You'd better borrow one of my overcoats. You can't be seen in public in a blood-stained suit, even at this time of the night, or rather, least of all at this time of the night. Even the most dim-witted policeman would stop you on suspicion of being Jack the Ripper reincarnated.'

On the following morning, late editions of the popular newspapers carried reports of two murders in Clerkenwell. The 'bruised and battered' body of a 19-year-old woman had been found in the well of a tenement building off Britton Street, and the newspaper accounts made it clear that the victim was a 'common prostitute'. A half-sovereign had been found in the pocket of her dress, so the motive had not been the usual one of robbery.

The other death, which was more shocking to the readers, was that of a 12-year-old boy, who had been discovered in an unoccupied flat in Roseberry Square, Clerkenwell. According to the caretaker, whose suspicions had been aroused by the flat's open door, the boy's naked body showed dozens of stab wounds and his face was horribly mutilated. He was quoted as saying that 'he'd seen some terrible things in India, terrible, but nothing as bad as this. His own mother wouldn't recognise the poor little devil'.

* * *

On the same day, a car had arrived outside James's rooms and he had been taken to an emergency meeting at Watergate House, where, since it was a Sunday, few people were to be seen.

During James's account of the previous evening's events at the Old Vienna, Vernon Kell sat quietly, rolling a pencil gently to and fro on his desk and staring into the space beyond James's left shoulder with a slight frown on his face.

But he reacted sharply when Lody's name was mentioned. 'And you're sure the man's name was Lody?' James nodded. 'Carl Lody?' He nodded again. 'Describe him to me.'

'He's probably in his thirties. Quite thin, and he looks fit, athletic. One of those bright, intelligent faces. You wouldn't mind being next to him on a long train journey.'

Kell looked at Maundy Gregory, who was seated to James's left. 'We know quite a lot about him, don't we?'

'Yes, sir, he's used other names. He usually claims he's a Swiss, who sells watches, plus scientific instruments for some German manufacturers.'

'And he works under the direction of Steinhauer presumably?'

'Yes. Should we bring him in?'

'No, let's feed him more information and, when the time comes, we'll try to give him something which will wrong-foot the Boche, put some of their ships or their soldiers in the wrong place at the wrong time. Maybe we'll bring him in then.'

'Or persuade him to work for us?' James suggested.

'A double-agent? Yes, that might work,' Kell said, 'though from what I know of Lody he's a German patriot, through and through.'

Gregory spoke in his expressionless voice. 'Even the most ardent patriot has been turned by the traditional thirty pieces of silver.'

Kell looked hard at Gregory and, his voice charged with contempt, said,

'I suppose you're one of those people who thinks anyone can be bought, are you, Gregory?' He didn't wait for a reply and asked James when he expected to see Neumann again.

'He told me he'd make contact as soon as he could,' James said. 'But he must be lying low for a while.'

'He and his associates have certainly left Clerkenwell. The Old Vienna was burned out by the way. It's a good job you left in a hurry, before those thugs got hold of you.'

'Yes, sir, I didn't linger.'

'Well, at least our ruffians are patriotic,' Gregory said. 'Anyway, you lingered long enough to break someone's nose, I hear, and apparently you cracked another fellow's ribs.'

'No. Neumann did that. How did you know?'

'You're not the only man we've got working under cover,' Kell stated with a smile.

'No, we keep an eye on you,' Gregory said grimly.

'Now, Clifton,' Kell said, 'as soon as Neumann is in touch, let us know and we'll decide what to do next. But Lody is the man we want to watch very carefully. He's one of Germany's most valuable assets over here and he's clever. He's also dangerous. Please remember that.'

16

Ken Bradshaw, the chairman of Blackburn Rovers, had rarely crossed the borders of his native county; to him, Manchester was big enough, noisy enough and had a level of sophistication, not that he would use such a word, which was heady enough for him. So, when he received a letter inviting him to a meeting at the offices of *The Daily Mail* to discuss the matches against the Corinthians, he was at first apprehensive, especially when he saw that he would be sitting down with two men with handles to their names, the Lords Northcliffe and Kinnaird. However, Bradshaw's strength of character was founded on his typically northern belief that he was as good as any other man, whether or not he had 'Lord' in front of his name; he also had an unswerving conviction that his team was the best that the footballing world could offer.

Nevertheless, he felt a certain sense of awe when he arrived at the imposing doors of number 2 Carmelite Street, the home of *The Daily Mail*, and this increased as he was shown into the oak-panelled boardroom. A massive and ornate table dominated the room and, as he paused on the threshold, a stocky man surged energetically towards him. He was wearing a dark-blue suit and a red tie with white spots on it; Bradshaw also registered the man's bright grey-blue eyes and pale face before his hand was grabbed and shaken vigorously.

'Mister Bradshaw, good of you to come all this way. I'm Northcliffe and I will chair the meeting.' He waved at the other three men, who had risen politely to their feet in greeting. 'You know Kinnaird and this is your fellow-chairman, Arthur Dickson from the Corinthians, and Mister Tippett, who's here representing Lord Kitchener.'

Bradshaw was relieved that the celebrated Lord Kitchener was not there; he wondered how he would have coped with a man of such distinction, though it would have been a wonderful story to tell his many friends and acquaintances in Blackburn. Northcliffe waved him to a chair across the table from Dickson. Another man, also dressed in a dark suit, sat at a desk in the corner of the room. Pale, self-effacing and expressionless, he took shorthand notes of every word that was said.

After the introductions, Northcliffe spoke quietly. 'We all know why we're here. The government needs to recruit huge numbers of young men to fight this war against Germany. We need their courage and loyalty as never before. We must appeal to these young fellows, and one of the most effective ways to do so is through sport. There are well over half a million men who play football in this country. Am I correct, Lord Kinnaird?' He acknowledged Kinnaird's nod of assent with a quick wave and then continued. 'If they all volunteered tomorrow, we would be well down the road to meeting Lord Kitchener's immediate target.

'But we must put the message across to these brave young men in the right way and these two games between our two finest football clubs will help us to do that.'

Northcliffe, his nervous energy overflowing into restlessness, stood up and grasped the back of his chair. He pushed at the lock of fair hair which flopped over his forehead, but it fell back immediately.

'Gentlemen, with the resources of my newspapers, and especially *The Mail*, behind the two games, with our ability to engage the interest of the common man, simultaneously to inform and amuse him, which is a far more effective tactic than bludgeoning him with facts and sermonising, we will be able to make an impact that goes far beyond the games themselves.'

Arthur Dickson raised his hand to gain attention and said, 'But I trust that *The Times* will write about our games. It always reports them.'

'Of course, Mister Dickson, but it's the mass market we're after. My objective is to get the whole nation talking about these great games. And, by talking about them, the seeds will be planted. These wonderful footballers are putting on a show for us, they will say, and we must respond, we must support our country in its hour of greatest need. As you know, my newspapers always have and always will stand for the power, the supremacy and the greatness of the British Empire.'

The newspaper proprietor was now standing behind his chair and waving his arms to emphasise the points he wanted to make.

'Please don't think me cynical,' Lord Kinnaird said, 'but are you not over-estimating the sense of duty that our young men possess? It's my experience that *panem et circenses* are their usual preoccupations.' Bradshaw looked up in surprise and wondered what language old Kinnaird was speaking.

Northcliffe appeared to consider Kinnaird's comment for a moment or two and then spoke. 'For my part, I've no wish to drift into cynicism either, but if you put the right message to people in the right way, you can sell them anything. So, these won't just be a couple of football matches, they will be two great occasions, they'll be full of excitement. We'll offer prizes to our readers, let's see, ten pounds if they nominate the scorer of the first goal, twenty pounds if they name the final score, and so on. My people will work on it. Now, one of my writers has some ideas on how to put some fun, some glamour, as our American cousins put it, into the games.'

Northcliffe seized a telephone by his elbow and said, 'Edith, send Green in, will you.'

The door opened at once and a tall man with a florid face and a luxuriant head of grey hair entered and stood at one end of the table. 'Good morning, Chief,' he said to Northcliffe and then nodded to the others. 'Good morning, gentlemen.'

Northcliffe spoke again. 'Green here is a master at generating publicity for our newspapers. He adds the fizz to the champagne, you might say.'

'Thank you, Chief,' Green replied, 'most kind. Money first. The company will of course meet all the expenses involved in putting on the matches, travelling expenses for the Blackburn players and a suitable match fee for each man. Similarly, any costs incurred by the Corinthians will be covered and we'd like to give them all a small gift.' Green looked at Arthur Dickson and Lord Kinnaird. 'That won't, we hope, endanger their amateur status.'

'No, no,' Dickson replied. 'They're allowed to accept small gifts.'

Green continued. 'We propose that most of the money collected at the gate should go to various war charities, with a fee to Blackburn Rovers and a donation to the Corinthians as well.'

'We need to offer a special trophy,' Northcliffe said.

'But there are two matches?' Kinnaird said.

'So we need an outright winner,' Dickson said. 'If each club wins one match, then the club with the most goals is the winner. How's that?'

'And if the matches are drawn and the goals are even, we can share the trophy,' Bradshaw, keen to make a contribution to the discussion, suggested.

Northcliffe held up his hand for silence. 'Gentlemen, aren't we making this too complicated? Yes, we should have two matches and I think that the first one should be played in Blackburn and should be seen as the overture to the main event in London, our capital city. In other words, the teams will show their paces for the entertainment of the good folk of Lancashire, and then play for the trophy at Crystal Palace, our biggest and finest ground. I am not in any way, Mister Bradshaw, trying to diminish the importance of your club's role in all this, but I'm simply being practical.'

'Yes, I understand your argument,' Bradshaw replied, 'and you have my agreement.' Having made his commitment, he then began to wonder how his fellow-directors would react to his giving way to the 'London toffs'.

'Excellent,' Kinnaird said with relief plain in his voice. 'Now, I have an idea. Perhaps the teams could play for the Sheriff of London Shield. It's a very impressive piece of silverware.'

'But it already has its own history, it's been around for twenty-odd years,' objected Dickson.

There was silence for a few moments and then Tippett spoke for the first time. 'Do you remember the Thomas Lipton Trophy? It must be gathering dust somewhere. It was only played for twice.'

'Oh yes,' Kinnaird said, 'Lipton had a grandiose idea of organising a so-called world football tournament. A ridiculous notion, it couldn't possibly work. Some tinpot club won it. From up north.'

Bradshaw spoke up strongly. 'It was West Auckland and they may be a small club, Lord Kinnaird, but they beat Juventus in the final the second time round.'

Kinnaird grunted loudly and Lord Northcliffe said, 'A capital idea, Mister Tippett. Can you track down the trophy? I can then ask Sir Tommy to put it up for our matches. He'll love the idea, he knows the value of publicity.'

'Talking of which, we have some other ideas to brighten up the occasions,' Green said.

'I'm sorry, but did I hear you correctly?' Dickson said. 'Two fine teams of footballers, the best in the land, will be taking the field, and you feel the need to brighten up the occasions.' Everyone could hear how affronted he was.

'I understand your irritation,' Northcliffe said soothingly, 'but we must do all we can to capture the interest of the public. By that I mean the wider public, as well as our sportsmen. So, let's hear what Green has to say.'

'Thank you, Chief. We want to involve some well-known people in the games. We hope, for instance, that King George will present the trophy to the winners.' There was a murmur of approval from everyone and Green continued. 'And we thought we'd ask someone from outside football, someone whom the public really looks up to, to do the kick-off at the matches.'

'Surely not Lloyd George,' Kinnaird said with a laugh.

'How about C B Fry?' suggested Dickson, 'or G O Smith?'

'Well,' replied Northcliffe, 'we were thinking of someone with a much wider appeal to the public. Marie Lloyd for example.'

'Marie Lloyd,' said Dickson, Kinnaird and Bradshaw, almost in unison.

'Yes,' said Green. 'The people love her and she kicked off a charity match last year at the Oval. She's very involved in charity work for the armed forces and their families.'

'This is making a bit of a circus of the whole thing, isn't it?' Dickson said.

'Exactly. You've put your finger on it, Mister Dickson,' Northcliffe responded. 'These aren't just games of football, they go beyond that into the realm of entertainment in its widest sense. Some razzmatazz, as the Americans put it. You should see how they stage their baseball and football games. Anyway, carry on, Green, I know you've got lots more to suggest.'

'Another of our ideas is to include at least one guest player in each team.'

'Can I just point out. . .' Dickson began, but Northcliffe immediately asked him to hear Green out.

'We have a suggestion for you, Mister Bradshaw. We hope that you can allow George Robey to play for you. He loves his football and he did play a few games for Chelsea and Millwall in his time.'

'In his time, maybe,' said Kinnaird, 'but he's in his forties now, surely?'

'Well, yes, but he's in good physical shape, I'm told. Anyway, Kinnaird, weren't you still playing the game when you were well into your forties?' Northcliffe said with a broad smile.

'Well, yes, but...'

'Quite. So, what do you think, Mister Bradshaw?'

In his agitation, the Blackburn man's accent became much more pronounced. 'Ah thinks the Corinthians would make bloody mincemeat of him, that's what ah thinks.'

Dickson jumped in quickly. 'I quite agree. We all want a grand game of football, not high farce. By the way, I trust that you're not hoping to foist some entertainer or other on the Corinthians?'

Green hesitated as he noticed the ice in Dickson's voice. 'Well, we were hoping to put forward Billy Wells, the boxer. He's another great favourite of the British public and I assure you that he's a fine footballer. He played for Fulham in his youth.'

Dickson spoke quietly and with exaggerated patience. 'There are several reasons why Wells cannot represent our club. First, he has to go through the process of qualifying for membership. That entails being proposed and seconded by other members and then, in order to qualify, he must play at least three games in a satisfactory manner. However, that process cannot happen because Wells is a prize-fighter, a professional sportsman, and we are an amateur club.'

There was a pause and then Northcliffe spoke up. 'I think, gentlemen, that we will admit defeat for the idea of having guest players. A shame, but it's not practicable. However, we will involve Robey and Wells and other similar people in some way, even if they merely attend the games and receive the plaudits of the crowds.'

He stood up to signal the end of the meeting. 'My thanks to you all for your valued assistance. I will now leave the matter in your very capable hands, though I will always be available to any of you if you need my help. We have just under three weeks to go until the first of our great matches and *The Mail* and *The Times* will announce this in a couple of days.'

As if by a pre-arranged signal, the door to the boardroom was opened by a secretary and Lord Northcliffe swept out of the room, closely followed by the man who had taken shorthand notes of the meeting.

17

Horatio Bottomley had presided over many financial coups in his career. Most of them had brought him great fortunes to dissipate on gambling, mistresses and other extravagant and enjoyable pursuits; none of them had benefited his investors in any way. Apart from the millions of worthless shares he had sold in companies without any assets, he had also made substantial sums by promoting, through *John Bull*, sweepstakes on the 1913 Derby (when the deranged suffragette, Emily Davison, had thrown herself to her death under the hooves of the King's horse), and on the Grand National in the following year. He had capitalised on his successes by running another sweep on the FA Cup. These latter ventures had been organised from a tiny office in Geneva, since lotteries were illegal in Britain.

When Bottomley read the story in *The Times* about the matches which were being planned between the Corinthians and Blackburn Rovers, he saw the potential for organising yet another betting coup. He summoned John Smithson, one of his most trusted business associates, to his rooms in Pall Mall. He had plucked him from the confines of a lowly position as a solicitor's clerk in the City of London. Intelligent but ill-educated, Smithson had thrown himself whole-heartedly into a world of easy money and extravagances which were beyond his wildest fantasies. He had been particularly useful in securing Bottomley's access to a network of illegal bookmakers all over the country. Like his mentor, Smithson was a prolific gambler and was also invariably in debt.

Having been a party to many of Bottomley's schemes Smithson was used to his infectious enthusiasms, but he had rarely seen him so elated. As he entered the richly-furnished sitting-room, Bottomley waved him to an armchair next to one of the tall windows and then, with his great bulk looming over Smithson, held that morning's copy of *The Times* in front of his face.

'Have you seen this, John?' He pointed to the headline on one of the inside pages. 'England's finest teams to play two matches. I'd heard this was being planned and it's a capital idea to make the country aware of the need for our young men to volunteer to fight the good fight.' He grinned at Smithson. 'It's also a grand opportunity for us to get our hands on lots of money by making and taking bets on the result. According to *The Times* the first match is just a minor part of the whole thing, an *hors d'oeuvre*. The big match is the second one for the Lipton Trophy.'

'But it's a two-horse race, Mister Bottomley. There's not much room to make a killing, is there? It's not like the Derby or the National, eh?'

Bottomley pressed a bell on the wall beside his huge mahogany desk and his butler entered a few seconds later. 'Ernest, bring us some champagne and some smoked salmon sandwiches. Oh, and some caviar on those toothsome little biscuits from Fortnum's. Have we still got some of the '04 vintage left?'

'Yes, sir.'

'Good, it's one of the best champagnes I've ever tasted, John. You'll enjoy it.'

'I always do, Mister Bottomley.'

As the butler left the room, Bottomley levered himself to his feet, walked to a table against a wall and chose two cigars from a large humidor. He cut off their butts, handed one to Smithson and then used a lighter in the shape of a horse's hoof to set it burning.

Bottomley sank into the armchair facing Smithson and said, 'We could make hundreds of thousands of pounds on these matches, John, believe me.' He paused as Ernest knocked and entered the room with a bottle and two glasses on a silver tray. After showing the bottle to Bottomley, he twisted the cork out of its neck and poured the champagne.

Bottomley resumed. 'We need to persuade the great British public, the ones that like a wager, that either Blackburn or the Corinthians are the red-hot favourites, and then make sure that the other side wins.'

'And how on earth will you do that?'

'The first part is easy, John. *John Bull* will have articles about the matches every day and we'll make a strong and informed case that one or other of them is the clear favourite. And we'll spread some money among all the journalists we know. That will persuade them to follow the *John Bull* line. The people at *The Times* will be no use to us, but many of the others will toe the line, especially the ones who would like to do more work for us.'

'As you said, that's the easy part. But how do we make sure we get the right result?'

'It's just a matter of applying pressure in the right places, John. Everyone has a secret, something he wouldn't reveal to his closest confidant, to his wife, his lover, his mother. Even you, John, I expect.'

If only he knew, Smithson thought, but he merely shrugged and drank some more champagne, as Bottomley continued. 'I'm probably the exception to that rule. People have called me all sorts of names, they've reviled me as a fraudster and a whore-monger and I've been in the bankruptcy court more than once. So, what do I care? My great strength is that people like me, and they trust me and they still give me their money because they think that I can double it or quadruple it for them.' He drank deeply from his glass and smiled thinly. 'They can't control their greed, you see, not many people can and they'd rather take a chance on me than contemplate missing out on a big pay day.'

He paused again and drew on his cigar and then poured them some more Pommery champagne. 'So, let's look at the Corinthians first. They're all in the upper echelons of society, so they've got the most to lose if any of their dirty little secrets are exposed. I know one or two of them. Their chairman for a start. Arthur Dickson. He's an estate agent, who sells a lot of the big stuff in the home counties. I wonder if he's ever done a deal on the side with a buyer, pushed the price down and then pocketed half the difference.'

'How am I supposed to find out things like that?' Smithson protested. 'It'll take months and we've only got days.'

'What about that detective agency, the one that gives us leads to rich people with money to burn? Use them. And I'll talk to Maundy Gregory. He works for Vernon Kell, so he's got access to lots of confidential information. We've got to be creative, John.'

As Smithson drained his champagne and prepared to leave, Bottomley said, 'One more thing, we know Richard Hildreth, don't we? He's been making a fuss, asking for his mother's money back. Not much chance of that, eh, John. But the point is that she must be feeling the pinch, so we can offer him a deal. If he co-operates, we can pay her back.'

'He's the goalkeeper, isn't he?'

'Yes, so that's a bit of luck. It's a crucial position, very useful from our point of view. Why should anyone suspect him if he deliberately fumbles a shot or has the misfortune to let the ball go under his body?' Bottomley grinned expansively as he poured the last of the Pommery into his glass. 'This is how I see it. We'll fix the first match at Blackburn, so that the Corinthians win. Some bribery will ensure that the Blackburn players don't put their hearts and souls into it. And if we have to, we'll apply some gentle blackmail. I'm sure that we'll find some of those professional footballers have skeletons in their cupboards. We'll make some good money for ourselves, but that will be as nothing compared to what we'll make on the really important game here in London. We'll build the Corinthians up as invincible, and then we'll "persuade" some of those gilded amateur players to throw the game.'

'I'm not sure about that, Mister Bottomley, these toffs won't necessarily react in the way we want them to, will they?'

'I've never been surprised by how human beings behave, John. It's usually predictable. Anyway, that's the grand plan, so let's give it a try, shall we?'

* * *

On the same day James received a telephone call from Vernon Kell, who asked him to attend a meeting that evening at Watergate

House. When he got there, the head of the secret service wasted no time in getting to the point.

'The Germans have been in touch. Indirectly. A letter, addressed to you, was delivered to the Josiah Morris office in Farringdon Road. And from Belmont's description it was clearly Neumann who delivered it.' Kell handed the letter to James. 'Here it is and, as you see, Neumann claims to be your cousin from Switzerland and wishes to meet you to discuss a family matter. He suggests that you should be outside the Lamb and Flag in Rose Street on Monday week at 10 o'clock in the evening. Do you know the place?'

'Yes. I believe that John Dryden was beaten half to death outside its front door.'

'Better be careful then, Mister Clifton,' Maundy Gregory said with a smirk.

Kell glanced with disdain at Gregory and said, 'We don't know what they're up to, but I suspect Lody is gathering as much information as he can before he leaves the country. We've had a report that a German submarine will pick him up off the Kent coast within a couple of weeks.'

'What do you want me to do?'

'Try and keep him and the others interested. For instance, we've got some details of troop numbers and movements for you to pass on. All of them harmless and some of them fictitious. But our main aim is to isolate Lody somehow, and then try to spirit him away without Neumann's suspecting anything.'

'Are you sure Lody will be there?'

Kell shrugged. 'No, but we hope so, and then we can at least try to persuade him to work for us.'

'I thought you regarded him as German patriot through and through, as incorruptible,' James said.

'Yes, but he might appreciate that it's better to be a live double-agent than a dead German patriot,' Gregory stated.

'There are still men of principle left in this world,' Kell said sharply.

James persisted. 'If I were Lody, I'd pretend to go along with your plans until I could get back to my own country.'

Kell nodded his agreement, but again stressed that they had to try to 'turn' him.

'What would happen if you simply arrested Lody, Neumann and the rest of them?' asked James.

'That wouldn't work to our advantage,' Kell replied. 'Steinhauer would close down the whole operation and then start again. No, since we know the identities of most of Steinhauer's agents, it's far better to keep them in play and under surveillance.'

'If Lody is catching a submarine back to Europe soon, we've precious little time to coerce him,' James said.

'Quite. But if he is there, you must do your best to lead him on. We'll be watching the three of you and we'll follow Lody and, when Neumann is out of the way, we'll snatch him. However, if things get nasty, Neumann is expendable.'

'Why not snatch Lody now?' James asked.

'Because we don't know where he is, do we, Gregory?' Kell said with an edge to his voice.

Maundy Gregory was expressionless as he looked at a far corner of the room. 'No. We can't keep track of him. He seems to use a cheap lodging house for a night and then off he goes. A couple of days ago, we thought he'd settled in a room in a tenement near Charing Cross, but by the morning he'd flown the coop.'

'So that's our problem, Clifton. When you meet them we'll put several men out there to watch and follow, and let's hope for the best.'

'Hoping for the best' didn't sound like the sort of protection that James had been expecting from the Secret Service Bureau, but he said nothing and resolved to be on his guard as never before.

18

Carl Lody had several attributes which were vital for survival when working under cover in a foreign country: he could make himself inconspicuous to the point of invisibility and he was extremely cautious. He accepted nothing at face value and assumed that nobody was as he seemed until he himself had done the most meticulous research.

The man he knew as Pieter Westermann had a plausible story and Lody had been impressed by the way in which he had stood shoulder to shoulder with Neumann and the other Germans when they were attacked at the Old Vienna. Neumann himself had been loud in his praise of Westermann. 'A real fighter,' he had told Lody enthusiastically. 'Just the sort of man we need.' In a perverse way Neumann's comments made Lody even more determined to make some thorough checks into the background of their new ally.

First of all he contacted his boss, Gustav Steinhauer, by telegraph and asked him to determine if there were any records in Berlin of a marriage, roughly twenty-five years ago, between a German woman called Westermann and an Englishman called Arthur Joyce; the second part of the inquiry concerned the birth of a boy called Peter or Pieter Joyce.

The reply came quickly back that nothing had been found that really fitted. Westermann was not an uncommon name in Germany and several Pieter Westermanns had been born in the years 1888 and 1889, but there was no trace of a father with the surname of Joyce.

It then occurred to Lody that, if the pair had not been married, they would not have registered the birth. Or the boy might have been born elsewhere in Europe; in England perhaps. Whatever the truth, he did not have the time to start a laborious search for someone who, he suspected, was using a false identity.

Lody decided that he would at least make some discreet inquiries at the offices of Josiah Wood and Sons. The company occupied a small Victorian building near Exmouth Market and at just after seven o'clock in the morning Lody, shabbily dressed and unshaven, was leaning in a doorway opposite. By eight o'clock four people had entered the building: a thin girl of about eighteen years of age who was probably employed to make tea, do the filing and carry out other such mundane tasks; a man of about the same age who could be the office messenger; a neatly-dressed woman who scurried busily up to and through the front door and who, Lody guessed, was the manager's secretary; and a man in his late-twenties, who was probably the office clerk. Finally, at just before half past eight, a man in his forties went into the building. He was smartly dressed in a dark grey suit, was rather portly for his age and had a small moustache. Yes, Lody thought, this was the manager of the firm, or possibly the proprietor; he wishes to present himself as a serious man of business and may well be a little vain.

At just after midday Lody, now shaven and dressed in a neat but inexpensive suit, went into Josiah Wood's offices and was greeted by the older woman, who was seated behind a typewriter at a wooden desk; the younger girl was busy filing a pile of papers into a row of cabinets in a corner of the office. To Lody's right, there were doors to two other offices.

Having greeted the woman, Lody presented her with his business card, which named him as Carl Fricker, a sales representative of the Gessner Scientific Instrument Company, based in Switzerland.

The woman read the card carefully and then looked at Lody over her spectacles. 'What can we do for you, Mister Fricker?'

'My firm needs some extra help with shipping its products into England. We're looking for a company which will take delivery of our goods at the port, clear them through customs, all that sort of thing, and then arrange transport to our warehouses.' Although Lody usually spoke English without a trace of a foreign accent, he did not neglect to give his voice a tiny 'continental' lilt, just for the woman's benefit.

'That's what we do, Mister Fricker. I'm sure we'll be able to help you. Where are your warehouses?

'One in London and one in Manchester, Miss, er?'

The woman flushed slightly as Lody gave her his well-practised smile. 'It's Mrs actually. Mrs Glover. I think you should speak to our Mister Belmont and discuss the details with him. He's very busy, but I'll have a word with him.' Lody nodded as if to acknowledge how heavily the burdens of commerce must lie on Mister Belmont's shoulders.

Mrs Green rose from her seat and smiled at Lody. My God, he thought, she actually fluttered her eyelashes at me. She went past him to one of the other offices and he registered her trim figure. Oh well, if I have to romance her a little, so be it. There might possibly be a modicum of pleasure in the process, even if she was no Mata Hari. The things he had to do for Germany.

A sharp 'come in' greeted Mrs Glover's knock on the office door nearest to Lody and she went in. He heard a murmur of conversation and then Mrs Glover held open the door and Belmont made his entrance.

Lody rose to his feet and shook Belmont's outstretched hand. 'Mister Fricker, very good to meet you. I can only give you a couple of minutes now. I'm a man of habit and I usually go out at this time for a stroll and a cup of tea.'

'Of course, I understand, Mister Belmont. A busy man should have a break from business every now and then. However, the shipment is urgent, a large number of watches and clocks, as well as some scientific instruments.'

'Swiss watches, eh. The very best, of course,' Belmont said ingratiatingly.

'Indeed, and the way the world is going this might be our last shipment for some time. So, could we perhaps meet later?' Lody hesitated. 'Would you care to have a drink with me? At five o'clock this evening? Would that suit you? There's a tavern just down the road and it looks pleasant enough.'

In fact, Lody had an aversion to London's public houses; he found them noisy, dirty and generally unappealing. It was difficult to find a beer to his taste and, as for a decent glass of wine, that was unattainable. However, he wanted to get Belmont out of his office and on to neutral ground, where he could ply him with alcohol.

'The King's Head? Is that the one?' asked Belmont.

'Yes, it's to your taste?'

'Certainly. I'll be there at five. Mrs Glover, will you please show Mister Fricker out.'

There was another handshake with Belmont and his secretary fluttered her eyelashes at Lody again as he gave her a slight bow at the front door.

* * *

By five o'clock that evening the King's Head, a spacious pub with a circular bar in the middle of the room, was already beginning to fill up with eager drinkers. Lody had stationed himself at a corner table near the entrance and was sipping, without much pleasure, a small glass of porter when Belmont arrived at a few minutes past the hour.

'Let me get you a drink, Mister Belmont,' he offered. This business of going to the bar to get a drink was another practice which Lody found irksome. 'What would you like?'

To Lody's surprise Belmont said, 'They do a nice glass of hock here. That would suit me.'

Lody returned with a bottle and two glasses and pushed his porter to one side. He told Belmont that he'd made an excellent choice, even though he thought that the hock was too sweet and it wasn't cool enough. It was preferable to that sour beer, though. They toasted each other and Belmont then asked Lody a series of questions about the size of the shipment, at which port it would arrive and where he wanted it to be delivered. Lody had done his research on the subject, but concluded by telling Belmont that he would get all the final details from his head office in Zurich within a couple of days.

Lody had thought hard about how to broach the subject of Pieter Westermann. If the man was an informant and he mentioned him, alarm bells would sound immediately in Belmont's mind and he would pass on his suspicions to the Secret Service Bureau. But if Westermann really was a shipping clerk employed by Josiah Wood, then presumably Belmont would not mind volunteering that fact.

Filling up their glasses again, Lody said casually, 'I can't quite recall who recommended your firm, but it may have been one of our embassy officials.'

'Glad to hear it,' Belmont interrupted with a smile. 'A personal recommendation is the best kind to have, is it not?'

Lody nodded his agreement and continued. 'But I hope you won't mind if I say that I didn't realise your company was quite so small. You and Mrs Glover and the young girl who does the filing.'

'And we do have another clerk, he was in the small office. Young Bill, he's a good worker.'

'That's all?'

Lody saw a slight frown crease Belmont's forehead and it was because he was now in a quandary. He was eager to secure what sounded like a profitable piece of business for his firm, so he was prepared to reassure this potential customer that he had other workers at his beck and call; in fact, he would inflate the numbers if necessary. On the other hand, this might be a test devised by that odious man, Maundy Gregory. He wished his nephew, who was doing some menial job at New Scotland Yard, had never introduced the fellow to him. The small monthly retainer paid to him by Gregory simply wasn't worth the trouble.

Belmont had been told by Gregory not to volunteer Westermann's name unless he was asked a direct question about him; and even then to be as vague as possible about the 'work' that Westermann did for his company. Belmont therefore said as he drained his glass, 'Well, we also have one or two casual workers, part-timers who are always available to help out when we have a lot of work on.'

'Do they have names? It's nice to know who you will be dealing with.'

'Yes, of course. There's Westermann, for instance. Pieter Westermann. He helps us occasionally.'

'A German? Not that we mind where he comes from,' Lody said quickly. 'We Swiss are neutral, thank heavens.'

'He's half-German, I believe.'

'So, he speaks German?'

'Oh yes, I think so.'

'And he lives in London?'

'Yes, he does.'

'Nearby perhaps? It would be nice to meet him.'

'I'm not sure where he lives, Mister Fricker. He moves around, you know what these young people are like.'

'I do indeed,' Lody said with a smile. He emptied the remains of the bottle into their glasses and they drank to the business they would do together in the future.

19

In view of the demands made on cabinet ministers in time of war, John Tippett was surprised to be summoned to a meeting with Lloyd George to discuss what seemed to be the minor matter of two games of football. He was even more puzzled when Winston Churchill walked into the room. However, he gave a concise account of the progress already made; how Lord Northcliffe was busy publicising the games, and that Old Trafford in Manchester and Crystal Palace had been reserved for them.

'Excellent, Tippett, excellent,' Lloyd George said. 'So we have the two best teams in the country, the two best grounds, and we also have an imposing trophy, courtesy of Tommy Lipton. Now we need to decide the result, that is, the best result for our purposes.' His eyes sparkling with mischief, the Chancellor looked expectantly at the other two men.

Taken aback, Tippett repeated the question. 'The best result, Chancellor?'

'Yes, we are organising these games for one reason only. Not to entertain the public, not to raise money for war charities, even though those are significant by-products. Our only motive is to encourage the flow of recruits into a flood. So, in my opinion, we should consider which result would do the most for our cause. What do you think, Winston?'

Before replying, Churchill drew deeply on his cigar, exhaled a cloud of smoke and tapped some ash into the ashtray in front of him. 'Leaving aside any ethical questions about fixing the result of a football match, I suppose we should consider this from two points of view. The burden of actually fighting this dreadful war will be shouldered by the ordinary soldier. He's the man who will grit his teeth and charge into the maelstrom for king and country. So, there is an argument for encouraging him by hoping for a Blackburn Rovers victory. It's encouragement for the common man, as represented by their footballers, their people. Without being too fanciful, the spectators may well say to themselves "what they can do, we can do". The players may be heroes for an afternoon on the field of play, but the ordinary citizen knows that they are really just like them, they live around the corner or a couple of streets away in the same sort of house.'

'Yes, in an over-crowded back-to-back, cold in the winter and too hot in the summer, and with a privy in the yard,' Lloyd George said forcefully. 'With wages that, after paying the rent, barely leave enough to feed a family properly.'

'Agreed, David, we're all aware that there's a long way to go before we see a more just society. And it may be a dream, but if we don't dream, we'll achieve little. But I must put to you the other argument. A nation needs leaders and, more than at any time, it needs them in time of war. And who will lead these brave young men into battle?'

'Men like the Corinthians,' Tippett said quietly.

'Exactly, and the soldiers in the ranks must have complete confidence in the men who command them, they must be prepared to follow their officers wherever they lead them.'

'So, you are suggesting that the so-called gifted amateurs should continue to reinforce their traditional superiority over the common man,' Lloyd George said.

'I think it's a bit harsh to put it that way, David. I am trying to be realistic, and I'm also playing devil's advocate.'

'You've put the arguments well, Winston, of course.' Lloyd George, deep in thought, tapped his teaspoon on the table and then rose and strolled over to the windows which overlooked Whitehall. He turned to face the two men. 'Logic tells me that you're right to stress the importance of leaders. They turn the course of history, and we all must accept that there's a natural hierarchy in society. Only a few can lead and the rest must follow. But in this case my heart tells me that we must enthuse the working men of this country in the cause of war, and one of the ways to do this is by letting them have a victory, however insignificant.'

'But we mustn't forget that there's a moral and a practical problem in decreeing that Blackburn should win the games,' Churchill said.

'The moral problem first, please, Winston.'

'At its simplest, what's the point of sport if you win by unfair means? The objective is a fair contest between two teams or two individuals for that matter, and cheating negates that.'

Tippett spoke up. 'It's not the victory, but the contest.'

'I wondered when someone would quote the Baron de Coubertin,' Lloyd George said. 'It's a laudable view of sport, but we are concerned here with war and I would only want to go to war with men who want to win, whatever the cost.'

'Whatever the cost?' queried Churchill. 'That's what worries me. Our motives for entering the war are supposedly honourable. We promised to protect Belgium if her territory were violated and we are keeping that promise. Must we now forget our principles? Must we lose our moral authority?'

'I'm glad you said "supposedly honourable", because we know that we are fighting to protect our trading interests around the world, though it suits us to cloak this in a mantle of duty and honour. And we have to win this war, by fair means or foul. For example, we already have a propaganda unit at work, we're using the talents of writers like Conan Doyle, Chesterton, H G Wells, Kipling and many another to blacken the German name, to spread stories of their atrocities in Belgium, that they've killed babies and children, raped their mothers and sisters, tortured their menfolk and burned their villages. It's not pretty, Winston, but it has to be done.'

'Yes, that's the tragedy of it, isn't it? "In war, truth is the first casualty", as Aeschylus put it.' Churchill paused and then resumed. 'But there is still the practical aspect of fixing these games. You're a football man, Tippett, what is your view?'

'I think that the Corinthians would resist any interference with all their might. They play the game for fun, and always with great skill and determination, but they would be appalled by such an idea. You've only to look at their attitude to penalties.' He looked expectantly at the two politicians.

'Go on, Tippett,' Lloyd George said, 'you've taken us beyond the bounds of our sporting knowledge.'

'Their view is that a true sportsman, a gentleman in other words, would never intentionally commit a foul, it could only be an accident. So, if a penalty is awarded against him, it is tantamount to calling his honour into question. Therefore, the Corinthians don't believe that the penalty should be in the rules of football, and they won't take advantage of such a rule. If they're awarded a penalty, their player will deliberately miss it.'

'That all sounds rather self-righteous,' Lloyd George said. 'And what if a penalty is given against them?'

'Their goalkeeper stands aside and offers the opposition an unguarded net.'

'Heaven help us,' Lloyd George muttered. 'Nevertheless, Tippett, you must go to their chairman, that fellow Dickson, and tell him what we are considering and why. You know the argument, reasons of state, the morale of the common soldiery, and so on.'

'I don't think it will have the slightest effect, sir.'

'Neither do we,' Churchill said. 'Anyway, my honest opinion is that it doesn't matter a damn who wins these games. Everyone knows that the officers of the British army exercise very little influence. It's the corporals and the sergeants who run the show and, if they've got any sense, both the officers and the rank and file do their bidding.'

Tippett hesitated before airing his opinions in front of two such formidable politicians, but steeled himself and spoke. 'Gentlemen, may I make a suggestion to you? Would it not be best if each side were to win one game? So, whichever team wins at Old Trafford, we must then persuade the chairman of that team to ensure that in the return match in London his players give way in the national interest.'

Lloyd George smiled at Churchill and said, 'This young man will make a politician, Winston, don't you think?'

'I do indeed, David, but let's hope that Blackburn win the first game, because their chairman will be a lot easier to persuade than that fellow Dickson.'

20

James and the other nine Corinthians who had gathered at the Hurlingham Club in west London had enjoyed themselves greatly during the morning. As Arthur Dickson looked on, they had warmed up with a few laps of the makeshift football pitch, done some faster running and finished with a practice match of five against five. It was strenuous, although heavy tackling was banned, since the chairman wanted them all to be ready in good condition for the first game in just under two weeks' time. Finally, they played a few sets of tennis, during which Max Woosnam showed why he had won his blue at the game.

As they were all leaving the club, Richard had seized James by the arm, waved a taxi down, ushered him into it and told him that he was taking him to lunch. 'We're meeting Emily at the Hyde Park Hotel, because you haven't been properly thanked for saving my baby sister from that brutish policeman the other day.'

'But you've done enough,' James protested. 'You sent me some champagne.'

'Emily wants to see you. She thinks that you're avoiding her.'

That was certainly true. In his reply to Emily's letter he had tried hard to echo her light-hearted but honest tone. He did not want to embarrass her and assured her that he had not taken her proposal seriously. He added that he realised she was still in a state of shock after the policeman's assault on her, and that shock made people behave in uncharacteristic ways. But he also emphasised how flattered he felt.

On reflection, however, he thought that he should have let his heart control his head. He should have picked her up in his arms, borne her off to the nearest jeweller's shop and bought the engagement ring; and then he should have put the announcement of their forthcoming wedding in the following day's edition of *The Times*. Sometimes instinct was the best guide and marriage to Emily had seemed so right. So, why had he been such a damn fool? Why hadn't he asked Emily to be his wife?

Since then James had begun to question whether the two of them would ever re-establish their old relationship. They had always been so close; they did love each other, even if it had been a platonic love.

But there was no denying that he was apprehensive about meeting her again so soon and he wondered whether he would betray the awkwardness he felt. Would she?

As they drew up outside the hotel Richard said, 'You're an old and valued friend, James. I know I don't have to say this, but I'm going to anyway. If you ever need any help, I want you to ask me first.' Before James could reply, his friend busied himself with finding some money for the cabbie and then he urged them both up the steps and into the hotel.

Emily was already seated in the restaurant at a table under the windows which overlooked Hyde Park. If James had felt the slightest tinge of embarrassment, it was dispelled as soon as he approached her. She rose to her feet and, to the surprise of the other diners, curtsied deeply and theatrically, while saying, 'At last, my noble knight in shining armour.' She then burst out laughing. So did James, her brother, and almost everyone else within earshot.

A waiter poured them champagne and Richard pointed out that it was Pol Roger, and not Horatio Bottomley's favourite tipple, Pommery.

'You still haven't resolved your mother's difficulties with him, then?' James asked.

'No,' Richard said shortly. 'And now he's setting himself up as a sort of cheerleader for the war effort.'

'In the pages of *John Bull,* I suppose.'

'Yes, but more than that,' Emily said, 'he's actually addressing public meetings, to urge men to volunteer.'

'And, though I hate to admit it, he's very successful at it,' Richard said. 'They turn up in their thousands to hear him.'

'Well, he is a fine speaker, as we all know,' Emily said, 'but he's now calling himself the Recruiting Officer for the British Empire.'

'You can't keep a good confidence trickster down,' James said.

Even if some of the faces at the neighbouring tables were more sombre than usual, the three young people made the most of the occasion. As they left the dining room and Emily went to retrieve her belongings from the cloakroom, James recalled again Kell's remark that they must all 'hope for the best' and he had a sudden and unexpected flash of apprehension about what might await him that evening at the Lamb and Flag.

He spoke quietly to Richard. 'You said that you would help me, if I needed it, Richard.' His friend nodded eagerly. 'Would you be willing to help me tonight? I need someone to, er, watch over me. It sounds strange, I know, but I must meet two men. Germans, who might have some information of use to the government. I don't trust them and if I get into trouble your presence would reassure me.'

James gave Richard the name of the Covent Garden pub where he was meeting Neumann and Lody and described them to him. 'Not a flicker of recognition, Richard, and wear some old clothes. And if we leave the pub, follow us discreetly.'

As Emily returned, Hildreth nodded his agreement. Since James did not have complete confidence in Vernon Kell and distrusted Maundy Gregory as much as he did the two Germans, he felt heartened that a close friend would be watching over him. The bonus was that, like most accomplished goalkeepers, Richard was strong, agile and fearless.

* * *

Sitting opposite Horatio Bottomley in his rooms in Pall Mall, John Smithson began his summary of what he had uncovered about the backgrounds of the Blackburn Rovers players. The detective agency favoured by Bottomley had an office in Manchester and had done all the hard work for him.

'The chairman, Ken Bradshaw, has a good business,' Smithson began. 'His bakeries make money and he doesn't seem to spend much. He likes a drink, especially after a game on Saturday, and he has an occasional bet on the horses. He's married with four kids and doesn't appear to stray from the marital bed.'

'He's an example to us all, then, John, and especially to this nation of shopkeepers.' A genuinely puzzled look flitted across Bottomley's florid face. 'But what's the point of having money if you don't spend it? The economy will go to hell if we don't spread our money around.'

'Well, quite,' Smithson said hesitantly. 'Anyway, Bob Crompton is as straight as a dye. A model professional.'

'Good heavens, he surely can't be that boring,' Bottomley said, with wonder in his voice.

Smithson shrugged. 'That's the story. Anyway, there are one or two players who might be useful to us, players with questionable habits.'

'Women and gambling, I suppose.'

'Yes. Albert Sedgemore, he's the other strong man in the Blackburn defence, along with Crompton. He's a naughty boy. Very keen on the ladies. Married of course, with one child and another on the way.'

'That's nice, John. It's his wife who's pregnant, I trust.'

'Yes, Mister Bottomley, it is his wife. And it's just as well that she doesn't know about his girlfriend. The girl's seventeen years of age and lives in Manchester and he's promised to leave his missus and live with her, as soon as his wife's recovered from the birth.'

'Oh dear,' Bottomley said with a heartfelt sigh, 'they always fall for that one, don't they?'

'So they do. But Sedgemore would be best advised to stick with his missus, because she happens to have three brothers, who've all been in bother with the police. Mrs Sedgemore is part of a vicious family, they're all ruffians and petty crooks, and they'll go looking for Albert if he upsets their little sister.'

'And he won't be hard to find, will he? Good, so he's an easy target.'

'And the other two are Tommy Wiggins and Billy Dodds. They're also regulars in the team and just as regular in making losing bets. They each owe the bookies more money than they can ever hope to pay back. And as you know, Mister Bottomley, those gentlemen aren't usually prepared to wait forever for their money.'

'So we'll offer to pay off their debts, eh, John? And they will return the favour by falling rather short of their normal high standards in the first game.'

'That should do the trick.'

'But, John, tell the bookies not to restrict their credit in the meantime. Give those losers enough rope to hang themselves, eh? Tell the bookies not to worry, Horatio Bottomley will guarantee the money.'

There was a knock on the door and the butler announced the arrival of Maundy Gregory, whom Bottomley greeted effusively. 'Maundy, so good of you to come over. Sit down, dear fellow. Have a drop of champagne. Thirsty weather, eh?'

Gregory lowered his square frame carefully into a chair and the butler prised open a new bottle of Pommery and filled three glasses. After he'd left the room, Bottomley said, 'As I mentioned to you on the telephone, Maundy, we need some information about certain members of the illustrious Corinthian football club. With your wealth of contacts, I was sure you could help us. In fact, you're the first person I thought of.'

'I would normally be more than happy to do so, Horatio, but I must be careful. Most of the information to which I have access belongs to the government. It's confidential and I don't wish to spend the rest of my days staring at the four walls of a prison cell, or indeed to end my days by being on the wrong end of a firing squad's rifles.'

'Oh, come, come, Maundy, let's not be melodramatic. I'm not asking for any secrets. Just some background on one or two people. You and Kell must have a huge amount of stuff, most of it peripheral, harmless. But, it could help us to, er, forecast the result of the final game between the Corinthians and Blackburn.'

As he drank some more champagne, Gregory allowed the shadow of a smirk to flit across his face. 'So you've got some bets going, have you?'

'Yes, and we want to make sure that they're winning bets. And we'll put plenty on for you, too.'

'That's risky, isn't it, Horatio, even for you. How on earth do you fix a game of football? There are twenty-two players out there and you can't control their actions. It's not like a horse race, when you can nobble the jockey who's riding the favourite for a few pounds. Or a boxing match when you can bribe one of those bruisers to lie down. I don't like the sound of it, Horatio. Football is by its very nature unpredictable.'

'Not if you apply the right kind of pressure at the right time and in the right places.'

Gregory shook his head in disagreement. 'We collect information on foreigners, on Germans, on Russian anarchists and on those Irish bastards, anyone who might harm our country. We don't spy on our fellow-countrymen.'

Bottomley spoke sharply, his habitual half-smile suddenly absent. 'Maybe not, but I'm sure your great friend, Basil Thomson, can help us out with some juicy tit-bits.'

Smithson noticed that Gregory paused as he took his glass from the table and that there was a barely perceptible tremor as he put it to his lips. 'What's Thomson got to do with this? He's the head of the Special Branch and I work for Captain Kell in the Secret Intelligence department.'

'You're being disingenuous, Maundy, aren't you? Because you and Kell report directly to Thomson and the business of his department is to dig the dirt on people, to uncover the sordid little secrets that they'd prefer to keep well hidden. Isn't that so?'

Gregory remained silent, his face blank. Bottomley continued. 'And you and Thomson have quite a close relationship, I'm told.'

'He's Kell's boss, so I only have a tenuous relationship with him. I do what Kell tells me to do. I report to him, not to Thomson.'

'That's not what I hear, Maundy. I hear that your contacts in the more exotic parts of London life, or of London low-life to be more accurate, are very useful to Mister Thomson. I believe that he has some very queer tastes and that you provide the means to satisfy them.'

Gregory rose laboriously to his feet. 'I won't listen to any more of your bloody nonsense.'

Bottomley also got up and patted Gregory on the shoulder. 'Stay awhile, Maundy, calm down and have another glass of fizz. Don't act as if your dignity is affronted because I won't buy it. I know too much about you.' He grinned at Smithson. 'Enough to get him hanged, eh, John?'

Smithson grinned back at Bottomley and raised his eyebrows. 'Well, maybe not hanged, Mister Bottomley, but certainly banged up in prison. And the other inmates don't like perverts, I'm told.'

'Don't threaten me,' Gregory said heatedly. 'You, Bottomley, should've gone down for fraud years ago. God knows how you got away with it. Now you've taken to blackmail and trying to fix football matches. You must be mad.'

'Look, Maundy, be sensible about this. It's not like you to lose your head. You can do us a good turn, with no risk to yourself and you will make a lot of money for yourself. And you need money, don't you? There are those unusual interests of yours. Perhaps we should call them sophisticated pleasures. And they don't come cheap, do they? You see, we know how much you owe those money lenders in Regent Street. They might appear to be civilised and understanding, but they're not. They're crooks, they're violent, in fact they're as nasty as any blood-sucking money shark you might find in Whitechapel. But, we will rid you of your debts and reward you with enough money to keep you in comfort for many a long year.' Bottomley held out his hand to Gregory. 'So, Maundy, will you help us?'

Gregory looked at the floor for a moment or two. His face was even paler than usual and a patina of sweat lay upon it. He got to his feet and shook Bottomley's hand as a mark of his capitulation.

Bottomley walked over to his desk, rummaged about in the piles of paper and found what he wanted. He handed one sheet to Gregory. 'That's a list of the Corinthians. The chairman and their most prominent players, the ones who'll turn out against Blackburn. Have a look at it, there's a good fellow, and then tell me if any of the names ring any bells. Well, cracked bells, if you like.' He laughed loudly at his own joke.

'Nothing much here,' Gregory said, after taking a few moments to scan the names. 'Arthur Dickson, for instance. He's sold houses and estates to half the toffs in the south of England, and to the idiots who aspire to be toffs, of course. I doubt we'll find anything untoward about him and anyway he's just a figure-head, he can't influence the team on the pitch. Ah, but here's Mister Clifton, we know him. James Clifton from the Foreign Office, yes, he's doing some work on the side for us. Kell found him. He's a fluent German speaker. A very superior kind of being is our Mister Clifton. I really don't know why Kell needs to use these bloody amateurs.'

'Gifted amateurs, Maundy, is probably what you mean. They're the backbone of our nation. But from the acid tone of your voice I assume that Master Clifton isn't one of your boon companions?'

'No.'

'If he works for your department, you should be able to set him up. You're skilled in the arts of subterfuge, so get him involved in something questionable, which we can use to temper his enthusiasm for victory against the northern foe.'

'It's a very enticing thought,' Gregory said with a rare show of animation. 'Ah, and here's another name that's cropped up somewhere in our files. Rupert Wavell. I've heard some rumours about him.'

'What rumours?' Smithson asked.

'Nasty ones. He's filthy rich and been spoiled rotten, especially by his mother.'

'Tell me more.'

'I seem to recall that he likes to knock the daylights out of prostitutes.'

'I thought he got his kicks on the football field,' Smithson said with a laugh. He glanced at Bottomley as if seeking his approval.

'Really, John, no puns, we're discussing some serious business. Talking of which, why isn't Wavell's father on our list of investors? Let's get after him. Anyway, Maundy, find out what you can. If it all works out, you'll be very well looked after, I promise you. This could be a highly profitable venture for us all.'

21

A few miles away Kurt Neumann and Carl Lody were drinking cups of weak coffee in a damp room with one small window. It was a store-room, part of the basement of a house in an alley between Brick Lane and Commercial Street. It was inhabited by a large Jewish family, several generations of which were crammed into the upper floors. Lody had paid the patriarch a few shillings for access to the room, which had the advantage of having its own entrance; he had also eased open the lock on the back door and this gave him another means of escape if he needed it.

'What a hole this is,' Neumann said. 'It stinks.'

'I would of course prefer to be in some comfortable rooms in Belgravia,' Lody replied. 'However...'

'Quite. Who's upstairs?'

'A Jewish family.'

'Ach, bloody Jews.'

Lody grimaced with distaste at Neumann's remark and said, 'Do we trust this Westermann?'

Neumann was about to drink some coffee, but stopped the cup on its way to his mouth and put it down. 'Do we trust him? What sort of a question is that, Carl? He risked his life for us, if you remember. But for him we might not be sitting here.'

'Yes, he fought well, I acknowledge that,' Lody said testily.

'And he's given us some useful information.'

'Useful maybe, but did he give us anything that we didn't already know?

'I must tell you, Kurt, I've been wondering about him since I first met him. That Berlin accent, it's almost too good to be true. He could be an actor, who's learned all the right intonations.'

'You're too suspicious at times, Carl,' Neumann said.

'Perhaps that's why I'm still alive.'

'Well, I think you're completely wrong about Pieter. I'm a good judge of people and I think he's genuine. A man's true character comes to the surface when there's a crisis and Pieter reacted like a true German – with courage. And I like the man, he's not only brave, he's obviously intelligent.'

'I like him, too, Kurt, but so what? If he wants to gain our confidence, he's going to try his best to make us like him, isn't he?'

'So you think he's been planted to spy on us?'

'Possibly. I asked Steinhauer to check the records in Berlin, whether they could find any trace of a woman called Westermann marrying an Englishman called Arthur Joyce about twenty-five years ago.'

'And?'

'Nothing. Nor was there anything in the records about the birth of a son to a couple called Westermann or Joyce.'

'Maybe they weren't married.'

'Yes, that had of course occurred to me,' Lody said impatiently. 'Anyway, a couple of days ago I visited that shipping company he's supposed to work for.'

'In the Farringdon Road, where I delivered the letter for Pieter?'

'That's the one. Josiah Wood. And I talked to the manager, a fellow called Belmont.'

'I hope your cover story was water-tight, Carl,' Neumann said sarcastically. 'They might check up on you.'

'I hope they do, Kurt. The Gessner Company is registered in Zurich and a man called Carl Fricker works for it. I assumed his identity just for an hour or two.'

'Good, and what did you find out?'

'Well, it worried me that I had to drag the name of Pieter Westermann out of Belmont. I've never worked in commerce, but if I were trying to secure a nice piece of business I think I'd be eager to impress my potential customer with the size and efficiency of my company. Yes?'

Neumann nodded his agreement. There were some clumping footsteps from the floor above and then a burst of chatter in a strange language. 'Yiddish,' Neumann said, disgust plain in his voice. 'It should be banned.'

Lody ignored the comment and continued. 'The strange thing was that Belmont didn't seem sure if Westermann spoke German. Again, if I were running a shipping agency, I would be very keen to tell people that I employed someone who's bilingual. Agreed? And he didn't know where our friend lived. Now, that's a little odd, isn't it?'

Neumann rose to his feet and tried to stretch, but his hands bumped against the stained ceiling. 'You seem convinced that Pieter is a British intelligence officer, but I'm not, so what should we do?'

Lody was silent for a few moments. 'I can't make up my mind about him, but he doesn't look as though he's in the game for the money, does he?'

'We're meeting him on Monday,' Neumann replied. 'So let's question him very closely. He's young and, if he is an informer, he's an inexperienced one. He might give himself away.'

'Agreed. And if he does give himself away?'

'I'll deal with him. You mustn't get involved. The vital thing is to get you on that submarine in four days' time.'

'Yes. Saint Mary's Bay on the Kent coast is the meeting point. One hour before midnight.'

* * *

The Lamb and Flag was only moderately busy at just before ten o'clock on a Monday night. As he bought himself a pint of ale, James saw that Richard was already in position at a table close to the door. Drink in hand, James went past him and lounged as casually as he could manage on the pavement near the same door.

At a few minutes past the hour Neumann walked towards him down Rose Street and to James's relief Lody was by his side. Both men greeted him and shook his hand; out of the corner of his eye he saw Richard put down his glass. He wondered where Kell's men had concealed themselves and was glad that he was carrying his Luger in his jacket pocket, though he wondered if he would ever be capable of using it.

Neumann's massive hand lay on James's left arm and he said, 'Pieter, there's someone we want you to meet. Nearby. So let's move on, shall we.'

'Aren't we going to have a drink?' James asked.

'No time.'

'Who are we going to meet?'

'Another of our group. It's important.'

James had no alternative but to agree, especially since Neumann's grip on his arm had become emphatic. Lody was in position on his other side as they hurried him past the end of the pub and down an alleyway. They were almost running and James hoped that either Kell's men or Richard, and preferably all of them, were following them. They took several sharp turns and then went through a door into a dingy building. Lody opened a door in the corridor and James saw, in the dim light of two oil-lamps, that they were in a makeshift office; the furniture amounted to an old pine table and three chairs.

'Sit down, Pieter,' Lody said sharply. James tried to take the chair nearest the door, but Neumann waved him away. 'Over there, in the corner, near the desk.'

'This is rather dramatic,' James said, his voice as even as he could manage. 'Do we need all this cloak and dagger stuff?'

'We are spies in a foreign country, and we are at war.'

'Talking of which, Pieter, do you have any new information for me?' Lody asked quietly.

James reached into his inside pocket and handed over some notes he had written down about the movements of supplies to various military depots.

Lody scanned them quickly, looked meaningfully at Neumann and said, 'There's nothing much to attract our attention here, Pieter, is there?'

James noticed the hostility in Lody's voice. 'It's not easy, Herr Lody. The English think they see German spies everywhere. I have to be careful.'

Neumann moved across the room and put a hand on James's shoulder. It was almost a fatherly gesture, but James was reminded again how alarmingly large and powerful the man was at close quarters. 'Pieter, we both appreciate the work you're doing for us, but we have a few questions for you. You understand, I'm sure, how careful we must be.'

James nodded and asked about the man they were supposed to meet.

'He'll be along later,' Lody replied. 'But I'm curious to know how long you've worked for Belmont.'

'Just a few months. I needed some interesting work and Mister Belmont thought my ability to speak German would be useful.'

James intercepted a look that passed swiftly between the two men and Lody said, 'Belmont wasn't even sure how well you speak our language, Pieter. How do you explain that? Does he really know you?'

'Of course he does. He can be a bit vague sometimes.'

'So vague that it took him a while to remember that you worked for him. This is worrying. There are some discrepancies in your story and Kurt and I wonder whether you are who you say you are.'

James shook his head in disbelief. 'I'm as German as both of you, despite my English father, that I promise you.'

Neumann turned away and, with his back to James, spoke in a low tone to Lody. James took the opportunity to ease his right hand into his pocket, grasp the handle of the Luger and release the safety catch. He suddenly accepted that he might soon be trying to shoot his way out of trouble.

Lody stopped talking and abruptly waved Neumann aside. 'Look, Pieter,' he said, 'this conversation has gone on long enough. I suspect that you are working for Captain Kell. Is that right?' A gun had suddenly appeared in Lody's right hand and James recognised the stubby shape of a Luger.

'I don't understand. Who is Captain Kell?' James began to wonder how quickly he could pull his own gun from his pocket and fire it. Not as fast as Lody could fire his, he feared.

Neumann spoke sharply to Lody. 'This isn't the way, Carl. You mustn't get involved. Give me the gun. I'll deal with Pieter.'

To James's surprise, Lody handed over the Luger; it looked like a child's toy in Neumann's huge hand and James thought this was his one chance to save himself.

James knew that he had no chance to draw and then fire his own gun, so he tilted it upwards in his pocket and hoped it was pointed at Neumann's body. Before he could fire, the door burst open with a crash and a muscular figure hurtled into the room and smashed into Neumann. Richard had arrived. James, unnerved, pulled the trigger of his Luger and a bullet thudded into the wall opposite. He was then crushed into the corner under the combined weight of Neumann and Richard as they grappled noisily; unable to move, he saw Lody race for the open door.

Neumann had his hands around Richard's throat and James could hear his friend's gasps as he fought for air. He pushed hard with his feet against the wall and just managed to create enough space to free his hand and wrench his gun from his pocket. With only a foot or two of leverage, he brought the Luger down on the back of Neumann's head with all his pent-up fear and fury. The German yelled and shifted his weight to counter this new threat and, with a little more room to manoeuvre, James hit him a crushing blow on the temple. The German groaned deeply once and lay still. Richard levered himself from under the man's inert body.

'Nice friends you've got,' he said as he massaged his neck. 'That was nearly as bad as playing in the Eton wall game.'

'You arrived in the nick of time, Richard, thank God. How did you know what was going on?'

'Fortunately, the door was very slightly ajar and I heard everything. But it was touch and go, eh?' Richard gestured at Neumann. 'I wouldn't want to face him in a straight fight, man-to-man. What do we do with him?'

'Maybe you should kill him,' said a voice from the doorway. It was Vernon Kell. He didn't seem to be joking. 'He's no use to us, in fact he'd be an embarrassment.'

'Did you catch Lody?' James asked.

'Yes, thank the Lord. He's on his way to a prison cell.' Kell looked at Richard. 'Thank you for intervening. We don't want to lose Clifton, I can assure you, despite our poor performance tonight.' His voice grew brisk. 'You two ought to leave now. We'll tidy up.' He walked to the door and spoke briefly to someone in the corridor. 'OK, off you go. James, you concentrate on your football for the next couple of weeks.'

As they prepared to leave, Neumann stirred from his position on the floor, moaned and sat up. He looked at James and said, 'Pieter, I wouldn't have killed you, I promise...'

Kell spoke sarcastically, 'No, of course not.' Then to James and Richard he said, 'OK, off you go, you two, while we clear up.'

In the corridor the two men passed a policeman in plain clothes and they hurried out of the building. That's when they heard a single pistol shot. They stopped in their tracks and James suddenly wanted to be sick.

Richard spoke quietly. 'As I said, James, you've found some nice new friends, haven't you.'

James swallowed hard as he remembered how Richard had said that he'd 'heard everything'. Had his friend really known how much danger he was in? 'Er, Richard, I didn't realise that you spoke German.'

'I don't. Well, I've got a smattering. I can order a beer, that sort of thing.'

'So how did you know when to do your rescue act?'

'I could tell from the smaller fellow's tone of voice that he wasn't inviting you to his box at Ascot and, luckily for you, I had enough line of sight to see what the big chap was up to. When he pointed that gun at you, I thought it was about time to take a hand and I charged in.' Richard grinned at James and patted him lightly on the shoulder. 'It's what goalkeepers do, isn't it? We're told often enough that we're crazy.'

22

How can people live in such a bloody depressing place, John Smithson thought, as he tramped down the narrow street of dilapidated houses, back-to-back dwellings which had been slung together in their hundreds of thousands during Britain's industrial revolution, bleak shelters in which the workers would live out their miserable lives.

Smithson was accompanied by a man called Jack Crossley, a craggy and taciturn ex-police sergeant, who now worked for the detective agency used by Horatio Bottomley. He was there in case of trouble and Smithson had no doubt that he would cope with any that arose. Out of curiosity Smithson led the way to the end of the road where there was a piece of wasteland about half the size of a football pitch. It was bordered by the rank waters of the Leeds and Manchester Canal and beyond that lay several cotton mills, only one of which seemed to be in use. The demand for cotton had faltered during the past few years and that explained the presence of several men on the street, now unemployed and unlikely to find another job. Oh well, Smithson thought unkindly, they'll just about do as cannon fodder in Flanders.

A few children, clad in torn hand-me-down clothing, played a desultory game of football in the dust. The ripples of weak sunlight served only to emphasise the dreariness of the scene. Smithson could see the imposing tower of one of Blackburn's churches in the distance and wondered if God was having the last laugh over Mammon. In another direction he saw a tall chimney which was belching smoke. He pointed to it and said, 'What the hell is that?'

'That's the Audley Destructor,' Crossley replied. 'The town's incinerator.'

Smithson couldn't wait to get back to London, but Horatio Bottomley had sent him to Blackburn on an important errand. With a week and a half to go before the first match between the Corinthians and Blackburn Rovers, he was there to 'persuade' three of the Blackburn professionals that their best interests would be served by 'helping' Bottomley with his grand scheme.

'Just talk to the three of them, John, man to man, and explain how good old Horatio will look after them if they co-operate. It's an easy choice, John, a rational one. But by all means put all our cards on the table and let them know how unpleasant it will be if they don't see sense and help us out.'

The first man in his sights was Tommy Wiggins. Smithson kicked some rubbish off the front step of number twenty-seven Linden Street and knocked on the door, which hadn't seen a lick of paint for decades. He waited for a minute or so and then knocked again, louder. He heard a faint scuffle of feet on the other side of the door and a woman's reedy voice said, 'Aye, what d'you want?'

'Tommy Wiggins, if possible, madam,' Smithson replied. 'Is he in?'

'Nay, he's down't pub.'

'I see. Which pub is that? Is it near?'

'Aye. The Kings 'Ead, down the road.'

Smithson thanked whoever it was behind the door, though he assumed that it was Wiggins's wife, and set off down the street.

'D'you know the pub?' he asked Crossley.

'Aye, it's a bloody midden.'

It was a two-storey ale-house, as unprepossessing as the houses which surrounded it. The Temperance Society could have used it to illustrate the degradation that drunkenness inevitably brought in its wake. Cautiously, even though he had Crossley to protect him, Smithson entered the pub and registered the broken-down chairs and tables and the cracked benches lining the walls. The barman was wearing a dirty vest that only just covered his huge belly. Three men sat at a table by the bar; they had half-full pints of beer in front of them and were playing cards for a few pennies scattered on the table.

'Good afternoon,' Smithson said cheerfully to the barman. 'Is Mister Wiggins here by any chance?'

The barman jerked his head towards the three men. 'Aye, there 'e is, one of our star footballers. 'E's the one with the moustache and the thirst.'

The man with the moustache raised his eyes briefly from his cards. 'Christ, you need a thirst to drink the piss they serve up in 'ere,' said Wiggins.

'You know what you can do, Tommy, if you don't like it. But nobody else'll give you beer on the slate, will they, lad?'

'Can I buy everyone a drink?' Smithson asked placatingly.

The three men made short work of what remained in their glasses and the barman pulled three more pints for them, one for himself, and one each for Smithson and Crossley.

Smithson noticed how warily Wiggins was looking at Crossley and assumed that he thought that the bookies had sent them to collect their money. 'So what's to do, lads? I don't suppose this is a social call, is it,' Wiggins said sarcastically.

'No,' Smithson replied. 'It's business. I'm up from London to talk to you and one of the other players. Billy Dodds.'

'That's me,' said the strongly-built man with curly black hair who was sitting opposite Wiggins. 'You a journalist? We charge for interviews, don't we, Tommy?' They both laughed.

Smithson grinned back at them. 'You're not far off because I work a bit for the newspapers,' he said, exaggerating his involvement with that side of Bottomley's activities, 'and I might have a business proposition for you.'

'There's some brass in it, is there?' asked Wiggins.

'There could be, but I need to talk to you in private.'

'Sounds important, eh, Tommy,' Dodds said. 'It's not a transfer to Chelsea, is it?'

'Tell you what,' Wiggins said, 'we'll go 'ome for a cuppa tea, if that lazy cow of mine can get up off her arse to make it.'

The two men downed their pints, nodded to their companion, who had not said a word, and headed for the door.

When they reached Wiggins's house, he marched into the main room on the ground floor and yelled, 'Mary, where the 'ell are you?'

'I'm here, Tommy,' said a small voice from the back of the house, where, Smithson assumed, there was a scullery.

'We've company, so let's have some tea.'

Mary came to the doorway and stood there shyly; she was a small woman, not yet twenty and the size of the bump beneath her grey smock suggested to Smithson that she was nearing the end of her pregnancy. She had a pretty, fine-boned face and her eyes were startlingly blue. Smithson wondered why she had become involved with an uncouth bastard like Wiggins.

Dodds spoke up. 'How are you, Mary love? How's the babby coming on?'

'Oh, he'll be fine, Billy, not long to go now.'

'Come on, woman,' Wiggins interrupted, as he threw himself into a chair by the fireplace, 'let's get a move on, we've business to do.' He waved his arms vaguely at the room. 'Sit down, lads.'

Smithson took a wooden chair at the table and Dodds another, while Crossly remained standing near the front door.

'So, what's to do then?' Dodds asked.

'It's a fairly simple matter,' Smithson replied bluntly. 'You and Tommy here are in the shit with several bookies, but especially with the Grogan brothers in Manchester. You owe them nearly a hundred pounds between you.'

'And what the fuck's it got to do with you?' Wiggins said loudly. His face had suddenly flushed and he started from his chair.

'Take it easy, lad, and listen to what Mister Smithson has to say,' Crossley said. 'It might be to your advantage.'

As her husband subsided into his seat, Mary Wiggins carried a tray into the room and put a pretty flowered teapot, with matching milk jug, sugar bowl and teacups on to the table. No doubt the tea set had been a wedding present, thought Smithson. In silence, she poured out the tea and began to ask who wanted sugar.

'We'll sort that out, love,' said Dodds. 'Why don't you go upstairs and have a lie-down?'

She looked at him gratefully, made her way to the stairs by the front door and went up to the next floor.

'I'll start again,' Smithson said. 'You two owe the bookies a lot of money, and bookies can be very unpleasant if they don't get paid.'

'I can deal with those bastards,' Wiggins said heatedly. 'They don't bloody frighten me.'

'Don't be bloody daft, Tommy,' said Dodds. 'Listen to the man.'

Smithson nodded his thanks and sipped his tea. 'I might have a way out for you. I have a business associate in London who is prepared to pay off your debts in return for your help.'

'D'you hear that, Billy?' Wiggins sneered. 'We've got a new friend. So who's this Good Samaritan then? And what sort of help does he want?'

'Let's just call him Mister B, you don't need to know who he is. And the help he wants is when Blackburn play the Corinthians up here on Saturday week.'

'Oh yeah,' said Dodds, 'I can see where this is heading. You want us to try and throw the game, is that it?'

'You've smacked the nail right on its head, Mister Dodds,' said Smithson. 'Yes, we want to make sure Blackburn lose.'

'Christ,' Wiggins said disgustedly, 'lose to those bloody toffs? We'd be laughed at, we'd 'ave to stay off the streets.'

'If you don't pay the bookies, you'd be well advised to leave the country, not just stay off the streets,' Smithson replied. 'Anyway, don't underestimate the Corinthians. They're good. It's even money on the first game.'

'Aye, that's right,' Dodds said, 'they've some grand players.'

'How the 'ell can we lose the game on our own?' Wiggins asked. 'The rest of the team'll be trying their bollocks off. You know what Bob bloody Crompton's like for a start.'

'And if he or the chairman get a sniff of what we're up to, we'll never play football for Blackburn again or for any other bloody club,' Dodds said. 'And I 'ave to tell you, Mister Smithson, that football's my life. I get a decent wage to 'ave fun, there's nowt better.'

'Nobody will find you out,' Smithson reassured them. 'You just need to play a bit below your best, lose a fifty-fifty tackle, miss an interception or a shot on goal. People will just say you had an off-day. It happens, doesn't it?'

'Aye, but if the other nine play like bloody heroes, we'll still be struggling.'

'You won't be the only ones not giving a hundred per cent,' Smithson said.

'Who else?' Dodds asked.

'Never you mind. But there's another of your players who's agreed to help. Oh, and by the way, my associate, Mister B, will put some money on for you as well, on one condition...'

'Yeah?' said Wiggins aggressively.

'You don't go near a bookie until after the game. Is that clear?' Smithson, a naturally cautious man in some respects, had decided to contradict Bottomley's instruction to let them have more credit with the bookmakers.

'I won't be going near a bookie ever again. In fact, I wish I'd never gone near those bastards in the first place,' Dodds said. 'They sent someone round to our house a couple of weeks back. Some thug. 'E were looking for me. The missus were bloody terrified. She's been giving me grief ever since.'

'Why should we trust you, anyway?' Wiggins asked.

'Because my associate has already promised the bookies that he'll settle your debts, so they're off your backs for the time being. But, if you let him down, he won't keep his end of the bargain.' In the sudden silence Smithson looked at each man in turn and then said, 'This is just about the best offer you're going to get, isn't it?'

Sullenly, Wiggins muttered his agreement and Dodds reached across the table and shook Smithson's hand. 'OK, Mister Smithson, I'll do my best to keep my end of the bargain. All I can say is God help me if this ever gets out.'

'Never mind God,' Wiggins said, 'it's Bob Crompton you should worry about.'

∗ ∗ ∗

As they walked back towards Crossley's car, Smithson said, 'Two down and one to go. Can we get to Sedgemore today?'

'Aye, if he sticks to his routine. Today's one of the days he has a cuppa with his mum. Mind you, he doesn't stay long with the old duck because he's keen to get his mitts on his fancy piece straight after. Come on, I'll show you.'

Half an hour later Crossley parked his car opposite the Belle Vue Guest House, a thin four-storey Victorian house, which had seen better days several decades before and was unlikely to see them again. He nodded at it and said, 'One of Sedgemore's mates runs it. Love is blind, eh, Mister Smithson.'

Smithson peered at the building and said, 'Amen to that, but who on God's earth would stay in a place like that?'

'You'd be surprised. Commercial travellers for one. Actors and entertainers, people like that.' He winked at Smithson. 'Oh, and private detectives.' He nudged Smithson's arm. 'Here they come. Look at 'em, a real couple of love-birds, eh.'

'She's a racy little bitch, isn't she. Shall we have a word now, or later?'

'Let 'em have their fun. We'll catch him in the room with his dick wet. How's that?'

'Er, he's a big rough lad, isn't he, Mister Crossley?' Smithson said nervously.

'You leave him to me.' Crossley patted his jacket pocket. 'I've got a cosh in here if he cuts up rough.'

He's really enjoying this, Smithson thought, as they watched the tall figure of Albert Sedgemore approach the house. He was arm-in-arm with his girlfriend, a buxom young woman with large breasts. The two men remained in the car for ten minutes and then crossed the road and went through the front door of the house. A sofa with faded red upholstery lay on one side of the hallway and straight ahead was a battered wooden desk. Behind it, some hooks were screwed haphazardly into the wall and a few keys hung from them. There were doors to a couple of rooms on the ground floor, and a steep stairway curved upwards.

Crossley rapped on the door nearest to the desk and asked loudly if anyone was at home. Half a minute later they heard the sound of footsteps and a voice grumbling, 'Aw right, aw right, I'm bloody coming,' and then the owner of the voice appeared. He was in his thirties and had several days' growth of beard; the buttons of his stained flannel shirt couldn't quite contain his paunch, and he was rubbing the sleep from his eyes. Ah, mine host, thought Smithson, and what a welcome he brings with him.

Crossley didn't waste any words as he curtly asked where he would find Albert Sedgemore.

'Who?' the man asked, feigning surprise. 'Who's he?'

'A big bloke, brown hair. Plays football,' Crossley answered. 'He's here with his bit of skirt, and I want a word with him.'

'And who the fuck are you?'

'Jack Crossley, recently a sergeant in the Manchester police, that's who I am, so tell me which room Sedgemore's in.'

'Not 'ere.'

'That's funny. I watched him walk into this shithouse with his whore a few minutes ago. Now, don't piss me about, my friend, because I can have a few words with some old friends in the Manchester police and this fuckin' flea pit'll be closed down within hours. It's nowt more than a brothel anyway.'

The owner was a man who'd spent his life being defeated. He looked sadly at Crossley and jerked his thumb over his shoulder and said, 'Down the corridor. Room three at the back.'

Smithson followed Crossley down the corridor, which had a sharp smell of decay and unwashed bodies. The detective tapped sharply on the door of room number three and, after a pause, a voice said, 'Is that you, Brian?'

'No, it isn't, Mister Sedgemore. It's Jack Crossley.'

'And 'oo the 'ell are you?'

'Someone you'll want to talk to, so open the door, lad.'

'Fuck off. I don't know you and I'm busy.'

Crossley tested the door, which was locked, but Smithson reckoned that the flimsy frame wouldn't last long if an able-bodied man applied his weight to it. He noticed that Crossley had his hand in the pocket where he kept his cosh.

'Look, Sedgemore, we aren't going away, so you might as well come out now. I know you're in there with your fancy piece, but I'd rather talk to you about it than to your wife's brothers. What do you think, Albert?'

There was a muttered conversation from the room and some rustling as some clothing was donned. Crossley motioned to Smithson to stand clear and did so himself as the door was flung open and Sedgemore's tall figure charged into the corridor. 'Right, you bastard,' he began but, although he was nearly as big as Crossley and much younger, he was no match for him. The former policeman grabbed him by the arm, twisted it behind his back and smashed him face first into the wall.

'Now, calm down, Albert, or I'll have to hurt you. All we want is a little chat. Let's go and sit in the hall, shall we, and have our few words.' He forced Sedgemore's arm higher up his back and Smithson heard a loud grunt of pain from the footballer. 'Agreed?' asked Crossley and Sedgemore mumbled 'Aye' in return.

Crossley released him and pointed down the corridor, while showing him the cosh he carried. 'Any bloody nonsense and I'll lay you out, understand?' He stayed a pace behind the footballer as they went along the passage and smacked the cosh meaningfully in his hand.

As they entered the hallway, the owner was hovering by the table. 'What's goin' on?' he asked feebly.

'Nothing to concern you, my friend, so you can piss off and leave us to our little meeting,' Crossley said. The man scuttled through a door and Crossley motioned to Sedgemore to sit down on the sofa, which sagged to the floor as it took his weight.

'Right, Albert,' Crossley said, 'Mister Smithson here has a proposition for you. Listen carefully, lad.'

Smithson did not mince his words as he told Sedgemore that his business associates in London required a win for the Corinthians in the forthcoming match. Only a win would do and he, Sedgemore, was being asked to play his part in securing the desired result.

Predictably, Sedgemore pointed out that there were ten other Blackburn players, who would be giving their all to win the game.

'Not so,' Smithson countered. 'There are two other players in your team who won't be at their best, if I can put it that way. Like you, they'll just miss the occasional important tackle, just fail to cut out a pass, misplace a clearance and so on. You know how it's done, Mister Sedgemore, don't you?'

'No, I bloody don't.'

'Well, you'd better learn,' Crossley said sharply. 'And quick.'

'What if I don't want to get involved. I'm an England player, for fuck's sake, I've got a reputation.'

'You should've thought about that before you started tupping that young lass back there,' Crossley said. 'And all this while your wife is up the stick, you rotten bastard. Your wife's called Amy, isn't she, Albert? And she's got three brothers, is that right? I remember them, they're right bloody villains, they beat people up for a living, but they do it for fun, too.'

'What've they got to do with all this?'

Smithson shook his head in disbelief and nodded to Crossley to continue. 'Look, lad, if Amy's brothers get to hear about yon lass down the corridor, you'll be lucky to escape with just a couple of broken legs. Your career in football will be over and I wouldn't give much for your chances of staying alive for long in this neck of the woods.'

'So there's your choice,' Smithson said. 'Are you going to help us or not?'

23

On the Wednesday before the first match the Corinthians met at the Hurlingham Club in west London for lunch. Arthur Dickson summarised the details of their journey to Manchester; due to the exigencies of travel during wartime, they were to catch a train on Friday afternoon, stay overnight at the Midland Hotel and return to London on the Saturday evening. He then wished them well and emphasised the importance of the two games in helping to reinforce national morale 'in the face of our mortal enemy, Germany' and in assisting His Majesty's Government to recruit soldiers to play their part 'in the most important game any of us will ever experience'.

Under the direction of the Corinthians' captain, Guy Willett, the team then did some fast walking and exercises, ran several laps of the pitch and finished with thirty minutes of six-a-side football.

Dickson sat on his shooting-stick and watched with approval. It seemed to him that the Corinthians were in fine fettle; they all looked fit and strong and moved the ball with speed and intelligence. Blackburn Rovers might be the current Football League champions, but his team would give them a very tough game.

As the practice match drew to its close, he was surprised to see John Tippett walk towards him from the direction of the clubhouse. He had last seen him a couple of weeks' ago at Lord Northcliffe's office when they had discussed the two forthcoming games. Dickson looked back on that meeting with a mixture of scorn and wonder.

After the usual greetings and inquiries about each other's health, Tippett steeled himself to tell Dickson the reason for his presence. The British government was still adamant that Blackburn must win the second game in London, and Lloyd George, as uncompromising as ever, had entrusted Tippett with the unpleasant task of informing the Corinthians' chairman of that decision. In vain had Tippett repeated his arguments that the Corinthians were the very embodiment of sporting integrity. With some asperity Lloyd George had simply said, 'Tell Dickson that there's a war on and he must do his duty like everyone else.'

Tippett watched the game for a few minutes and then said tentatively, 'How do you think the Corinthians will fare against Blackburn?'

'I'm sure we'll have two very close matches and, as long as they're played in the right spirit, I don't really mind who wins.'

Tippett seized his chance. 'My masters, in particular Mister Lloyd George, have something to ask of you then.'

'Ask of me?'

'Yes, Mister Dickson, of you in your role as chairman of the club.'

'Go on.'

'For reasons of state it is felt that the most favourable result of the match here in London would be a victory for Blackburn.'

'Most favourable,' Dickson repeated and, feigning puzzlement, continued, 'Please explain yourself.' The chill in the air was immediate and almost tangible.

'The main purpose of the matches is, as you know, to recruit young men to the armed forces,' Tippett said tentatively. 'The men who will become officers are already volunteering in great numbers, as we would have expected.' He gestured towards the players. 'They're men like your Corinthians. But we need millions of ordinary men to volunteer, the rank and file, and it is thought that they'll be encouraged to sign up if they see the professional footballers of Blackburn prevail.'

'The good yeomen will rush forward, will they, Mister Tippett, and show us the mettle of their pasture?'

Tippett tried to ignore the sarcasm. 'Yes, they will identify with a victory for the common man.'

Dickson grunted and shouted out, 'Fine tackle, Archie,' as one of the Corinthians won the ball and passed it quickly to Rupert Wavell. 'Have I heard you correctly? Are you really asking me to tell my Corinthians not to try?'

'Not to try as hard as usual, perhaps.'

'Don't be mealy-mouthed, Mister Tippett. You're asking us to cheat and I have no hesitation in rejecting the idea. For one thing, you will under-estimate the intelligence of the so-called common man at your peril. He loves his football and understands it, and if a game has been rigged in favour of one side or the other he will spot it right away. And he'll make his feelings known. My final comment on this wholly improper suggestion is that no Corinthian would ever countenance such a deception. If he could, he wouldn't be a member of our club. I'm sure you can understand that, Mister Tippett.'

'I can, but my political masters won't. They are more concerned with reasons of state, with trying to win this war in which we're all embroiled.'

'I appreciate that subterfuge has a big part to play in war, so that should suit the wily, or should I say devious, Lloyd George.'

'He's a brilliant man.'

'Agreed. I heard someone call him a wizard the other day.'

'The Welsh Wizard, that's right.'

Dickson raised his eyebrows. 'I thought that the Welsh Wizard was Billy Meredith.' *

Tippett smiled at Dickson's pleasantry, but wondered how Lloyd George, whose temperament was volatile at the best of times, would react to this outright refusal to co-operate

*Meredith was one of football's foremost players, whose career spanned thirty years from 1894 to 1924. A winger, he made over 700 appearances for the two Manchester teams, and was capped 48 times for Wales.

* * *

Later that day John Smithson received a note from Horatio Bottomley; he was asked to join him that evening in the bar of the Ritz Hotel for 'a quiet chat'. Since Bottomley would no doubt be capable of attracting a noisy crowd to a Trappist monastery, Smithson wondered how he would manage to arrange such seclusion, especially at the ever-popular Ritz.

Bottomley occupied a table in the corner of the bar, his customary bottle of Pommery champagne nestling in a bucket of ice before him. When Smithson had settled into a chair and a glass of champagne had been poured for him, Bottomley leaned towards him and said quietly, 'A progress report, please, John. I know you've collared those Blackburn players, but have we laid our bets on the Corinthians to win on Saturday?'

'Wiggins, Dodds and Sedgemore will do their best, or rather their worst, for us on Saturday and that should ensure a victory for our Corinthian friends. And we've spread the bets around.'

'Even money?'

'Yes, Mister Bottomley, some at evens and some at five to four against.'

'That's good. How much do we stand to win?'

'Over two hundred thousand at the last count.'

Bottomley drew deeply on his cigar, expelled a cloud of smoke and then drank some champagne. He smiled broadly. 'Good work, John. And we'll pile all our winnings on Blackburn to win the final game in London.'

'All the money?'

'Yes. We can't lose.'

'I've heard that refrain before, Mister Bottomley.'

Bottomley waved a greeting at a noisy group of men, who had just entered the bar. He leaned over the table and said, 'I have some news which will dispel your apprehension, John, and it's from an important and, I might stress, highly confidential source.' He bent as close to Smithson as his formidable belly allowed and dropped his voice to a conspiratorial whisper. 'Our government, in the shape of Lloyd George himself, has decreed that Blackburn must win the London game.'

'I'll have a large bet with you, Mister Bottomley, that the Corinthians will tell that Welsh bugger what to do with his decree.'

'Maybe, but we have plenty of insurance. In the form of Maundy Gregory for a start.'

'That man gives me the creeps.'

'I daresay, John, but he is fully committed to our cause and he has some intriguing information about some of those Corinthians and he will use it to the great benefit of us all.'

'I still wouldn't trust Gregory to buy me a newspaper, let alone negotiate with any of those Corinthians. They may be toffs, but some of them are intelligent toffs. They'll give Gregory short shrift.'

'Don't under-estimate him. He's clever and unscrupulous and he'll have some help.' Smithson grimaced and Bottomley continued. 'It's all right, John, I know what you're going to say, but you don't have to get involved with him. You've done your bit with our friends in the north.'

'So who's the lucky man?'

'He has a colleague, David Parker, who works for Basil Thomson. As you know, Thomson is the Assistant Commissioner at Scotland Yard and the head of the CID. Vernon Kell reports directly to him, so it all fits together very neatly.'

'What do we know about Parker?'

'Not a lot, but if he's a friend of Gregory's...'

'Do we have to cut him in on the profits?'

'No. Gregory will pay him out of his share.'

* * *

After having breakfast with his mother, Richard Hildreth left their home in Portman Square at just after ten o'clock. He walked at a brisk pace north along Baker Street until he reached the Outer Circle, which is the boundary of Regent's Park. Although goalkeepers were not expected to be as fit as the other ten players, Richard prided himself on being in as good a physical condition as the rest of the Corinthian team.

Twice around the Outer Circle was a walk of just over five miles and it constituted an important part of his regime. It was another sunny summer day and he was already warm as he passed Macclesfield Bridge. He breathed deeply, worked his arms vigorously and then ran on the spot for several seconds, much to the amusement of a group of children in the care of two uniformed nannies. He smiled back at them; he felt privileged to be alive, even if his mother's financial problems were taking their toll on her. On that very morning he had caught a glimpse of a letter from her bankers and it had clearly caused her some distress, though she had refused to discuss its contents with him. He was worried about her and, after the matches with Blackburn Rovers and before he joined his regiment, he was determined to uncover the full extent of her problems and try to resolve them. His first priority would certainly be to extract her 'investment' from Horatio Bottomley.

It was a busy summer scene with cyclists bowling along, perambulators being pushed and walkers ambling in the sunshine. Despite all the activity Richard became conscious of someone behind him, someone breathing hard as he strove to get alongside, and his curiosity compelled him to glance back. The man was nearly as tall as Richard, but more heavily built.

His broad and sallow face was filmed with sweat as he sought to overtake Richard, who, since he did not know the man, strode onwards.

'Mister Hildreth,' the man said, his voice a little shrill from his exertions, 'Could I speak to you, please?'

Richard slowed down and spoke over his shoulder. 'Who are you? I don't think I know you.'

'No, you don't.' The man drew level and Richard caught a whiff of something odd on the man. Some kind of eau de toilette perhaps. He searched his mind for a reference and thought it reminded him of his unmarried Aunt Florence. Was it rose water?

'I need to talk to you in private.'

'So write to me and make an appointment,' Richard replied. 'I'm busy. This is the time of day when I take some exercise and I don't want to forego it.'

'I think I should tell you that I work for Mister Basil Thomson, head of the Criminal Investigation Department at Scotland Yard.'

'I'm very impressed,' Richard said sarcastically, 'but you still need to make an appointment.'

'My name is Inspector David Parker. Here's my card.'

Richard slowed up and, as he took the card, he noticed how big Parker's hands were. He also saw scar tissue on the knuckles and traces of grime under his fingernails. Scented toilet water and dirty fingernails; that was an odd combination. Parker was not a man he would care to welcome into his own home, he thought.

'This is rather an unconventional approach, Inspector Parker, isn't it?'

'It's an unconventional situation, Mister Hildreth.' He pointed at a bench. 'Let's sit down for a minute or two, please.' Having established his status and authority, this sounded more like an order than a request.

When Parker had sat down, Richard ostentatiously chose the other end of the bench. As he settled himself he tried to appraise Parker as quickly and unobtrusively as he could. His clothes, for example, appeared to be more expensive than those normally worn by a police inspector; the dark suit was well-cut, his shirt and necktie were made of silk, and his shoes looked hand-made. Rather fussily, a coloured handkerchief flowed from the breast pocket of his jacket.

'I won't waste your valuable time, Mister Hildreth,' Parker said, the sarcasm evident in his voice and his tone emphatic. 'There are a number of people, some of them important people within the government, who require a win for Blackburn Rovers when you play them in London in just over a week's time.'

'Well, certain people had better hope that the Rovers play better on the day than the Corinthians, had they not?'

'That's not a satisfactory answer. We require a guarantee of the result and you are one of the players who can provide that guarantee.'

'What do you want me to do? Let me guess. Throw the ball into my own net, I suppose?'

'Nothing as crude as that, but no doubt you'll do what you have to do.' Parker looked grimly at him and Richard noticed the hardness in his eyes; this was a man who was used to getting his own way. He also saw the dull red patches on each of Parker's cheeks; he was also a man whose life was lived close to the edge of violence.

'What I'll do, Inspector, is what I always do, play the game to the best of my ability, in a fair and sporting manner.' Richard knew he sounded pompous, but he didn't care.

'You people live in a different world, don't you, Hildreth?' There was a pronounced sneer from Parker and Richard noticed that the respectful 'Mister' had been forgotten.

Parker moved closer on the bench and Richard got another dose of his toilet water, tinged now with the smell of his sweat. 'Just you listen to me, Hildreth. You've got two very good reasons for doing what you're told.' Parker shook a thick index finger almost under his nose. 'First, there's that brother of yours in Ireland.'

'What of him?'

'He's a bloody traitor to his country, that's what.'

'What on earth are you talking about?' Richard was genuinely mystified by the accusation. 'My brother Adam, a traitor. Are you mad?'

'He was quoted in *The Times* a few months back, he's a great supporter of home rule for Ireland, isn't he?'

'Yes and so are many others, here and in Ireland. There's Asquith for a start, and Churchill. Until this war began it was one of the government's policies to push through home rule. Does that make all these people traitors?'

'No, but it would if any of them was involved in supplying guns to the Irish Volunteers, guns which might be used against British soldiers.'

'Where did you hear such nonsense?'

'It's in a report from one of our under-cover agents. A few weeks ago your brother assisted a man called Erskine Childers in landing a large quantity of Mauser rifles and ammunition at Howth Harbour near Dublin.'

'Erskine Childers? The novelist? So why haven't you arrested him?'

'We have other plans for him.'

'Oh, no doubt,' Richard said sarcastically. 'Maybe he'll put you and your fantasies in the sequel to *The Riddle of the Sands*.'

'I would be very careful, if I were you, Hildreth.' Parker's index finger was in action again, waving under Richard's nostrils. 'We can start proceedings for the arrest of your precious brother tomorrow, if we want. However, if his well-being isn't a big enough incentive for you, let's have a chat about your mother.'

Richard glared at Parker and told him to leave his mother out of the discussion.

Parker spoke quietly in return and without his accustomed sharpness. 'You can help her, as well as Adam. We know that her finances are in a mess. In fact, she'll have to leave that fine house of hers in Portman Square soon if she doesn't recover some of the money she invested with Mister Bottomley. Isn't that so?'

'We'll sell some of our estates in Ireland if we have to.'

'In wartime? Some chance. But let me continue. Our government wants Blackburn to win this game and such a result also suits our mutual friend Bottomley. He's a great patriot, as you know.'

'Oh yes, patriotism is usually the last refuge of scoundrels like Bottomley.'

'You're in no position to treat him with contempt. On the contrary, you should be grateful for his generosity. If you co-operate he'll return your mother's investment to her. All of it, plus ten per cent. Would that persuade you to help us?'

His mind in confusion, Richard got to his feet and said, 'I'll let you know what I think later.' He strode swiftly off in the hope that a strenuous walk would calm his thoughts. What was Bottomley up to? If he were willing to return his mother's money, one thing was certain – that a great deal more money would be heading in Bottomley's direction and presumably in Parker's.

Parker remained seated for a minute or two. His long experience of dealing with crooks and informers told him that

Hildreth's final remark meant that he would, in the end, toe the line. All that talk of honour and sportsmanship that these toffs went in for and they were just like any of the thieves and ponces with whom he dealt every day of the week.

24

The train journey from London to Manchester was more prolonged than usual and, therefore, more tedious. The railway network was strained to breaking point as the extra trains carrying troops and the supplies essential to a country at war had to be accommodated. The dining car, in which the Corinthians would normally have taken lunch, was no longer in service, and their party of twelve players, the chairman and a committee member called Hubert Soames, was served a frugal lunch of sandwiches and beer.

The Corinthians were crammed into two adjoining first class compartments and the presence of twelve young men attracted many glances. Some were curious, some knew about the game and realised that they were members of the famous amateur club, but others looked at them with contempt, as if wondering why these men, clearly in their physical primes, were not fighting for their country in the trenches of Flanders.

As the train lurched slowly past Wolverhampton, Arthur Dickson entered the compartment which held eight of the players, including James and Richard, Rupert Wavell and the captain, Guy Willett. He stood uncomfortably by the sliding door and said, 'Gentlemen, I wanted you all to know that I've recently been the subject of a certain amount of pressure from our government with regard to these matches we're about to play.'

'Pressure?' asked Willett. 'In what sense? We're playing a couple of games to help recruit men to the army and navy, so why should there be any pressure?'

'Because, Guy, our government, in its wisdom, wants to ensure that Blackburn wins the game in London.'

'For what reason?' Willett asked.

'A victory for the working man, for the men who will bear the brunt of the fighting, is considered to be desireable.'

'How much are they willing to pay us?' Wavell drawled from his seat by the window.

'That's not funny, Rupert,' Dickson replied.

'My apologies, of course, Mister Chairman. In other words this idea has been dreamt up *pour encourager les autres*,' Wavell said in an exaggerated French accent.

'I just wanted you to know,' Dickson continued, 'that I told that fellow from the War Office, Tippett, what he could do with his suggestion. Well, Lloyd George's suggestion actually. And I wanted you all to know what's been going on. However, it did occur to me to ask if any of you had been approached to, er, throw the game.'

Dickson looked around the compartment and, since no one responded, he prepared to leave.

'What about you, Richard?' Wavell asked with a smirk. 'You're our goalkeeper and, if I were trying to fix a game of football, you'd be my primary target.'

Richard grinned amiably at Wavell and said, 'If someone offers me a large bag of gold sovereigns you, Rupert, will be the first person to whom I will turn for advice.'

A few minutes later, Willett asked if anyone had seen that day's edition of *The Daily Mail* and produced a copy from his suitcase.

The headline read: TITANIC CLASH AT OLD TRAFFORD IN PROSPECT. Underneath there were photographs of the two teams and the report was as follows:

'The best sporting stadium in Great Britain will tomorrow play host to the two finest and most accomplished football teams in the world. The first of two special matches (the second will be at London's Crystal Palace next Saturday) will be played in front of a record crowd of over 70,000 spectators.

'The matches are being played to bring into focus the needs of the British Army, Navy and Flying Corps in their historic fight against the German foe. Our brave boys, battling against overwhelming odds in hostile foreign fields, NEED YOUR HELP. Able-bodied men are needed. DO YOUR DUTY AND VOLUNTEER.

'Lord Northcliffe, the proprietor of *The Daily Mail*, has put his full weight behind these prestigious fixtures and this is his personal message: "Men and women of England, I felt it my duty to help to organise this, the first of two magnificent games of football. Football is Britain's national game and you could not find two finer teams to represent it than our brilliant League Champions, Blackburn Rovers, and those exemplars of sportsmanship and sporting integrity, the Corinthians."

'We thank Lord Northcliffe for his message of support and we should point out that all the profits from the two games will be donated to Armed Forces' charities. There will be collections before each game, and numerous recruiting points have been set up both outside and inside the grounds. GOD SAVE THE KING.'

* * *

Most of the Corinthians would have welcomed a quiet dinner in the Midland Hotel and a few hands of cards before retiring to bed. This was, however, denied them because the Lord Mayor of Manchester had invited them all to a formal dinner with several dozen local dignitaries. After the meal a number of speeches of welcome were made and it was after eleven o'clock when the players were able to drift away to bed.

As they collected their keys at the reception desk, Richard spoke quietly to James. 'Can you spare me a moment, James? Over there, in the sitting room?' He pointed to a high-ceilinged room to their left and led the way to a table in a corner; it was well away from a group of businessmen who were happily engaged in emptying a bottle of whisky as rapidly as possible.

James looked expectantly at his old friend. Was it some news of Emily? Had she got engaged to someone, perhaps? Or was it Richard's mother? He knew that she had been a source of anxiety to him for many months.

Richard, usually relaxed and with a smile rarely far from his lips, seemed untypically ill-at-ease and James prompted him light-heartedly. 'Well, what is it, Richard? Women trouble? Money trouble?'

There was no answering smile. 'You recall Dickson's remarks earlier about fixing the second game?' James nodded. 'Well, I had a very strange conversation recently with some fellow from Scotland Yard, name of Parker, an Inspector. He said he works for Basil Thomson, the head of CID.'

'Does he indeed? I can probably get some information about him for you.'

'Good. I can only tell you this in strictest confidence.' Richard shook his head with some embarrassment. 'Christ, James, why am I saying such a crass thing to you? Let me tell you what actually happened.'

Richard summarised the offer he had received from Parker and James said, 'So, Bottomley's involved in some betting conspiracy, eh?'

Richard nodded and then told James how Inspector Parker was also trying to blackmail him about his brother's supposed gun-running activities.

'Adam? Running guns? What utter nonsense. Have you contacted him?'

'Not yet. I'll send him a note tomorrow.'

'Adam's never been that interested in politics, has he?'

'Hardly at all, though he's professed his support for home rule for Ireland.'

'So have I.'

'Quite.'

'So what will you do?'

'Nothing, as yet. But we might try to use your many contacts, James, to find out more when we get back to London. Meanwhile, it's bed for me and let's look forward to an enjoyable game tomorrow.'

* * *

Manchester United's football ground at Old Trafford had been built for an unprecedented cost of nearly £100,000. The inaugural game was played against Liverpool on 19 February, 1910 and a journalist was so overcome by his enthusiasm that he described the United Football Ground as 'the most handsomest, the most spacious and the most remarkable I have ever seen'.

The Corinthians, when they arrived there about an hour before the kick-off, would no doubt have agreed with that overwrought scribe. The covered South Stand had plush seats which would have suited a London theatre, let alone a football ground, and the banks of terracing stretched around the other three sides. The stadium was already filling up and it seemed that *The Daily Mail* had been right to predict an audience of 70,000 people.

To the Corinthians who had played for their country a large crowd usually meant a thousand or two spectators, even if the traditional New Year's Day game against their fellow amateurs, Queen's Park, generally drew 20,000 onlookers to Hampden Park in Glasgow.

They had been shown around the ground by the United chairman, Mr J H Davies, and had been much impressed by facilities which were lavish for their day: there was a billiard room and a recreation room for the players, a gymnasium, a massage room and large plunge-baths in each changing room.

'This is the way forward for the game of football,' Davies said proudly and the Corinthians had agreed enthusiastically. After all, the man had invested a lot of his own money in the new ground and deserved every encouragement.

Such an occasion at such a stadium induced some nervousness among the amateurs as they sat in their dressing room, although the mood was lightened by the ebullient Max Woosnam, who said, 'Remember, it's the same for the Blackburn lads, they've rarely played in front of a crowd this size either. We'll love it, there's nothing like the noise of a crowd like this. It will galvanise us, I promise you.'

'Galvanise or paralyse?' asked Rupert Wavell.

'You do your usual thing, Rupert,' said the captain, Guy Willett. 'It's a wide pitch, so run at their defence and then slide the ball into the gaps for Hugh and Henry and Edwin.'

'Then we've only got Sedgemore and Bob Crompton to contend with. Still they're human, just like us,' Richard said with a laugh.

'Human? That's debateable,' Woosnam replied.

* * *

Finally, it was time for the teams to make their ways on to the pitch. The Corinthians, technically the away side, were first to appear; in their usual under-stated style, they strolled out, in their long-sleeved white shirts and dark-blue shorts. To the casual spectator the impression was of a bunch of fellows who had met by chance and decided to form a makeshift football team.

Despite their air of studied nonchalance, several of the Corinthians experienced a sense of shock and then of exhilaration as they saw the solid walls of spectators on all four sides of the stadium. The applause was polite as they waited for the entry of their opponents. As soon as the first blue and white shirt was glimpsed in the tunnel leading to the pitch, a huge wave of sound rolled over the stadium. James had never heard anything quite so thunderous and the hand-clapping and cheers seemed to go on for several minutes. There was no doubt which team had the support of the crowd.

Then it was time for the players to line up and shake hands with the Lords Northcliffe and Kinnaird, with Sir Daniel McCabe, the Lord Mayor of Manchester, and with the Mayor of Blackburn. Finally, to another clamorous round of applause, George Robey shook hands with each player in turn; he knew every man's name and wished him well in the forthcoming game.

The players peeled off to different ends of the ground and hit a few shots at their respective goalkeepers. Then the two captains, Guy Willett and Bob Crompton, who had played together on several occasions for England, met in the centre circle where the referee tossed a coin for the choice of ends. To Crompton's surprise, Willett, who had called 'heads' correctly, said, 'We'll kick off, Bob, so you have the choice of ends.'

'Right, that's fine, Mister Willett, we'll defend the west goal.'

Willett had decided to use a tactic designed to give the Corinthians an immediate attacking advantage. As the referee's whistle blew, Hugh Pryce-Morgan tapped the ball to Edwin May, who laid it back smoothly along the closely-cropped turf to Max Woosnam, who had as strong a kick as anyone in football. The Corinthian forwards hared up the field while Woosnam kicked the ball, high and long, towards the opposing penalty area. The tactic paid an immediate dividend, since the strapping figure of Albert Sedgemore only half-cleared the ball and it fell at the feet of Archie Ludlow, who was about ten yards behind the Corinthian forwards. He moved it neatly towards Wavell on the right, and his lofted pass skimmed over Bob Crompton's head and was taken on the run by Pryce-Morgan; by this time Willett had surged into the penalty area and Pryce-Morgan's pass inside gave him enough space and time to control the ball and hit a low shot past the Blackburn goalkeeper's right hand. The Corinthians were a goal ahead with less than a minute of the game played.

For a moment the crowd was silent, shocked by the suddenness of the Corinthians' strike on the Blackburn goal; many of the privileged spectators in the South Stand had hardly settled into their seats and had even missed the goal. Then the applause rang out, generous in its volume, and the teams lined up to re-start the game. James, on the left of the field, knew that a forceful riposte would come from the League champions; he noticed that Crompton was talking animatedly to all the Blackburn players within earshot.

Moments later James collected a clearance from Richard and exchanged passes with Herbert Grosvenor as they moved up the field. Grosvenor's pass into the edge of the Blackburn penalty area was slightly too strong and James took the full force of Crompton's tackle. The Blackburn captain timed his challenge to perfection, shoulder to shoulder with James, won the ball and moved it forward to Billy Dodds. James could not remember ever being tackled so hard; he felt as though Crompton had compressed the very marrow of his bones. As he struggled to his feet, Crompton put out a hand and helped to haul him upright. 'You OK, lad?' he asked and, when James nodded, he patted him on the shoulder and ran back to his position. James had anticipated a demanding game against the champions, but he now realised just how onerous a task lay ahead.

On Monday, 7 September, *The Times* published the following account of the match.

ASSOCIATION FOOTBALL

CORINTHIANS v BLACKBURN ROVERS

This was an outstanding game of football, played in late summer sunshine on the excellent pitch which the United Ground provides. An enthusiastic crowd was treated to a veritable feast of footballing skills by the great apostles of the amateur game, the Corinthians, and the polished professionals of Blackburn Rovers, the current League Champions.

After a short patriotic address from Lord Northcliffe, the game could not have commenced in a more dramatic manner, as M Woosnam sent a long pass into the heart of the Blackburn defence, Sedgemore made an indecisive clearance, and some neat inter-passing between A R B Ludlow and R Wavell enabled the Corinthians' captain, G W Willett, to plant an incisive shot into the corner of the Blackburn net.

The response from the Rovers was swift. Marshalled admirably by their captain and full-back, Crompton, a player equally powerful in both defence and attack, the blue and whites mounted a series of attacks along both wings, where Barnett and Simpson showed both fleetness of foot and great persistence. It was unfortunate that Wiggins at centre-forward did not convert the chances offered to him. It must be said that the Corinthians' defence was robust, with M Woosnam much to the fore in clearing his lines. However, minutes before half-time, Crompton angled a long cross-field pass to Hopkins, who evaded J A Loxley's tackle and put the ball just beyond R J S Hildreth's athletic dive and into the Corinthian net.

The drama had further to run before the curtain came down for the interval, and the focal point was the nimble and elusive running of R Wavell on the Corinthians' wing. Having seized the ball just beyond the half-way line, he raced past Moss, the left full-back, wrong-footed Sedgemore, who was uncharacteristically slow to react to danger, and cut the ball back perfectly into the stride of M Woosnam, who struck a thunderous shot into the roof of the Blackburn net.

At half-time we were reminded of the serious purpose that lay behind this enjoyable sporting occasion. As the band of the Lancashire Fusiliers played a selection of military marches, a collection was taken for armed forces charities.

Your correspondent was not alone in expecting the pace of the game to slacken during the second half, but we lesser sporting beings know not what reserves of strength and determination are possessed by these exemplars of the modern game of football. The quickness and neatness of the Corinthians, personified in the play of A R B Ludlow and J Clifton, its robust enthusiasm as shown in the play of M Woosnam and G W Willett and the subtleties of R Wavell and E deG May were answered fully by the outstanding skills of Crompton, Barnett, Simpson and Parry. For twenty minutes no advantage accrued to either side, but then the Corinthians went further ahead when H B Pryce-Morgan dribbled swiftly into the Blackburn penalty area, eluded a challenge from Sedgemore and slid the ball under the diving goalkeeper.

Now came the moment when the League Champions looked for inspiration and they needed to look no further than their herculean captain. Crompton knew that only deeds, not words, would restore his team's fortunes. Repeatedly he surged forward to support his forwards and, having won the ball in a resounding tackle on the redoubtable M Woosnam, he threaded a pinpoint pass into the stride of Dodds who, indifferent in performance thus far, could not fail to score.

Despite all the pressure exerted by the champions, they could not draw level and in the final few minutes the Corinthians demonstrated why their style of football is revered in the four corners of the civilised world. The ball travelled from their goalkeeper, R J S Hildreth, to J A Loxley and then via a succession of crisp and accurate passes involving half the team to R Wavell, who dashed through the middle, showed a clean pair of heels to the lumbering Sedgemore and struck the ball clinically past the Blackburn custodian.

Thus, a rousing contest ended with a deserved victory for the Corinthians by four goals to two. It was a sporting encounter which embodied everything for which an onlooker would hope: great skill, manly endeavour, graciousness and sportsmanship. One might say that the players showed all those qualities which are most valued in a human being and which will be needed in full measure during the trials facing our country in the months to come.

It is humbling to report that the many recruiting booths stationed around the United Football Ground were besieged for several hours after the game by men eager to sign up for the armed forces.

* * *

After the game Dickson burst into the Corinthians' changing room; he was followed by one man clutching a crate of champagne and another bearing a tray of glasses.

'That was a most impressive display of footballing skill,' Dickson said. 'I'm proud of you all. Now, let's fill those glasses and drink a toast.' When everyone had a glass in his hand, he said, 'Here's to the Corinthian Football Club, and long may it prosper.'

After the toast had been drunk and drunk again, Guy Willett said quietly to Richard and James, 'I don't want to decry our performance today, but I thought that one or two of the Blackburn players weren't at their best.'

'Wiggins, perhaps?' Richard said.

'And Sedgemore,' added James.

'Yes. Mind you, everyone's entitled to an off-day,' Willett said.

'Not that you'd want to make a habit of it, with Bob Crompton as your captain,' Richard said.

As Willett wandered off to speak to Dickson, James said, 'Are you thinking what I'm thinking?' Richard nodded.

25

Horatio Bottomley was one of life's great optimists. When his schemes came to fruition, he regarded such an outcome as the due reward for his energy and perspicacity; and a setback, however serious it might appear to others, was a mere interruption to the inevitable upward progress of his business or social life.

Ebullience should have been his middle name and when Smithson entered Bottomley's Pall Mall flat he received the very warm welcome that he had anticipated. Although it was only the middle of the morning a magnum of Pommery champagne sat in an ice-bucket on the desk in front of Bottomley, who waved his glass expansively at Smithson.

'John, welcome. Sit yourself down and have a glass of fizz.' He grasped the bottle and poured the champagne carefully into a goblet and handed it to Smithson. 'The Corinthians did us proud on Saturday, did they not? And we're well on the way towards making a bundle of money. I see that the newspapers are all predicting another victory for our amateur heroes at Crystal Palace.'

'Yes, Mister Bottomley, we'll get good odds on Blackburn.'

'Excellent,' Bottomley grinned widely at his associate. 'You'll get the bets on today?'

'Most of them.'

'And the Corinthians whom we have in our sights know what they have to do?'

'Well, more or less, Mister Bottomley.' Smithson avoided Bottomley's gaze by picking up his glass and drinking from it.

'More or less, John, what the devil does that mean?' He spoke emphatically and was no longer smiling.

'Gregory sent that fellow David Parker to deal with Hildreth, but he's not sure that the bait was taken.'

'Well, those two had better make sure, hadn't they. I will emphasise to Mister Maundy Gregory that this game on Saturday will make or break him.'

'It's all right, Mister Bottomley, he and Parker claim that they have a cast-iron plan to make sure that Clifton and Wavell do what they're told. They won't have any options but to co-operate, that's what Gregory said. So whatever Hildreth does or doesn't do isn't important.'

'I hope he's right,' Bottomley said grimly, as he drained his glass and reached across his desk for the magnum.

* * *

A few hours later Maundy Gregory met David Parker in a rarely-used office in an obscure corner of the New Scotland Yard building. Whereas Parker was his usual slightly menacing self, Gregory seemed ill at ease, even if he tried to keep his face as expressionless as usual. He perched himself on the edge of a dusty desk; Parker, a file in his hand, stood by the half-open door, in order to ensure that nobody came upon them suddenly.

'What's the latest news on Hildreth?' asked Gregory.

'I spoke to him this morning and told him again that he'd better co-operate with us. It's in his interest.'

'And?'

'He seemed much more amenable, especially when I told him that his lovely young sister, Emily, is being watched by the Special Branch.'

'Is she?' Gregory asked sharply.

'No, but she is on a list as a strong supporter of those bloody suffragettes. She's quite pretty... if you like that sort of thing.' Parker cracked his knuckles and grinned, as if in anticipation.

'When do we move on the other two? Time's getting short, you know, John.'

'I do know it and I'm as anxious as you to make sure our bets are safe. I'll be able to retire on the proceeds. I've got my eye on a nice little house near Sandwich.' Gregory grunted. 'And the answer is that we're watching Wavell. He can't go more than a couple of days without knocking some cheap little whore about, so we're hopeful we'll catch him at it tonight.'

'Good. And Clifton?'

'That's easy, we'll tie him in to that queer bunch at the Foreign Office. You know some of them, Maundy, don't you? Andrew McCormack? Percy Allott? They're regular customers of the queer boys who sell themselves around those pubs in Soho, aren't they?'

'You keep me out of it, Parker.'

'I will, Maundy, don't worry. And we must also guard the reputation of our mutual friend, Basil Thomson, mustn't we?'

* * *

Rupert Wavell had enjoyed an excellent dinner with his parents at the Café Royal. The accounts of the game in the newspapers had all praised him to the skies for his skill and panache. 'Electrifying', 'one of the great Corinthians', and 'worthy to be compared with the great Billy Meredith as an attacking winger' were some of the comments about him. His parents basked in the reflected glory as people, both known and unknown to him, came to his table to offer their congratulations and to wish him well in the second game. Wavell had rarely seen his mother so happy, and he felt a pang of conscience when, at just before ten o'clock, he made ready to leave.

'It's still quite early, Rupert dear, isn't it?' she implored him.

'Yes, Mama, but I must get some rest. I'm still exhausted after that game and we have another one on Saturday.'

Wavell managed to extricate himself a few minutes later and left the dining room to another round of congratulations from the other diners. There was even a scatter of applause as he reached the exit. He loved his mother, but more and more these days found her constant attentions to be cloying. He shuddered to think what her reaction would be when he told her that he'd been accepted into the Royal Flying Corps; he had been taught to fly by Claude Graham-White at Hendon Aerodrome and had decided that a war conducted from those filthy trenches was not for him. He would far rather be airborne, above the fray, no matter how dangerous were those flimsy aeroplanes.

Tonight, however, Wavell only had one thing on his mind, and that was some close combat with a whore. Recently he had thought it wise to stay away from his previous haunts in Clerkenwell and in a street off the Horseferry Road in Victoria had found a brothel which catered for his unusual tastes. It was run by a former merchant seaman and his wife; they had first met when she was plying her dubious trade on the waterfront in Marseilles. Between them they managed to provide a good selection of women, several of whom were ready to indulge customers like himself who 'liked a bit of rough stuff'.

Tom and Annette welcomed him into their sitting-room and offered him a glass of gin, which he declined.

'How are we, sir?' Tom asked with an obsequious smile that exposed the blackened stumps of his few remaining teeth. 'What's your pleasure tonight, Mister Gladstone?' Wavell never used his own name in such places and it was part of the fun to assume the names of famous public figures.

'Is Fleur available?' he asked and Tom nodded and gave Wavell another of his grisly smiles.

'In her nanny's uniform, Mister Gladstone?'

It was Wavell's turn to nod and Tom told him to take one of the back rooms on the first floor and he would send her up.

Wavell stripped to his underwear and threw his expensive clothes into the four corners of the room. When Fleur entered the room he said, 'Clear this place up, you lazy bitch,' and smacked her hard across the face. He saw a mixture of contempt and hatred in her eyes and thought that she'd made a very good start to the entertainment that was to follow.

Less than an hour later Wavell left the brothel and had only taken a few paces towards Horseferry Road when a solidly-built man in a dark suit appeared from the shadows of a doorway. Very much aware that there were plenty of men in such localities who were capable of extreme violence to gain a shilling-piece, Wavell stopped, backed away and prepared to flee. He was confident that he could outrun anyone on earth. However, another man, smaller but younger, was blocking his escape route. He might have to stay and fight and hope that he could still get away with a minimum of damage.

'It's all right, Mister Wavell, no need to panic,' said the older man quietly. 'We are police officers and we merely want to talk to you for a moment.'

'Talk to me?' Wavell said suspiciously. 'Why? What possible reason can you have for accosting me in this way, my man?'

'I'm not your man, as you put it. I'm Inspector Parker of the CID and we want to speak to you about a criminal assault on a prostitute called Fleur.'

Wavell stared at Parker for several seconds and then said falteringly, 'But I paid for her services, Inspector. It's just a game I like to play...'

'You should stick to football, sir, I'm told you're good at that, too. I wonder how your fine Corinthian friends will react to the news that you're in court for assaulting a common prossie, eh?'

Wavell suddenly realised that this wasn't about his beating up a whore. Did the man want money? After all, many of the police were known to be corrupt, to be bribeable. He reached inside his coat pocket for his wallet. 'Erm, Inspector, perhaps I could offer some sort of recompense. Would that settle the matter?'

'Don't add the attempted bribery of a police officer to the charges, Mister Wavell. No, we'd better talk this over at the police station. There's one just down the road.' Parker spoke to the other man. 'Jim, go and get that prossie, Fleur, and bring her to the station and tell that ponce Tom to come and see us in half an hour or so.'

When they reached the police station, Parker walked straight past the policeman at the front desk and led the way into a cell. Wavell's nose wrinkled involuntarily as it registered the virulent smell of urine and vomit. 'Sit down, Mister Wavell. We'll just wait for Fleur to arrive and then we can listen to what she has to say before we decide what to charge you with.'

Wavell took one look at the stained wooden bench and remained on his feet. He assumed that his mother would be able to extricate her beloved son from another of his 'little scrapes'; no doubt his father knew someone at the top of the Metropolitan Police tree and she would then march into action.

'This is Sergeant Dobbs,' Parker said, as the man called Jim, preceded by Fleur, appeared in the doorway. 'And of course you already know Fleur.'

She looked venomously at Wavell and he gazed back, noting her almost-closed left eye and her swollen lips.

'Did this man assault you, Fleur?' asked Parker.

'Yeah, that's the bastard.'

'Did he pay you?'

'Nah, just a tip after. A few bob.'

'And you wish to complain of assault?'

'Yeah, I bleedin' well do. 'E's ruined me face.'

'Oh, it's not too bad, Fleur.'

Parker suddenly closed on Fleur and, as Dobbs trapped her arms behind her back, he smashed his fist twice into her face. She screamed with the pain and the shock; her nose had broken and her right cheek was split open and was pouring blood.

'That's better, eh, Jim. Fancy you doing so much damage, Mister Wavell. The magistrate won't like it, he won't like it at all. And you such a toff, too. OK, Jim, clean her up a bit. Then write a statement about the assault and make a list of her injuries. That ponce can take her home then.'

When Dobbs had dragged Fleur out of the cell, Parker grinned at Wavell. 'I enjoyed that. You know what it's like don't you, Wavell? Your fist or your boot crunching into some cheap prossie.'

Parker was sweating with pleasure and Wavell looked away as nausea swept upon him. God, did he look like that disgusting thug when he had his way with his whores? He knew that he'd gone pale with shock and his voice shook as he spoke. 'You must be mad. You won't get away with this, Parker, I'll make a complaint and you'll be thrown out of the force.'

'Really? I don't think you realise how much trouble you're in, Wavell. I'll make these charges stick if I have to. But there's a much more serious matter concerning you. It's about the murder of a prostitute on the second Saturday in August. You were with her that night, in that pox-riddled brothel on the corner of Shoe Lane and Plum Tree Court. Or in your case I suppose we should call it a knocking-shop.' Parker smiled grimly at his joke and continued, 'Yes, I can pin that murder on you, Wavell, because I've got several witnesses. You took her out of that dump on some pretext or other and beat her to death.' He paused and looked hard at Wavell. 'As I said, Mister Wavell, I can make the charges stick, if I have to.'

Wavell heard the heavy emphasis on the last phrase and looked up, unable to disguise the hope suddenly flaring in his eyes. 'Am I right in thinking that you don't have to press these charges, Inspector?' His habitual drawl had almost returned as he continued. 'So what do you require of me?'

'Don't try too hard in the match on Saturday, Mister Wavell. You're going to have one of your off-days.'

* * *

'You're from Captain Kell, are you?' James asked. To his surprise, two men had accosted him as he left the Foreign Office and introduced themselves as Inspector Parker and Sergeant Dobbs. James knew that this was the odious Inspector Parker who had attempted to blackmail Richard, but did not intend to reveal that he knew anything about him. He held out his arm to stop a taxi; he was in a hurry to get to the Queen's Club for lunch and some practice with the rest of the Corinthians.

'No, sir,' Parker replied, 'we're not from Captain Kell, though I have worked with him in the past. No, this is a personal matter. Do you mind if we ride with you in the taxi?'

'That's up to you,' James said, without bothering to hide his impatience. He looked pointedly at his watch. 'I am already late for lunch.'

James gave his directions to the cabbie and they all climbed into the taxi. 'So, if it's not to do with Kell, what's this about?'

'It's about your private life, Mister Clifton.'

James had a sudden and awful thought that his liaison with Mrs Kitson-Clark had come to light and that he was to be implicated in a divorce. However, he hadn't seen her for two months or more and these men were policemen, not private detectives.

'My private life is exactly that. Private,' James said emphatically.

'Not if you're involved with a bunch of queers and perverts, it isn't.'

James tried to reach over and rap on the cabbie's window; it was clear that the man was even more of a maniac than he or Richard had suspected and he should get out of the taxi at once. Parker thrust him back roughly into his seat.

'Stay where you are. We know there's a little group of you in the Foreign Office who play games with the little queer boys from around Soho and Clerkenwell, and you're one of them, aren't you? You and Percy Allott and Andrew McCormack and others I could mention.'

'You're off your head, Inspector. I don't know those men and I have no interest in boys of any kind, let alone queer boys, as you call them.'

'Early in August, on a Saturday night, on the eighth of August to be precise, you were followed by one of our CID officers. You were involved in a brawl at the Old Vienna restaurant. It's got a very nasty reputation, all sorts of criminals and queers go there. Later you were seen to be engaged in conversation with a young lad somewhere near Roseberry Square. And you gave him some money, I assume for services to be rendered.'

James recalled the poor lad to whom he had given money and he also remembered the man who had appeared to be following him on the night that he, Neumann, Lody and the other Germans had been attacked. 'Yes, I was at the Old Vienna, and yes, the place was attacked by some thugs and we were all lucky to get out of there unharmed. As for the boy, he was half-starved and I gave him a few pennies for food. I was in that part of London on the instructions of Captain Kell. Ask him, if you don't believe me.'

'Why should I believe you? What I do know is that this young lad was only twelve years old. And he was found murdered in a disused flat in Roseberry Square the next morning. You were seen by a police officer to give him money and you were seen with blood on your face and clothing that night.'

The taxi had negotiated Hyde Park Corner and had trundled into Knightsbridge and James said, 'I'll be reporting this conversation to Captain Kell, I can assure you.'

'Don't bother. We're acting under the direct orders of Basil Thomson. He wants your little band of perverts arrested and dealt with – in the interests of national security.'

'National security?' James said sardonically, 'that covers a multitude of evils, doesn't it.'

'Be very careful, Mister Clifton. If you'd like to shut up and listen, I can show you an easy way out of this mess. Or, just as easily, we can drop you into the mire from a great height.'

James at once realised what was to come. Just like Richard, he was about to be blackmailed. He also realised that a number of people, not just Bottomley, must have an awful lot of money at stake if they were taking such pains and such risks to ensure that the Corinthians lost Saturday's game.

26

James was uneasily aware that he was quieter and less communicative than usual during lunch and was relieved when Max Woosnam read out a few extracts from that day's edition of *The Daily Mail*. Even though the two football matches had been the brain-child of Lloyd George, Churchill and other members of the Cabinet, this did not deter Lord Northcliffe from claiming the credit and the headline on the front page of the newspaper read: 'THE BRAVE MEN OF LANCASHIRE RESPOND TO THE DAILY MAIL INITIATIVE. THOUSANDS OF NEW RECRUITS FLOCK TO THE COLOURS.'

'Well, that's put Kitchener and Lloyd George in their places,' Woosnam said, 'and here are a few pearls from other famous people. What you'd expect from Kinnaird – "looking forward to a grand game in a grand cause". And there's C B Fry of course – he goes on about the manly virtues adhered to in sport carrying a man through the travails of war. Billy Wells is here, too. His message to both teams and to the British nation is that the contest is never over until the bell sounds for the end of the final round. A fight is never over until one man's hand is raised in victory.'

'That's rich, coming from our horizontal heavyweight,' said Richard.

'Miss Marie Lloyd is more flippant,' Woosnam continued. 'She says "a little of what you fancy does you good", so keep up the good work. And George Robey orders both teams "to kindly temper your skills with a modicum of reserve in case the spectators are overcome with excitement". And Arthur Balfour sends his best wishes to both teams.'

'It's all very interesting, Max,' said Guy Willett, 'but we must get out there and practise.'

'One more, Guy. This is from Lady Ottoline Morrell. Apparently she's a great supporter of football, and of Burnley in particular.'

'Ah, Lady Utterly Immoral,' Wavell interrupted. 'A great advocate of free love – with either sex, I'm told.'

'She claims here to be Burnley's mascot,' Woosnam said, 'and hopes that Saturday's game will be as enthralling as her team's victory in the Cup Final earlier this year.'

'One goal to nil, wasn't it?' Willett said. 'Hardly enthralling.'

'It was for the Burnley players,' Woosnam said. 'Lady Ottoline joined them in their dressing room afterwards.'

'And probably in the communal bath,' added Wavell.

'Let's get her to support us,' Richard laughed.

'On that note, let's get out there for some practice,' Willett said firmly.

* * *

James happily lost himself in the comforting rituals of a Corinthian training session, which ended as usual with a six-a-side game. After they had washed and changed, some tea was served in the club and James spoke quietly to Richard and asked him to join him outside for a few minutes.

Without any preamble he said, 'I've just met Inspector Parker.'

'Ah, and what did he want with you?'

'The same as you, in essence. He told me not to try too hard on Saturday, or he would expose me as one of a group of perverts in the Foreign Office.'

'And are you?' Richard laughed at the expression on James's face. 'I'm sorry, James, but you of all people. He must be mad.'

'Yes, or rather no. Not mad, but presumably a part of the same conspiracy. He went on to tell me that he had solid evidence to prove that I murdered a young lad, a male prostitute in fact, a couple of weeks ago.'

Richard looked aghast. 'God Almighty, James, this is even more serious than I thought. These people must be up to their necks in things you and I can hardly imagine. What on earth should we do?'

'First of all, we must be sure that we know what's really behind all this. It's obviously some kind of betting conspiracy.'

'Presumably one of gigantic proportions.'

'Yes,' James agreed. 'Since we know that Bottomley is involved, it probably runs into hundreds of thousands of pounds, maybe millions.'

'So, Bottomley and Parker are a part of this and Parker works for Basil Thomson. Is even he beyond reproach? And what about that fellow you worked for briefly? You will recall that he killed a defenceless man...'

'Yes, Captain Kell, ruthless in defence of his country. And he's as sound as a bell, I believe. However, I wouldn't extend that compliment to Thomson.'

'But what is the link between Bottomley, Parker and, possibly, Thomson?'

James looked thoughtfully towards the backs of the houses on Palliser Road that formed one side of the Queen's Club's boundary. 'I'd put my money on that devious bugger, Maundy Gregory, being one of the prime movers. I'm sure that he had me followed when I was working for Captain Kell. I don't know why, but it certainly happened.'

'So, you and I must do something and do it quickly,' Richard said.

'Yes, but if we've been threatened, isn't it logical to ask if any of the other men have been, too? Are any of them susceptible, like us?'

Richard looked through the windows of the room where the rest of the Corinthians were taking tea. 'They're all as right as rain,' he said, 'except, perhaps...'

'Except, perhaps, our brilliant right winger, Rupert Wavell. He seems to have a colourful private life, to mix with some peculiar people and I doubt it's gone unnoticed by Gregory and his associates.'

* * *

James remembered how, a few weeks before, Richard had described Wavell as 'elusive'. Slippery was a more appropriate epithet, he thought, as they tried to persuade Wavell to talk to them about an unspecified but important problem that affected all of them. Wavell made a series of excuses: he was having drinks with his father and some business associates, and afterwards he had promised to join some fellows at the Turf Club for dinner and a game of cards.

Finally, James, exasperated beyond politeness, abandoned any notion of tact and said, 'Look, Rupert, both Richard and I are being blackmailed by this very unpleasant Inspector Parker. We suspect, for reasons which I won't bother to list, that you might also be one of his targets.'

Wavell began to protest, but James overrode his words. 'Both rumour and my own observations tell me that you have, how shall I put it, an unconventional private life.' Wavell tried again to speak, but James continued. 'Don't interrupt me, Rupert, because this is too important to us, to all of us. We've got to act and act quickly, to scotch this danger. Now, will you help us?'

Wavell paused for thought and then nodded resignedly, 'I'll do what I can to help.'

An hour later, the three Corinthians entered the Oxford and Cambridge Club in Pall Mall and James turned to Richard. 'If you agree, I'm going to telephone my father. His connections in the Foreign Office are second to none. He also knows Captain Kell quite well, and other people in the Metropolitan Police. He could be here in less than two hours and I know he will be a great help.'

Richard nodded his agreement, but Wavell looked uneasy.

'Rupert,' James said sharply, 'are you in accord with us?'

'This is a delicate matter. Er, your father...'

'Is the soul of discretion,' Richard said.

* * *

While they waited for Mr Clifton's arrival, it was agreed that James was the right person to give his father a summary of the problems which confronted each of them, except that Wavell had been very reluctant to tell them anything. In the end, Richard had said, 'Look, Rupert, we know that you've been approached by Parker, just as we were, and I can assure you that nothing you tell us can possibly shock us. After all, I've been told that my brother Adam will be denounced as a traitor to his country and James has been accused of a homosexual murder.'

'I daresay,' Wavell had replied, 'but it's my private business. I'll help you, but only on my own terms.'

'That's not good enough,' James said firmly. 'We are your friends and we need your whole-hearted support.' Several people were sitting at nearby tables and James rose to his feet and said, 'Let's go into the dining room for a moment. What I have to say demands some privacy.'

Reluctantly, Wavell followed them into the deserted dining room and James said, 'Rupert, we are certain that, like us, you are being blackmailed to throw the game on Saturday. So, you must tell us why so that we can devise a plan to stop Parker and his associates.'

'No,' Wavell said. 'The matter is confidential and must remain so.'

Richard saw James's demeanour change. He became very still and his face seemed to go taut, not with anger but with a deep-seated resolve. No one who knew James doubted his moral and physical courage; but Richard also knew that there was a hard and uncompromising side to his character that only showed itself in a crisis. When such a mood overtook him, it was dangerous to resist him.

James spoke very quietly. 'You've led a charmed life, Rupert, but it's now time to grow up and think of others. You can't avoid your moral obligations any longer, or hide behind your mother's skirts for that matter. We will not give in to blackmail, we are going to take on these criminals and we are going to beat them. Do you understand me?'

Wavell looked at the floor. 'You are being bloody insulting, James, and the answer is still no.'

'Excuse us a moment, please, Rupert,' James said and he led Richard across the room and out of earshot.

When they returned, Richard took over. 'James has made it plain what he wants from you, Rupert, and I support him. Therefore, if you refuse to help us, I'm going to ask Guy Willett to remove you from the team. That would be a shame, because soon we'll all be going off to war and it'll be our last game together for a while. But, Rupert, I assure you that's what I'll do and Guy will certainly back me up.'

'You'd do that? To me?'

'Yes, without the faintest regret. You're with us or against us, it's that simple.'

Wavell shook his head in sad disbelief and, often faltering and sometimes looking away in embarrassment, he told them about his conversation with Parker. In the end, he even allowed himself to speak, albeit uneasily, about his emotional problems. 'The only way I can feel at ease with a woman is if I am in complete control… then I have this awful compulsion to ill-treat her.'

James saw tears brewing in his eyes and spoke quietly. 'To beat her up?'

'Yes, that's so. That's why I've never contemplated marriage, even though half the mothers in London seem to be very keen to have me as a son-in-law. Ironic, isn't it?'

* * *

Henry Clifton did indeed arrive at the club within a couple of hours. Looking animated, his face bright with anticipation, he strode into the bar and ordered a whisky.

'Sorry to have disturbed you like this, Father,' said James, 'but we need your advice.'

'Not at all,' his father replied. 'I'm intrigued by what you said, or rather, didn't say on the telephone. Oh, and flattered too that you young fellows would wish to consult me.' Clifton took a sip of his whisky and soda. 'So, gentlemen, tell me more.'

When James had finished his summary of the situation, his father sat silently for a while. He sipped his whisky, drew hard on his Turkish cigarette and said, 'You're all convinced, are you, that this is a conspiracy by Bottomley and others to carry out a betting coup?' They all nodded and Henry Clifton continued. 'But about a week ago, James, you also told me that the government was putting pressure on your chairman, Dickson, to ensure that the Corinthians lost the second game. So, should we rule out government interference?'

'That's true,' Richard said, 'but surely that's just a coincidence. I can't believe that our own government would be a party to some crude form of blackmail.' Richard seemed genuinely shocked by the idea.

'Governments always do whatever is expedient to achieve their ends, especially in wartime,' Clifton replied.

'I can see that normal conventions are abandoned during time of war, but I find it difficult to believe that men like Lloyd George and Kitchener and Churchill would condone such behaviour.'

'Very well,' Clifton replied. 'So, let us agree for the time being that this is a betting conspiracy and try to find some solutions to the problems. We have very little time before the game itself, only three and a half days, so I assume that you agree with me that the best defence can only be attack.' He smiled at them all. 'I can already see a light gleaming in Richard's eyes, so let's start with him. There are three elements to your story. First, let's discount this man Parker's remarks about Emily. Since the war began, the suffragette movement has more or less gone into hibernation. By the way, I'd be prepared to bet that, as soon as the war is over, women will get the vote anyway. Second, there's the accusation about your brother, Adam, which he denies. I happen to know Erskine Childers quite well and I know where to find him. And, tomorrow morning, I will ask him to pen a letter in which he will confirm that Adam had no part in that gun-running episode.'

Henry Clifton drew deeply on his cigarette and Richard waved at a waiter for more wine and another whisky.

'As for your mother, what we must do is recover her money from that scoundrel, Bottomley, before Saturday. I must give that some thought because, to do that, we have to turn the tables on him in no uncertain manner.'

'That's a tall order,' Richard said, doubt weighing heavily on his words. 'He's a fraudster and a bankrupt, and he gets away with it every time, because he's clever and very plausible.'

'Yes,' Clifton said, 'and whatever he gets up to, the public still seem to adore him. Maybe that's how we'll ensnare him, we'll play on his lust for popularity. I'll put on my thinking cap.'

'Next, there's my situation,' James said. 'I never thought I'd be involved in some sort of homosexual scandal and I promise you, Father...'

'No need to go on, my boy. I know you well enough by now. In the past I've worked with Percy Allott and I know that he's, well, a bit odd. But I've never thought of him as one of those vicious men who consort with those desperate waifs who sell their bodies for a few pence.' Clifton sighed. 'I will go and see him tomorrow at the Foreign Office and find out whatever I can, that is, if he's willing to tell me anything at all.'

Clifton then spoke directly to Wavell. 'Your problem, Rupert, seems similar to that facing James. You visit prostitutes occasionally, have been accused of assaulting one of them and Parker's threatening to pin a murder on you. It's obvious that the same group of people are orchestrating this and we need to get a lead to them. Of course, the police have a lot of contact with prostitutes and with those who run brothels, since they're supposed to prevent such offences against public morality.'

'Except that they don't,' Wavell said. 'On the contrary, they have a vested interest in prostitution. They use these women and they also benefit in the way of bribes.'

'So, do you think that the prostitutes or the madams would talk to us? Or would they be too frightened to name names?'

'No, they wouldn't talk to men like us,' said Wavell, 'and yes, they'd be terrified of the reprisals that would certainly follow.'

'Nevertheless, we've got to give it a try,' Clifton said. 'Elizabeth used to visit a women's refuge somewhere in the East End. I'm sure she'd furnish us with an introduction and we'll take it from there.'

Briskly Clifton stood up and his eyes were alive with the challenge they would all face in the short time left to them.

James thought his father looked ten years younger. 'Let's all meet tomorrow. I'll reserve a room here for a couple of nights, so this club will be our campaign headquarters.'

27

After dinner that evening Henry Clifton tentatively suggested to his wife that he, assisted by either James or Richard, should talk to some of the women at 'that women's refuge of yours in the East End'. He was unprepared for her vehement reaction.

'First, Henry, it's not my refuge, as you put it. It's run by a brave and determined woman called Annie Wilding. Her aim is to help girls whose lives have been marked by poverty and degradation, to help them lead normal lives again.'

'I appreciate that, Elizabeth, but we just want to get some information from them.'

'For a highly intelligent man, your naiveté sometimes amazes me,' Mrs Clifton said severely. 'Why on earth do you think that these poor women, who've suffered at the hands of all sorts of men, would tell you anything?'

Henry Clifton chose not to reply, but instead sipped from his glass of whisky.

'If you tell me what you want to know and why, I might find a way of helping you,' Mrs Clifton said.

'Well, it's a rather unedifying story, I'm afraid.'

'I'll try to stand the strain,' Mrs Clifton said sarcastically.

Henry Clifton laid out the bare bones of the story for his wife: that there was a plot to blackmail some of the Corinthian players to secure a major betting coup and that the blackmailers included some senior members of the police force.

'So, James and Richard are being blackmailed.'

'I didn't say that.'

'Oh, really, Henry. And when you have these names you'll try to turn the tables on these squalid people, is that the plan?'

'Yes, Elizabeth, that's the idea.'

'Fine, we'll do what we can. Annie Wilding will help us.'

'Us?'

'I'll take Emily with me. The girls all like her.'

* * *

It was easy enough for Henry Clifton to arrange a meeting with Erskine Childers, who, in order to capitalise on his sea-faring knowledge, had exchanged his post as a parliamentary clerk for one in the intelligence arm of the Royal Navy. However, he insisted on a modicum of discretion and their meeting took place not in his office, but in the gardens between the Savoy Hotel and the Embankment.

Clifton was sitting on a bench and reading that morning's edition of *The Times* when he saw Childers approaching with his lop-sided walk, the result of a boyhood accident which had destroyed his ambitions to win a rugby blue at Cambridge.

The objective of the meeting was quickly realised, as the amiable Childers agreed to write a letter which would exempt Adam Hildreth from any part in the infamous gun-running episode at Howth Harbour.

'I'll send it over to you today,' Childers said. 'But what's this all about? I hardly know Hildreth, I think I've only met him a couple of times, and briefly, too.'

'I can't tell you too much, Erskine, beyond the fact that there's some dirty business going on and I'm giving my son, James, and two of his friends some help.'

'You're certainly the right man for the job, Henry.'

Clifton smiled his appreciation. 'I'm glad that you've clearly been forgiven for running guns to the Irish dissidents, Erskine, but I must ask you why you're not locked up a couple of miles down-river in the Tower.'

Childers laughed. 'You know the rules. I can't tell you any more than you already know.' He tapped the side of his nose with his forefinger. 'Wheels spinning silently and mysteriously within other wheels.'

'Point taken.' Childers began to rise from his seat on the bench, but Clifton raised his hand to detain him for a moment longer. 'There is something else I'd like to know, if you're prepared to tell me. Who supplied those rifles to you? It was a German company, I believe.'

'That's correct, but I don't think they'd be willing to sell you anything at present, do you?' They both laughed and Childers continued. 'It was a firm in Hamburg called Moritz Magnus. Armaments brokers, quite well-known in the business.'

'I see. And how did you pay them?'

'In cash. Swiss francs, of course.'

* * *

An hour later Clifton was sitting in a comfortable room in the Foreign Office and wondering how to persuade Percy Allott to talk about some of the more peculiar sexual activities which men could pursue in London. He appreciated that some of the most accomplished men in history had been homosexuals, and Oscar Wilde had been one of the more recent and notorious examples, but he found such practices abhorrent. Not that Clifton had any intention of revealing his views to Allott. His objective was solely to extract information from him in order to release his son from the threat of blackmail.

Allott was a few years younger than Clifton, who had known him for a long time. He also liked him. Allott had an acute intelligence, was amusing and invariably helpful. Seated behind his well-ordered desk, he was as always plainly but elegantly clothed; he wore a dark-grey checked suit, a crisp white shirt and a plain blue tie.

A quick smile fluttered across Allott's face. 'So, Henry, it's always a treat to see you and looking so well, too. I hope that I can be of service.'

'It's rather a delicate matter, Percy and I'm not going to wrap it up in diplomatic jargon because it's become too serious for that. My son, James, has been doing some work for the Special Branch...'

'Vernon Kell.'

'Yes, and he thinks he's uncovered traces of some activities which might endanger national security. He believes that there is a small group of men, some of them in the Metropolitan Police and some of them here in the Foreign Office, who are involved with prostitutes...'

'That's hardly a great crime, is it, Henry? And I don't see how it could be construed as a security problem.'

'I'm not making any moral judgements, but these prostitutes are male as well as female and some of them have been murdered.'

Allott shrugged. 'That's the risk they run. They're in a dangerous business. While I can certainly believe that the police might be involved with prostitutes, I think it unlikely that anyone here in the FO would be foolish enough to follow suit.'

Clifton looked steadily at him and Allott stared back. 'Nevertheless, a very good source told me that you might well have some information, inside information, one might say.'

'You were misinformed, Henry.' Allott's voice was cold and the focus of his eyes on Clifton's face did not waver. 'All I know about such matters is what any man in my position would know: newspaper stories, rumours, anecdote. As you know I have been happily married for over twenty years and have children. The seamy side of London life has never had any interest for me.'

'That wasn't what I meant to imply,' Clifton said swiftly. Allott looked ostentatiously at his watch and then studied the diary which lay open on his desk. 'I want any knowledge which you may have gleaned in your official duties about where such a group might engage in its dubious pleasures, where they might recruit these unfortunates that they abuse.'

Allott looked thoughfully at Clifton and tried to assess how much he knew. Since he was sitting there in his office, he assumed that he already had acquired some compromising information. Allott needed to protect his reputation and, since he respected Clifton both for his intellect and his integrity, he decided to take the risk of trading information in exchange for anonymity. He spoke quietly. 'I can give you some addresses, a couple of public houses where these people meet and I've been told about a male brothel in Clerkenwell. But you must give me your word, Henry, that you will never name me as a source, nor even acknowledge that this conversation took place.'

'You have my word, of course. Now, let's hear some names.'

Within a few minutes of Clifton leaving his office, Allott had spoken to Andrew McCormack and two other Foreign Office officials. His message was clear and unequivocal: stay away from certain pubs in Soho and a house in Clerkenwell.

* * *

At around the same time Elizabeth Clifton and Emily Hildreth were sitting in the communal living room of the East London Women's Refuge. This was housed in a dingy building, once a clothing factory, off the Bethnal Green Road.

Its founder, Annie Wilding, had been forced into marriage at fifteen years of age; her husband had then promptly forced her on to the streets to earn him a living. Just over a year later he had been found, with his throat cut, behind an ale-house in Brick Lane. Since his wife had been seen trawling for customers in the vicinity of Liverpool Street on the same evening, the police had discounted any theory that she might have murdered him. They didn't look too hard for the killer anyway; they were relieved to see the back of another drunken villain.

From those unpromising beginnings, Annie had, with the help of a sympathetic local schoolteacher, set about educating herself. While working the night shift in a pie factory, by day she devoured book after book in the public library. The schoolteacher required her to write down her thoughts about each book and then corrected her 'essays'.

In due course Annie had the confidence to initiate her grand plan. With the support of local churches and charities she had leased the old factory for a peppercorn rent and set up her women's refuge. Elizabeth Clifton had heard about the venture from a friend, had donated some money to the cause and had occasionally visited it to talk to the women staying there and to help with the cleaning and cooking.

Annie was in her mid-twenties, but looked older; if the travails of her life had put many lines on her face, her natural good humour softened her features. When cups of tea had been set before the three of them, Annie said, 'It's a treat to see you both again and I'll help in any way I can, Mrs Clifton, so tell me what you're after.' She had worked hard to learn how to 'speak proper' and her cockney accent only broke through when she became animated.

'Information, please, Annie. Of a rather specialised nature.' Mrs Clifton hesitated.

'Don't worry yourself,' Annie said, 'there's nothing you can say or ask that will shock me, you know.'

'No, I realise that. We wondered if any of your girls would know about any brothels which cater for men who like to inflict violence, or receive it for that matter.'

'Ah, the sadism trade. I've never really understood that nonsense. Are you sure Miss Emily should be listening to stuff like this?'

Emily smiled and said, 'It's all right, Annie, I've read my Krafft-Ebing and like you I'm not easily shocked.'

'Your craft what?'

'He wrote about sex, its problems and its perversions.'

'Blimey, sex is the cause of most of the problems in this world. Maybe that's what's wrong with Kaiser Bill, eh? Anyway, there's a couple of girls who used to go in for the funny stuff. I'll talk to them in a minute, but tell me why you're interested.'

'Someone we know is being blackmailed and we think the blackmailers are in the police force. What we need are names, of course.'

'That's asking a lot. These girls don't deal in names, I can't remember ever being properly introduced to any of the men I went with.' She grinned at Mrs Clifton. 'But I've heard some rumours. Give me a minute or two.' She handed each of the women a sheet of paper. 'Here's our latest appeal, by the way.'

A few minutes later, Annie returned. 'It's business as usual for the police, they're up to their ears in it all. 'Course, they're always looking for a bit of free entertainment, if you take my meaning, ladies, But the girls tell me that there's some high-ups in the police who go in for knocking the women about and for knocking young lads about, too.'

'High-ups?' queried Emily. 'How do you know that?'

''Cos one of them seemed to be the boss. The others called him "sir" and so on, and they deferred to him. And it didn't stop at just knocking the stuffing out of these poor little beggars.'

'Go on', said Mrs Clifton.

'Some of them have disappeared and never been seen again. Nothing unusual about that, it can happen if you're on the streets. But some of the poor mites have been found. Dead. You've probably read about them, well, no, I don't suppose *The Times* bothers with stuff like that.'

'Did they give you any names, Annie?' asked Emily.

'No, but they described one of them. An evil beggar, big, in his forties maybe, a bit of a dandy and that's unusual for a policeman, isn't it? And he seemed to act as a bodyguard to an older man, the important one.'

'And where do these men go for their, er, pleasures?' Emily asked.

Annie handed her a piece of paper. 'Here's some addresses and one of the girls said she'd heard they use a flat in the Clerkenwell area, but she doesn't know where it is.'

* * *

During a meeting of the war cabinet, the vital question of recruitment was as usual discussed. It was the eighth day of September and the government had still not met its initial target of recruiting a total of half a million men for its 'first new army'. The shortfall was partly explained by the gross inefficiencies of the authorities; the system was unable to cope with the crowds of eager volunteers besieging the recruiting centres. The army was barely organised to train these new recruits for combat, and many of them were surprised to be told to provide their own blankets when they reported for training. These soldiers were desperately needed too, since the British Expeditionary Force was on that very day helping to repulse the German advance on the Marne; a few weeks later it was to suffer severe losses at Ypres.

'Did that game of football have any effect?' Lloyd George asked Kitchener.

'Yes, there was a significant increase in recruits in the Manchester area for a few days after the game.'

'How significant?'

'Over ten thousand more volunteers.'

'So we should see a similar effect in London from Saturday onwards.'

'I hope so. We've had about fifty thousand recruits from London so far and that's nowhere near enough,' Kitchener replied.

'I see that Lord Derby has come up with an interesting initiative,' Asquith said. 'He appealed to the chaps who work in the City of London to raise a battalion of men and about fifteen hundred of them volunteered.'

'Yes,' Kitchener said, 'the Stockbrokers' Battalion. Derby is busy trying to organise these Pals battalions, as he calls them, in other parts of the country.'

'Well, that's an ideal concept for sport, isn't it?' Lloyd George countered. 'We'll get some posters around the Crystal Palace ground on Saturday.' He paused. 'By the way, gentlemen, I had a rather curious conversation with that old rogue, Bottomley, yesterday. Bumped into him outside Parliament. He told me that we could look forward to the result we want on Saturday. He assured me that Blackburn will win.'

28

Henry Clifton had used his contacts in the Foreign Office without hesitation, and they had rewarded him by unearthing a letter from Moritz Magnus in Hamburg. He had then made the short trip to an office in a back street in Pimlico. Clifton had used the owner's services on several occasions during his diplomatic life, primarily to procure documents for Russians who were in danger of their lives and needed to remove themselves and their families to more hospitable countries.

It didn't take him long to explain what he wanted and the man promised to deliver the document to the Oxford and Cambridge Club by six o'clock that evening. He refused to accept any payment for the service.

* * *

The document arrived on time, just as Clifton, for the benefit of James and Richard, had nearly finished his summary of the information he had so far gleaned.

'It's interesting,' he said, 'that one address in particular was named both by Allott and by the girls at Annie Wilding's refuge as a brothel frequented by the police.'

James kept his voice low. They had gathered in a corner of the library, but a man, apparently asleep in his armchair, was slumped nearby and James didn't want to risk his overhearing anything. 'So we can assume that it caters for men of differing tastes. Talking of which, here comes Rupert.'

Wavell was not his usual poised self; he looked dishevelled and, as he apologised for his late arrival, James noticed that his tie was slightly askew. 'Trouble with Mama. She hit the roof when I told her I'd volunteered for the Royal Flying Corps. She said she'd arranged a nice job for me in the Home Office.'

'That's what mothers do,' Clifton said. 'I know that James's mother hates the idea of his going off to war.' He paused. 'So do I. Anyway, before you all go off to hammer the Boche, we must try to unmask these damned blackmailers and then stop them in their tracks.'

'We need to catch them in the act, so to speak,' Richard said.

'That would mean watching Parker in particular for several hours a day and we haven't the time or the resources to do that,' James said.

'True,' Clifton replied, 'nevertheless, Parker seems to be a pivotal figure in all this, even if he's not the prime mover.'

'We know he's being used by Bottomley,' Richard said, 'but can we assume that Bottomley is involved in prostitution and murder as well?'

'I don't think so,' Clifton replied, 'but he has links that enable him to use Parker and, through him, the resources of both the Special Branch and the CID to carry out his betting coup.'

James tried to summarise the situation. 'So, Bottomley is a criminal insofar as he's engaged in fraud and blackmail, but the violence and murders are being carried out by others, who also have connections to Parker.'

'That's an excellent outline of what's going on,' Clifton said, 'and we must find out just how high up the chain of command we must travel to find Parker's accomplices. We must force the issue.'

'How on earth do we do that?' Rupert asked querulously. 'We've no idea how far these people are prepared to go.'

'Parker and Maundy Gregory,' said James. 'Special Branch and the CID.'

'Yes,' Clifton said, 'we have to talk to Vernon Kell. You and I, James, should do that, I think. Meanwhile, Richard, I've arranged for us to meet Mister Bottomley tomorrow morning.'

'Really?'

'Yes, I've planned a little surprise for him.'

As he had anticipated, Henry Clifton was unable to make an appointment to see Horatio Bottomley; his private secretary told him that Mister Bottomley was far too busy. However, Clifton knew that he was in London and would be throughout the day since he was addressing a recruiting rally at the Royal Albert Hall on that very evening; and, when he was in London, Bottomley invariably had lunch at Romano's in the Strand.

At just after midday, Clifton, with Richard in his wake, entered Romano's and saw that Bottomley was already established at his usual table at the far end of the main room. The head waiter intercepted them and when Clifton explained that he was meeting Mister Bottomley, he insisted on leading them formally over to the table.

Although Bottomley looked guardedly at them as they approached, politely he managed to heave his great bulk upright in order to greet them. 'Gentlemen, Horatio Bottomley at your service.'

Clifton introduced himself as a retired diplomat and slightly garbled Richard's introduction, in case his name rang any alarms in Bottomley's memory.

'Please, gentlemen, sit down and have a glass of champagne with me.' He looked at his watch. 'My guests are due here in a matter of minutes, but we can have a little time together. How can I be of assistance?'

'We need your help with some investments,' Clifton began.

'Ah, investment, the spice of business life. Where would we all be without it?' Bottomley asked, a smile spreading expansively across his fleshy features. 'There's an easy answer to that, eh, Mister Clifton. In penury, that's where we'd be.'

'Or Carey Street,' Clifton said, also with a smile.

Bottomley shuddered theatrically. 'Don't, Mister Clifton. I've had a close shave or two, as you know. All in the interests of maximising the returns for my investors. Calculate the risk and then be both imaginative and courageous. That's been the guiding principle of my business life.'

Clifton nodded in Richard's direction. 'This is one of my son's friends and he has a slight difficulty with an investment his mother made with you...'

'Now, Mister Clifton, I cannot discuss any financial matters without having the documents which are germane to the transaction in front of me. You will understand that, sir, will you not?'

'Up to a point, but this is actually a simple matter and we can resolve it in a few minutes, if you so wish. Richard, please tell Mister Bottomley what you require.'

'It is indeed a simple matter. A year ago my mother invested forty thousand pounds, almost all her available capital, with one of your companies. No interest has been paid, even though you promised a yield of eight per cent and, despite repeated requests, she has been unable to get her money back.'

'The economic situation has changed radically, gentlemen. We're at war and...'

'And you guaranteed an eight per cent yield,' Clifton said firmly.

'Yes, but...'

'Yes, but nothing,' Clifton interrupted and then paused as he saw Bottomley signalling to two men who had just entered the restaurant. 'Your guests?'

'Yes. Important ones.'

'Please ask them to wait.' Bottomley frowned at Clifton's demand and his florid face became a deeper shade of red, but he seemed to recognise the innate authority that the former diplomat possessed. He waved impatiently at the head waiter, who bustled importantly over to the table. Bottomley asked him to make his guests comfortable for a minute or two and serve them some champagne. Clifton continued. 'Mrs Hildreth would like her money back.'

'Pray, ask the lady to write to me and I'll do my best.'

'Today. My mother would like her money today,' Richard said firmly.

'Impossible.' Bottomley tapped the table with his forefinger and then drank some champagne. 'As anyone who knows me will tell you, I'm a convivial man and a tolerant one, too, but your behaviour, gentlemen, is testing even my temper. I'm on the brink of asking the proprietor to have you thrown out.'

'That wouldn't be in your best interests,' Clifton said. 'We can settle this business quickly and amicably, if you so wish, so please listen to Mister Hildreth.'

'Hildreth?' Bottomley said. 'Of course, I knew the name was familiar. You've a brother, I think. Adam? Is that his name? I've heard some odd things about him. Isn't he involved in supplying guns to the Irish rebels? Not exactly a patriotic activity in time of war, is it, Mister Hildreth?'

'I wonder where that absurd accusation originated?' Clifton said, with heavy irony. 'Could it perhaps have come from a contact at Scotland Yard? From Inspector Parker?'

'No, I don't know anyone called Parker and you would appreciate, as a retired diplomat, that it's never wise to reveal one's sources.'

'Very well, but first let me deal with this nonsense about Adam Hildreth's treachery.' Clifton retrieved a sheet of paper from the inside pocket of his jacket. He unfolded it and held it at eye level in front of Bottomley. 'Please read this letter. It's from Erskine Childers.'

Bottomley found a pair of spectacles in one of his pockets and read the letter. He looked sceptically at Clifton and said, 'Childers, eh? Not a man to be trusted.'

'But he will stand by his statement in this letter,' Clifton said. 'Now, Mister Bottomley, you seem reluctant to help Richard and his mother, so I want to ask you about your business connections in Switzerland. You have a company registered in Geneva, I believe.'

'You are well-informed. It was set up to handle the lotteries we run on sporting events like the Cup Final and the Derby.'

'And only such things?'

'Yes, that's what I've just said. Look, Mister Clifton, I have guests waiting and...'

'And they'll have to wait a minute or two longer. It's interesting to me that you are so dismissive of Erskine Childers, because you know him well and do business with him, don't you?'

'None whatsoever. What nonsense.'

'That's odd.' Clifton reached again into his pocket and waved another sheet of paper in Bottomley's face. 'How do you explain this receipt from a firm in Hamburg called Moritz Magnus? It's addressed to you, at your office in Geneva and confirms the receipt of two hundred and five thousand Swiss francs in payment for nearly a thousand Mauser rifles and 29,000 rounds of ammunition.'

Bottomley grabbed at the piece of paper, but Clifton whisked it out of his reach.

'That's a damned forgery, Clifton, and you know it.'

Clifton smiled briefly. 'Forgery would perhaps be more your game than mine. No, you were up to your eyeballs in the supply of arms to Irish rebels. Let us speculate what that will do to your reputation. Horatio Bottomley, the great British patriot. He will be no more when I release this to the newspapers tomorrow.'

If Bottomley felt the strain of the situation, he didn't show it. For a few moments he stared down at the table, then sipped some champagne and said, 'Now I understand why people say that diplomats are employed to go abroad and lie for their country.'

'That's more acceptable than what they say about Members of Parliament,' Clifton replied.

'Which is?'

'That they tell lies solely in their own interests.'

'Very amusing, Mister Clifton. I have to say that for the moment you seem to hold a good hand of cards, even if the deck is stacked. So tell me what you want from me.'

'The sum of forty thousand pounds plus interest must be returned to my mother's account today,' Richard said.

'Of course, glad to do that small service for the lady,' Bottomley blustered, his normal bonhomie restored in the blink of an eye. 'Forty thousand, plus interest, let's call it forty-five thousand. I'll give you a cheque now.'

'No cheques,' Clifton said firmly. 'They sometimes fail to clear. You bank at Coutts, just down the road. We will go there together now and you will instruct the manager to prepare a banker's draft. In other words, Mrs Hildreth will have a guarantee of payment, which cannot be countermanded. Richard will then take it to his mother's bank in the City.'

'What about that forged document?' Bottomley asked.

'It will be returned to you tomorrow.'

Bottomley led the way out of the restaurant, made his noisy and jovial excuses to his two guests, and ensured that the transaction was swiftly concluded at Coutts Bank.

As the three men paused outside Coutts Bank, Clifton said, 'You claim you don't know Inspector Parker, but Maundy Gregory is a good friend of yours, I believe.'

'Hardly a friend.'

'And Basil Thomson?'

'I know of him, of course. What's the point of all this, Mister Clifton?'

'To establish how involved you are with a very nasty conspiracy.'

Bottomley laughed. 'I'm just a businessman, oh, and a gambling man, of course. Talking of which, Mister Hildreth, if we get the right result on Saturday, a win for Rovers, I shall send you a little present.' He gave them both a stage wink, smiled broadly and surged along the pavement towards Romano's.

* * *

'Are you sure this isn't too much for you, Father?'

'Too much for me?' Henry Clifton laughed. 'I haven't enjoyed myself so much for years. Having to cease being a diplomat was a great blow to me, James. I suddenly felt useless, as if I'd been thrown on to the proverbial scrapheap long before my time. So, this is an opportunity to participate again, and of course it's all the better that I'm trying to help you and your friends.'

James was delighted to admit that there was a pronounced spring in his father's step, as they walked companionably along the Embankment towards Watergate House in the late afternoon sunshine, which put a little sparkle even on to the murky surface of the Thames.

Henry Clifton pointed at the Thames. 'It's comforting to think that Shakespeare looked out over this same stretch of water, isn't it?'

'Liquid history.'

'Yes, that sums it up.'

When they reached the headquarters of the Secret Service Bureau they were greeted by the same large and perspiring policeman and were conducted to Vernon Kell's office. There were two other people in the outer room, a man whom James recognised but didn't know and Jane Elkins, who smiled quickly at him and then resumed reading the papers that littered her desk. There was no sign of Maundy Gregory.

Kell greeted them both warmly as they entered his office. 'Good to see you again, Clifton, and you, James. You're looking fit, I hope that you give Blackburn another football lesson on Saturday.'

He waved them to some seats and stood expectantly behind his desk.

Henry Clifton took the lead and said, 'James and I have become embroiled in an unofficial enquiry and we need your help, Vernon. It's rather a delicate matter, so...'

'So it will remain within these four walls.'

'Thank you. How well do you know Inspector Parker?'

'Moderately well, since he works quite closely with Basil Thomson, to whom I report. Why?'

'Do you think he's the sort of man who'd be involved in a betting conspiracy?'

'That's highly unlikely, Henry. Parker is very well thought of and he has a fine reputation for tracking down and apprehending dangerous criminals.'

'Is he known as a violent man, sir?' James asked.

Kell looked carefully at them both from the other side of his desk. As he began to answer, Elkins entered the room with a tray on which there were three cups of tea and Kell continued. 'Parker is certainly forceful, if needs be, but violent? No. As I said, he's an officer of the highest repute.' He nodded his thanks to Elkins, who gave James another shy smile as she passed him.

'What about his private life?' James asked when Elkins had left the room.

'What about it?' countered Kell.

'Is he a man who might be involved in prostitution, for example?' Clifton asked.

Kell looked puzzled and then impatient. 'He has to deal with all sorts of crimes in the course of his working life, but I repeat that Inspector Parker is an excellent police officer.' He paused for a moment and his gaze focused on Clifton. 'Henry, you must be more specific. Although rumour and innuendo is the normal currency of my job, I don't have to tolerate it in connection with someone like Parker.'

Clifton nodded to signify his understanding and said, 'I've mentioned the betting conspiracy and we think it involves hundreds of thousands of pounds, maybe millions. Both Maundy Gregory and Inspector Parker seem to be implicated in it.' Kell began to protest, but Clifton held up his finger for silence. James marvelled again at his father's quiet air of command. 'And then it becomes serious, Vernon, because people we know are being blackmailed, they are being accused of heinous crimes, including murder.'

'I'm sorry to state the obvious, Henry, but why haven't you gone to the police with this?'

'Because everything leads to the police, in the person of Parker. Furthermore, we believe that he is acting on the orders of someone much higher up the chain of command.'

'How high?'

'The top.'

Normally imperturbable, Kell now looked ruffled; he stood up and walked a few paces to the nearest window and stood there, his hands clasped behind his back. 'No, Henry, you're mistaken. Thomson? Impossible. He's a man of great talent, a man of distinction.'

'I don't dispute that, but I've heard rumours about his personal life, unsavoury rumours.'

'Rumours, Henry,' Kell said sharply. 'I'm surprised at you. "Rumour is a pipe blown by surmises, jealousies, conjectures". So, what about some hard facts?'

James intervened. 'Both he and Parker are friendly with Gregory, I think.'

'Oh Maundy knows everyone there is to know,' Kell replied.

'Including Horatio Bottomley?'

'Of course, and the same applies to Bottomley, but more so. Who doesn't he know?'

Clifton looked searchingly at Kell, who had resumed his seat. 'What would you think of my suspicions that Gregory, Parker and probably Thomson are part of a group of men, including some from the Foreign Office, who indulge in perverse sexual practices?'

'Not a lot, Henry. In fact I find your suggestions outlandish. A gambling conspiracy, sexual malpractices, and you're levelling these accusations at men for whom I have the utmost respect. It's intolerable. If you ever find any evidence, real evidence, I'll listen to you. In the meantime, I've got some German spies to track down.'

Kell rose to his feet, but James forestalled him. 'Captain Kell, just one thing. What's happened to Carl Lody?'

'He was convicted of spying for the enemy and executed last week at the Tower.'

James swallowed hard and frowned.

'You liked Lody?' Kell asked quietly.

'I certainly respected him,' James replied. 'He seemed to have integrity, even though he was a spy.'

'Yes, you're right. A brave man, too. I couldn't help but shake his hand before he went before the firing squad.' Kell moved towards the door. 'I'll see you out.'

As they all walked into the outer office, Jane Elkins rose to her feet. 'I'll see the gentlemen out, if you wish, Captain Kell.'

'Thank you, Elkins.' Kell shook hands with his two visitors and retreated to his office, where once again he stood by the windows overlooking the gardens, although he didn't register them as he thought about what Henry Clifton had said to him. At various times over the years he had heard tittle-tattle about Gregory's personal life, but had disregarded it. Gregory had been instrumental in building up a remarkable dossier of facts, all kept in meticulous order on a Roneo carding system, about German spies, Russian anarchists and Irish dissidents; he had made himself indispensable to the Special Branch and Kell did not give a damn what he did when he was off-duty. However, any hint of scandal involving Basil Thomson would be dangerous, since his support was vital to the smooth running of Kell's department. He would have to monitor Henry Clifton's activities carefully, though he hoped that the matter would simply peter out. There were many more pressing claims on his attention.

Meanwhile, Elkins was leading James and his father down the three flights of stairs until eventually they reached the doors to the street. Unexpectedly, as James began to thank her, she joined them outside on the street. 'If you're looking for information about Inspector Parker,' she said, 'I can help you.' James nodded eagerly and she continued. 'Soon after I joined Captain Kell's department I had a drink with him. I should've known better. He drank a lot and I won't cause myself the embarrassment of recalling what he suggested that we did together. Anyway, he then started to boast about his influential friends.'

'Such as?' asked James

'That hateful man, Maundy Gregory and "the boss", he called him.'

'The boss,' Clifton repeated. 'Can we assume he meant Basil Thomson?'

'Yes, you can, sir. They get together, those three, almost every week. I've heard them talking, you see, they don't even notice I'm there any more. Apparently they have a meal and plenty to drink and then go up to Clerkenwell for some further entertainment. There's other men involved, sir, and Parker said most of them would rather have their fun. . . er. . . with boys, rather than girls.'

'Almost every week, you said, Miss Elkins,' James said. 'Do you know when the next evening's entertainment will be?'

'Yes, I heard Gregory talking on the telephone the other day. It's tomorrow.'

'Where in Clerkenwell?'

'I'll try and find out and let you know.'

'When do you have lunch?'

'From midday.'

'I'll be outside the Coal Hole in the Strand at midday tomorrow.'

29

After waiting for Jane Elkins outside the Coal Hole for nearly twenty minutes, James became uneasy. Perhaps she'd had second thoughts about giving him any information; after all, Gregory would make a very unpleasant enemy. Or maybe she'd simply been unable to unearth anything of interest. He glanced at his watch for the umpteenth time, deciding that he might as well give up and return to his own office when he saw her walking swiftly towards him.

'I'm sorry, sir,' she said breathlessly, 'there were no calls for Gregory until about fifteen minutes ago. It was tricky, he knows I usually go out for half an hour for my break at twelve o'clock, so I had to pretend to be finishing something for Captain Kell. He's a horrible bastard, that Gregory. Sorry, sir, excuse my language.'

'You don't have to call me sir,' James said with a smile. 'It's James, and I appreciate your helping us.' He gestured towards the door of the Coal Hole. 'Would you like a drink?'

'Oh no, Mister James. My mum would kill me if she found out I'd been in a pub. Let's walk, shall we?'

They strolled along the Strand towards Trafalgar Square.

'There's five or six of them apparently, and they start off at one of those pubs in Soho. Then they're having a meal at a place called the Crown and Anchor off Hatton Garden. The owner is one of Gregory's people.'

'An informant?'

'Yes. He passes stuff on about any foreigners that he thinks might be of interest.'

'And then what?'

'There's a house, well, a brothel where they'll sort out some, well, whatever they fancy, the younger the better, so I understand, and they'll take them off to a flat in Roseberry Square. Here's the address.' She gave James a slip of paper.

'How did you get this, Jane?'

'Gregory isn't the only one who knows where the secrets are kept. As I told you, I'm just a part of the furniture to them.' She smiled broadly and James could see that she was enjoying her role as a spy.

'Do you know whether Thomson is going to join them?'

'No, sir, I mean Mister James. He's a lot more careful than the others. Well, he'd need to be, wouldn't he?'

They had reached Trafalgar Square and Jane said, 'I must get back. It's full steam ahead with Captain Kell at present, as you can imagine.'

James looked at her, a neat and plain girl in nondescript clothes and wondered how he could possibly convey his thanks. Lamely, he said, 'You've been so helpful. I can't thank you enough. You didn't have to do this.'

'Oh yes, I did, Mister James, because that Gregory and that Parker are such nasty bastards. Oh dear, there I go again. You sort 'em out, won't you, but be careful because they're up to all the dirty tricks.'

* * *

'So what's the plan?' Richard asked.

It was the middle of the afternoon and he was sitting alongside Wavell and facing James and his father in a corner of the library at the Oxford and Cambridge Club. There was only one other person in the room.

'The plan?' James repeated. 'Well, I suppose we could try to catch Gregory and the others with their prostitutes and their young boys.'

'And then?' asked Wavell. 'Tell them that they're very naughty fellows and should be ashamed of themselves?'

Richard spoke sharply. 'Don't be so bloody facetious, Rupert. This is our chance to stop these thugs and remember that you are the person who has most to gain and most to lose, since you are being framed for murder.'

'Yes, I'm sorry, although it's some consolation to think that in a week or two I'll be above all this. High up in the sky in a Royal Flying Corps 'plane.'

'Be careful you don't fly too near the sun,' Richard replied sarcastically.

'What do you think, Father?' James asked.

'As Richard has said, this is your opportunity to turn the tables on them. Catch them indulging in their odious practices certainly, and then make it clear that you will ruin their reputations unless they forget their allegations against you. Well, against you James and you Rupert. Richard is now in the clear.'

'Thanks to you, Mister Clifton.' Richard turned towards the others. 'You should've seen Bottomley's face.' He grinned at the memory.

'I don't like the sound of this,' Wavell said nervously. 'If we're going to confront these people, there will be violence and I don't fancy our chances against Parker. He's a real brute and no doubt he'll have other police thugs with him.'

'You're right, Rupert,' Clifton said, 'you'll need some recruits. Three of you won't be sufficient.'

'Three of us?' Wavell said. 'Well, I'm not very keen on full frontal violence. I never have been.'

'That's odd, I thought that kind of thing was right up your street,' Richard said, a thin smile of distaste on his face.

'Now then, Richard,' James chided him, 'We mustn't taunt Rupert about his personal tastes.'

'Of course not, but he must pull his weight. There's no turning back now, not for him or any of us,' Richard said forcefully. 'But I agree that we need some support. Perhaps we could ask Max Woosnam to help? He's big and strong, and a battler if I ever I saw one.'

'No,' James replied. 'We shouldn't involve any more of our friends unless absolutely necessary. However, I think I know just the man for the occasion.'

* * *

As he bustled along the pavement on his short walk to the headquarters of the Household Cavalry, James realised that he would be asking a lot of Staff Corporal Cowie. Why should he help them? After all, he and James had only met briefly on two occasions, so they could hardly be described as bosom pals. Above all, Britain was a country at war, Staff Corporal Cowie was a serving soldier, and could be anywhere.

However, he was in luck; when he asked the soldier guarding the Horse Guards entrance if could speak to Cowie, he was admitted and asked what his business was with him.

'Captain Kell of the Special Branch has sent me along,' James lied. 'James Clifton. The Staff Corporal knows me.'

Another soldier was summoned, instructions to find Cowie were bawled at him and James was shown to a seat in the corner of the office.

Within minutes James heard the clatter of army boots tramping towards them and the door from the courtyard was filled by the formidable bulk of Staff Corporal Cowie.

'Mister Clifton, sir,' Cowie roared. 'A pleasure to see you again, sir. What can I do for you?'

'Could we step outside? It's an urgent matter and confidential.'

Cowie beckoned him through the door and they marched along a colonnade that formed the boundary of the first of the inner courtyards.

'I need your help, Staff Corporal, and I need it tonight.' James thought it best to come straight to the point. Mentally crossing his fingers he then gave the soldier as brief and concise a summary as he could manage of what he and Richard were planning, the difficulties they were likely to face and why they had to take such extreme measures.

When he'd finished, Cowie said, 'You'll appreciate that I work for His Majesty's army, won't you, Mister Clifton. I'm not some kind of mercenary.'

James grimaced. 'So, you can't help us?'

'I didn't say that, sir. Tell me about this feller Parker? An Inspector, is he?' James nodded. 'I've heard of 'im. A nasty bastard, very free with his fists. Knocked seven bells out of one of our lads a while back. The lad was only drunk, well, maybe a bit disorderly as well, but there wasn't no need for that.'

'So, would you be prepared to lend us a hand?'

''Course I will, but one or two questions, Mister Clifton. The opposition, 'ow many of them will there be, d'you think?'

'Parker will be there and he might well have a couple of his thugs along as protection. There'll be two others, but they won't be dangerous.'

'OK, so there's you and me and Messrs Hildreth and Wavell, but with your permission I'll bring one of me mates along. Stan Pearson. A good man and very handy if trouble starts. And what's our objective, sir, assuming we catch these bastards?'

'Just that. We catch them, identify them and threaten to expose their activities.'

'A spot of blackmail, in other words.'

'Exactly. Do to them what they're doing to us.'

'The best plans are always the simplest, eh, Mister Clifton. By the way, this queer brothel, it's in Clerkenwell, is that right?'

'Yes, off Northampton Square.'

'I think I know it.'

'You know it?' James couldn't keep the surprise from his voice.

'It's all right, sir, I'm not one of them. No, between you and me, a couple of our officers was beaten up and robbed in there. It was all hushed up of course.'

'But of course.'

'You sound shocked, Mister Clifton. Well, it takes all sorts, don't it? So, me and Stan'll see you later. We'll be in mufti and I'd suggest you and Mister Hildreth and Mister Wavell dress down a bit, old clothes, eh. Blimey, I'm lookin' forward to meeting them two, by the way. They can both play a bit.' He rubbed his hands vigorously in anticipation and led James back through the orderly room and on to the street. 'By the way, sir, have you still got that Luger?'

'Yes, I have.'

'Well, bring it along.'

'Are you sure?'

'Better be safe than sorry, Mister James, eh?'

* * *

Early on the same evening Gregory had a brief telephone conversation with Parker. He confirmed all the arrangements for the evening to come, beginning with their meeting at a pub in Gerrard Street.

'And is our mutual friend joining us?'

'Yes, he'll join us at the flat.'

'Not dining?'

'No. It wouldn't do for him to be seen in such a place. And, David, make sure you've got your two best men with you. Just in case.'

'In case of what, Maundy? In case the police raid the flat?' Parker laughed so uproariously that Gregory had to hold the telephone away from his ear for a few seconds.

'No, I realise that is not an eventuality.' Gregory invariably became pompous when he was mocked. 'But I think that girl Elkins was sniffing around the office today. She looked a bit nervous. Nothing I can put my finger on.'

'You wouldn't put your finger anywhere near her, would you, Maundy. That's not your cup of tea, is it?' Parker laughed loudly again and Gregory wondered how much gin he'd had to drink that day; when drunk he could be unpredictable and, therefore, very dangerous.

'No, David. Half-educated trollops from Shepherd's Bush are not my style. To continue, however, she seemed to be looking for something. I just wonder about her. Just intuition, I suppose.'

'Intuition? That's what detectives use when they can't find any evidence. Why don't you get rid of her, Maundy?'

'I can't. Kell has a high regard for her.'

'I suspect there's nothing to it. It's your imagination. Enjoy tonight's sport and then look forward to all that lovely money we're going to win on Saturday. But to relieve your mind I'll bring Sayers and Mills with me. They'll keep us safe in our beds, so to speak.' He laughed again.

Gregory grunted and put down the telephone.

30

At Cowie's suggestion, James's intrepid band met at a pub called the George and Dragon in the Farringdon Road. It was crowded and noisy, and the clientele seemed to James's eyes to belong to the lowest rung of the social order: labourers, street traders and petty crooks, with a number of prostitutes selling their wares amongst them.

Cowie introduced his fellow-soldier, Pearson, who looked as solid as Cowie, but younger and leaner. Their rough civilian clothes were not out of place in the pub, nor were James's, since he had found the suit he had used during his undercover activities for Kell's department. But Richard and Rupert looked as though they had merely forgotten to don the ties which would normally accompany their reasonably smart suits.

When they had all gathered around a table in a corner of the pub and James had bought some pints of beer, Cowie said, 'With your agreement, gentlemen, I'm going to send Pearson here to watch that queer dive where Parker and his friends collect their doxies. He'll follow them when they leave, just in case there's a change of plan and they go somewhere else with 'em. OK? But we'll go to the address in Roseberry Square and wait.'

The three Corinthians nodded their agreement and Cowie continued. 'As Mister James 'as told it to me, we want to catch these buggers in the act, so to speak, so me and Pearson'll smash the door in and lead the charge. Let's hope none of 'em's got a weapon and starts shooting. I'm only joking, gents, they're not Brick Lane villains who put no value on another man's life, or on their own for that matter. I know for a fact that Parker, for instance, prefers to use his fists and his boots, the bastard. He's put a few in hospital that way.'

'And then what do we do?' Wavell asked nervously.

'We'll herd them into a corner and Mister James can tell 'em how a full account of what they get up to will be on Captain Kell's desk tomorrow morning if they don't lay off with the sodding blackmail.'

'Parker and the other bobbies won't give up without a fight, will they?' Richard said.

'No,' Cowie replied, his voice grim, 'and Stan and me'll deal with them. Now, I've got a little present for each of you young gentlemen.' His broad back shielded the table from any curious onlooker as he laid three leather-covered coshes on the table. 'This is a very effective weapon if someone comes at you with a knife. Have it handy and make sure you hit 'em in the knife-arm with it. You're all fit and strong, so make it bloody well count, put 'em out of the fight. You can go low, o' course, and smack 'em in the ribs or in the knee. Either way, they won't come back at you, I can tell you that. OK?'

Pearson drained the last of his pint and told them he'd see them all at Roseberry Square, and James proposed one more drink before they left. Wavell had made no inroads into his glass of beer and declined any more.

* * *

At about the same time, Henry Clifton was sitting in the library at his club, a glass of whisky on the table before him. Earlier, he had gone to the dining room, but had merely picked desultorily at his food. This was so uncharacteristic that the head waiter, who had known him for many years, had inquired after his health.

By eleven o'clock Clifton had read every newspaper in the place, but the news of the war that dominated almost every page made him even more depressed. To try to lift his spirits he had found a copy of *The Pickwick Papers* in the shelves, but had laid that aside as well; he now sat motionless in his armchair, his eyes gazing at the shadows in the far corner of the room. He knew that his

213

fear for his son was irrational; James had plenty of support and tonight's little skirmish was as nothing compared to the dangers he would face in Flanders.

Nevertheless, he had asked James to return to the club, with his two companions, as soon as it was all over. He could hardly bear the waiting; he just wanted to see him again, whole and unharmed.

* * *

As the four men approached Roseberry Square, Pearson appeared from the shadowed depths of a doorway. 'I nearly missed 'em,' he said, 'but they're in a basement flat at number thirty-one.'

'How many of them?' asked James.

'Three young lads from the brothel, one of 'em can't be more than ten, and four others.'

'That must be Parker and Gregory, but who are the other two?'

'They'll be Parker's men,' Cowie said. 'Big blokes are they, Stan?'

'Yeah, solid.'

'Any sign of Thomson? He's an older man,' James explained. Pearson shook his head.

'He's probably waiting in the flat,' Richard suggested.

'They're bound to put one of the police on the front door,' Cowie said quietly, 'so the first thing we do is take care of 'im. Me and Stan'll do that. You gentlemen, you stay here out of sight until we call you over.'

Cowie spoke briefly to Pearson and they both ambled towards Roseberry Square. As they got nearer they began to argue noisily and Cowie stumbled into the railings above the basement flat at number thirty-one.

He grabbed the railings, peered down and shouted at a man who was lounging against the wall by the door. 'Eh, mate, can yer give us a light?'

'Piss off, I'm busy.'

'Oh, come on, I'm dying for a sodding smoke.' Cowie started down the stairs. 'I'll give you a fag, but just gimme a light.'

'Yeah, well make it quick.'

Cowie reached the foot of the stairs and registered some muted laughter coming from inside the flat. He shook a cigarette out of the packet in his left hand and, as the policeman reached out to take it, he smacked him under his left ear with his cosh and caught him as he fell. He dragged him away from the door, propped him in a sitting position and felt his pulse. Most basement flats used the space under the stairs to store odds and ends, and Cowie added to the rubbish as he shoved the man inside the shed and pulled the door shut.

He went quickly back up the stairs and waved James and the others over. Gesturing with his thumb down the steps, he said, 'He'll be out for ten minutes or more, but he'll be OK. Now for the difficult part.'

The five men moved stealthily down the steps and Pearson made another quick check of the policeman; he gave Cowie the thumbs-up sign.

'OK,' Cowie whispered, 'Stan will lead the charge and I'll be right behind him, then you gentlemen follow us. Get them coshes ready.'

They lined up and first of all Pearson gently tried to ease open the handle of the door. It was locked. He stepped back two paces, raised his right foot and crashed the sole of his heavy army boot into the edge of the door where it met the frame. The frame splintered but held and one more solid blow was required to burst open the door. The two soldiers leapt through the gap, one to the left and the other to the right.

James was right behind them. Beneath the dim electric light he saw a small boy cowering in the far corner with Parker looming over him; another boy was lying naked on a bed in the other corner with Gregory; and Basil Thomson, the head of the Criminal Investigation Department at New Scotland Yard, was sitting in an armchair with a third boy on his lap.

It might have been a scene in one of Hogarth's more lurid drawings and it was imprinted on James's mind's eye for many a long day.

Shrieks of fear and a bellow of anger from Parker erupted and, knife in hand, Parker's second bodyguard hurtled through a door at the side of the room. His mistake was to head straight for Cowie, who cracked his cosh across the man's right arm and then delivered a crushing blow to his ribs. The policeman dropped his knife and subsided to the floor with a groan.

Unexpectedly, Parker, having shoved the boy away from him, produced a revolver from his jacket pocket.

'You going to kill us all, Parker?' Cowie said with a sneer. 'That's a Webley revolver, ain't it, not the most reliable of weapons.'

'Well, you'll be the first to go,' Parker replied. James noticed that his aim was steady and, although he had a gun in his own pocket, he was not sure that he would be able to use it effectively. James decided, therefore, that if Parker fired at Cowie, he would rush him. He knew that Richard would be close behind, if not ahead of him.

'Put the gun away, Parker. Don't be such a damn fool.' Thomson had pushed the boy off his lap and on to the floor. He stood up. 'Put it down,' he repeated forcefully.

Parker's aim still did not waver and in the tense silence James could hear Gregory's breathing, heavy enough to be asthmatic; or perhaps it was just the sound of fear. 'Come on, David,' he said, 'violence isn't the answer.'

'On the contrary,' Parker replied, 'it can solve most problems, can't it, Basil?'

James, recognising the unspoken threat in Parker's words, glanced questioningly at Richard, who raised his eyebrows and shrugged imperceptibly.

'I think, Inspector Parker, that you should listen to your superior officer,' Wavell said, from behind James.

'You shut your mouth, pretty boy,' Parker shouted, 'or you'll be the next on the list.'

As Parker's gun arm wavered slightly, there was a sudden movement from Pearson, who hurled his cosh across the room and hit Parker in the mouth. The policeman staggered back, cursing, and Pearson was upon him, trapping the arm with the gun behind Parker's back and then wrenching it upwards until he was forced to drop it.

'Good work, Stan,' Cowie said, as he took charge of the gun and shoved it into the waistband of his trousers. 'Mister Richard, would you please bring that other gentleman in here.'

With Wavell's help, Richard dragged the still-dazed policeman from the shed into the room and propped him against a wall. Meanwhile, the three children had pulled on their bits of ragged clothing and were huddled in a corner together. They were wide-eyed with fear and the youngest was trying to stifle his sobs.

Cowie spoke to them. 'All right, lads, it's over for you. Get out of here quick and don't tell any tales about what you've seen.' James delved into his pocket and gave the children a few coins and then they left the room at a run.

Cowie and Pearson were holding Luger pistols and Cowie waved Thomson and Gregory closer towards Parker. 'Mister James, would you please find your Luger and take the safety off.' As if in a dream, he did what he was asked. Beside him, he sensed Richard's body stiffen with apprehension.

Cowie spoke quietly. 'You three are scum and you deserve to die howling with pain and sobbing for your mothers. I don't have time to arrange that for you, so we're just going to shoot you. Now.'

'You stupid bastard,' Parker said, 'you can't get away with this. You'll be hunted down within hours.'

'Don't pay any attention to him, Parker,' Thomson said. 'He's bluffing.'

'You'll see in a moment that I'm not, Mister Assistant Commissioner.'

Pearson moved towards Cowie, though his gun remained trained unwaveringly on Parker, and muttered something in his ear.

'My friend here has just pointed out that if we kill you three, we'll have to kill these two apologies for policemen as well. We're not murderers, even though I think trash like you should be executed.'

'As Mister Thomson said, they're bluffing,' Parker said, contempt clear in his voice.

Cowie moved swiftly until he was within a foot of Parker. James thought that he was going to club him with his gun. 'One more word from you, Parker, and I'll make an exception in your case. Now, Mister James here will tell you the conditions under which you'll be released.'

With a silent thank-you to whatever gods there were, James lowered his gun. 'I'm going to write a full account of what we found when we entered this room. It will be witnessed by these two friends of mine and then lodged at my bank. If you Gregory or you Parker try to blackmail any of us, the report will be delivered immediately to Captain Kell of the Special Service Bureau. None of you will attempt any retribution against Cowie or Pearson on pain of the report being put into Kell's hands. Is that understood?'

'No, it's not understood,' Thomson said. 'I don't know what's going on here.' He gave Gregory and then Parker a furious look. 'I suppose you two have been up to your tricks again and now you've involved me, you stupid, greedy bastards.'

There was silence for several seconds and James said, 'I still want to hear from you all. Do you understand, Assistant Commissioner Thomson?'

'Yes,' Thomson muttered; Gregory's assent was even more grudging.

'And you, Inspector Parker, please speak up,' James said, the warning clear in his tone.

'Yeah, if that's what you want.'

Cowie then spoke briefly to Pearson, who left the room and re-appeared in the doorway a few moments later with a length of wooden planking in his hand.

'We're going to make you safe and sound,' Cowie said to Thomson and the others, 'while we return to base. And remember that Mister James will have his statement written and witnessed within the hour.'

Parker looked menacingly at Cowie. 'I'll find you and deal with you, you bastard.'

'I doubt it, 'cos I'll be on the boat to France in a couple of days. Now, move yerselves.' Cowie gestured with his gun and all the men except Parker began to file out of the door.

Parker stared defiantly at Cowie, who said quietly, 'If you piss me about, Parker, I'll have the great pleasure of blowing some holes in your kneecaps. Now, move yerself.'

Slowly Parker moved towards the others. While Pearson stood guard, Cowie herded them into the shed under the stairs, slammed the door on them and rammed the wooden plank under the handle to make it secure. 'It won't hold 'em for long, but long enough for our purposes. Right, let's go.'

* * *

Cowie had exaggerated the speed with which James's statement would be prepared; it was about two hours later that it was written, witnessed and lodged in Henry Clifton's bedroom at the Oxford and Cambridge Club.

Relieved and delighted to see his son return unscathed with his two friends, he had insisted on the night porter bringing them all large glasses of malt whisky to celebrate.

As the first shafts of dawn were showing themselves in the sky, James with great relief regained his flat. There was a letter lying on the mat inside the front door and his heart pulsed a little faster when he recognised Emily's handwriting. He tore open the envelope. The letter ran to just a few lines:

My dearest James,

My only news of you recently has come from Richard, who continues to assure me that you are in good health and not in any danger. But I hate the thought that you and he are facing situations that even you, with your many talents, may find impossible to control. As you know, your mother and I did a little 'undercover work' on your behalf, though we were not privileged to be taken fully into your confidence.

I appreciate that, owing to this horrible war, we all have too much to do and I am uneasily aware of 'time's wingéd chariot hurrying near'. So, I want you to meet me tomorrow (Friday) for lunch so that we can talk quietly together. Midday at the Lyons Corner House in Coventry Street is the time and the place I have chosen (with care).

With love,

Emily.

James read the letter several times over and, physically exhausted and emotionally spent though he was, he found it very difficult to fall asleep.

31

When he reached his office at just after nine o'clock on the following morning Maundy Gregory was feeling exhausted to the point of paranoia. The twilight world, which he enjoyed with such perverse relish, seemed now to be full of danger.

It had taken the five of them nearly an hour to break out of that confounded shed. It looked makeshift, but it was sturdy enough for its purpose, and in the confined space the three policemen were unable to use their considerable strength to positive effect. After much cursing and banging, a man living in a room on the first floor had come down to investigate the commotion and had released them. It hadn't improved anyone's temper, and especially Parker's, when the man had nearly collapsed with laughter when they emerged one after the other from the shed. 'Blimey,' he had spluttered, 'you lot are a bit past it to be playin' hide and seek, ain't yer.'

Atkins's cheery 'good morning' elicited no response from Gregory beyond a venomous look; and to compound his suspicions of her he thought he glimpsed a knowing little smile on her lips. However, what caught his eye more was an envelope on his desk, which bore the Assistant Commissioner's stamp; the note inside ordered him to see Thomson in his office as soon as he arrived for work.

'Tell Captain Kell that I've gone to see Assistant Commissioner Thomson,' he snapped at Atkins. As he went out of the door, she made a rude and unlady-like gesture at his back.

Thomson was ostentatiously studying some papers when Gregory entered the large, oak-panelled office. He did not look up for over a minute, nor did he offer his subordinate a greeting or a seat and Gregory was left to stand in front of his superior's broad desk like a miscreant schoolboy.

'Well, Gregory, you and Parker excelled yourselves last night, did you not?' Thomson finally began. 'Because of your stupid and devious schemes, you managed to put us all in danger of our lives. Even worse, that fellow Clifton and his associates now have the means to blackmail me, to ruin my reputation, whenever they choose.'

'And mine,' Gregory replied quietly.

'Your reputation isn't worth tuppence, Gregory. Mine, on the other hand, is worth a great deal. So, you'd better tell me the full extent of your perfidy and I can then decide how to deal with you both.'

Gregory fidgeted uncomfortably under Thomson's gaze; he studied his fingernails and then looked down at the carpet. 'Things got out of hand, sir. We were trying to help someone, who has laid some very large bets on the result of the football game at Crystal Palace tomorrow. He asked us to persuade some of the Corinthians to assist us…'

'Persuade?' Thomson said, incredulity loud in his voice. 'You were blackmailing these men, you confounded idiots. And who is this gambler you were helping?'

'I'm not at liberty to say, sir.'

'Scruples, Gregory? I am surprised. Let's see, who are you close to, who has the resources and the lack of scruples to carry out a betting conspiracy on a major scale? The fraudster Bottomley fits the bill better than anyone, I would aver.' Gregory stood silently in the face of Thomson's anger. 'And how much do you and Parker stand to gain from this latest trickery?'

'Not a lot. A few pounds.'

Thomson laughed derisively. 'I know you too well, Gregory. You wouldn't do anything for a few pounds. I ought to have you and Parker dismissed from the service and that may well be Parker's fate. Unfortunately, you will probably survive, if only because Kell values your work.'

'And I've been of great service to you, Assistant Commisssioner, have I not?' Gregory said boldly. 'I'm the man who clears up the mess for you when things get out of hand. Yes, I'm very useful because your reputation is only intact because of me.'

'Be very careful, Gregory.'

'No, you be careful, sir. We stand or fall together. I know enough about you to get you hanged.'

'Get out of here.'

'Certainly. But there's just one more thing. I happen to know that our government wants the same result that Bottomley wants tomorrow, namely a victory for Blackburn. For reasons of state.'

'Reasons of state? What are you on about?'

'They want a Blackburn win because they think it will help recruitment, it will encourage *hoi polloi* to volunteer. So, you can console yourself that we were acting in the interests of the country as well as ourselves.'

'That doesn't excuse your criminal activities.'

Gregory turned on his heel and, closing the door with exaggerated care, left the office.

Thomson sat motionless for a minute or two and then strode into the adjoining office where his secretary sat. 'Have you managed to find Inspector Parker yet?'

'No, sir.'

'Well send a constable round to his home. I want to see him immediately.'

'Very well, sir.'

* * *

Like most young men of his upbringing, James was not particularly romantic. He acknowledged that romance had its place in the scheme of things; poets, novelists and painters needed to harness it and he had indeed a great love of the romantic poets, especially Lord Byron. It was, therefore, some sixth sense that guided him, at one minute past midday, to the table at which he and Emily had taken lunch at the Lyons Corner House just over four weeks ago, after he had rescued her from the melée outside number 10 Downing Street.

Emily was dressed in a simple light blue dress with a cream trim, but had teamed it with a jaunty straw boater. When he first saw her, James was struck anew by her loveliness, her self-assurance and the intelligence that glowed in her eyes.

She grinned at him when she saw him approaching and he, on reaching the table, bowed in an exaggerated way, seized her right hand and kissed it lightly. 'Miss Hildreth, fancy seeing you here,' he said, as he took his seat opposite her.

They sat in silence for a few awkward moments and then both began to speak at the same time. Embarrassed, they laughed, then stopped and to their relief a waitress arrived at the table. It was the same one who had served them before and she smiled in her motherly way at them and said, 'It's nice to see you again, miss, and you, sir. What can I get for you today?'

'Do you remember, James, what we ate last time?'

'Er, well, I...'

Emily shook her head admonishingly at him and the waitress smiled indulgently. 'I'll have the chicken and barley soup, please, and my forgetful friend will have the lamb chops.' As the waitress left with the order, Emily continued. 'Is your life back on an even keel now? Your problems solved? Because I know that Richard has somehow worked a miracle, with your father's help, and retrieved our mother's money from that scoundrel Bottomley.'

'Yes, that's very good news. As for me, I think all is well, but it was a close-run thing.'

'What was?' Emily asked pointedly.

James knew that she was unlikely to tolerate any evasions, so, leaning close to her and speaking quietly, he told her the gist of the story: the betting conspiracy, the blackmail attempt and an edited account of his and Richard's adventures of the previous evening. However, he refused to give any names.

'And where is the statement?' Emily was enthralled by the story.

'It's now safe in the vaults of my bank.'

'Thank heavens. But why didn't you and Richard talk to me about it? Or to your mother?'

'You both did your bit for us. The information you got from that women's refuge was invaluable. And the less you were involved the better. Some of these people are very unpleasant indeed.'

'Yes, I daresay, but you must have been at the end of your tether.'

'I can't deny that I was worried. But Richard was a tower of strength and so was my father.'

Their lunch arrived and they both picked at it without much enthusiasm. After a few moments Emily said, 'Do you remember what we talked about when we were last here?'

James chewed his food slowly in order to give himself time to compose himself. 'Well, we discussed some important things. Politics, the suffragettes, the war...'

'And?'

James became aware suddenly that the orchestra, as on the previous occasion, was playing a medley of tunes from *Hullo Ragtime*. He also knew that the next few moments would change both their lives. 'We talked about marriage.'

Emily smiled encouragingly. 'So, is it time to talk about it again?'

His food forgotten, James walked around the table, enclosed Emily's right hand in both of his and, to the delight of many of the customers and the amazement of others, sank to his knees and said, 'Wonderful Emily, will you marry me?'

'Yes,' Emily replied, 'wonderful James, I will marry you.'

The waitress, who was taking an order at a nearby table, smiled broadly at them and then a tear rolled down one of her cheeks.

* * *

Later that day Maundy Gregory was conducted to the entrance of Horatio Bottomley's flat in Pall Mall by the hall porter, who knocked on the door and then departed. To Gregory's surprise, it was John Smithson, not the butler, who invited him inside.

'Where's Ernest?' he asked.

'He's with his wife and family,' Smithson replied. 'One of his sons has been killed.'

'Poor man,' Gregory muttered dutifully.

Bottomley did not offer Gregory his usual effusive greeting, but asked him to sit down, while he remained standing by one of the windows. His normal ebullience was noticeably absent and Gregory wondered if years of indulgence in rich food, an unending supply of champagne and a succession of mistresses, and a life spent living on the edge of a financial precipice, had at last taken their toll.

'Maundy, where the hell is that fellow Parker? I need to speak to him and there are things I want him to do, but I'm damned if I can find him.'

'I saw him yesterday evening and he seemed in good order,' Gregory said cautiously.

'Do you want some champagne,' Bottomley asked irritably. Gregory shook his head. 'Now, is everything in place for our little gambling coup tomorrow? Clifton and Wavell, they'll do what they've been asked?'

Gregory knew that he had been summoned to Bottomley's flat solely in order to answer that question; after all, Bottomley stood to win a remarkable amount of money, even by his elevated standards. Even more important, Gregory himself desperately needed to satisfy his many creditors. However, he didn't dare reveal the truth, that the plan was in ruins. 'The plan was carried through, Horatio,' he lied. 'As you know, Parker told them both, in unambiguous terms, what would happen if they didn't co-operate.'

'No last minute difficulties?'

'Not that I know of. Why do you ask?'

'Because there is rather a lot of money at stake.'

Gregory realised that Hildreth had not been mentioned and that the goalkeeper's role was now vital to the success of Bottomley's scheme. A cold clutch of foreboding suddenly seized his stomach. 'The goalkeeper, Hildreth,' he said, 'his part in all this is absolutely crucial. Nothing's happened, has it?'

'No, no,' Bottomley said and Gregory recognised the bluster in his voice. It was how he would reassure one of his investors, just before relieving him of several thousand pounds. 'He'll be keeping goal for us, rather than for the Corinthians, don't you worry.' He laughed loudly.

'I'm relieved to hear it,' Gregory said drily. He also said a silent and earnest prayer that Blackburn Rovers would be on irresistible form tomorrow at the Crystal Palace. It was his only hope of salvation.

32

Bad news travels through society at a remarkable pace, but good news is transmitted almost as fast and by six o'clock on that Friday evening James had received half a dozen letters of congratulation on his forthcoming marriage and an invitation from Mrs Hildreth to take drinks and dinner at her home on that very evening. She added that his parents would be present so that the forthcoming union of the two families could be properly celebrated.

Richard had managed to uncover some excellent wines in the family cellar to accompany the seven courses which Mrs Hildreth's cook had produced at such short notice. James's father made a short and witty speech to wish the couple well and Richard replied with equal aplomb. In view of their commitments to the Corinthian cause on the following day, James and Richard had to leave the celebration earlier than they would have wished, but it had been an evening full of good humour, frivolity and, despite the country's involvement in war, of optimism.

After Richard had agreed, with a great show of mock-reluctance, to be James's best man, the Clifton family left together. Diplomatically, his parents preceded James to the cab, as he made his good-byes to Emily in the hallway. He clasped her to him and said simply, 'This is the best day of my life.'

'And mine. With so many more to come.' He kissed her, and they clung to each other as if unwilling ever to be parted again. James had an insane notion that he would like to dance her all around the square, in a re-creation of one of the sequences from *Hullo Ragtime*. Fortunately, he resisted the impulse, and walked slowly to the cab, looking back every few yards at Emily, who was waving and blowing kisses. Then he clambered unwillingly into the taxi, which headed south towards Sloane Street.

* * *

In the lounge of the Charing Cross Hotel, Bob Crompton, a glass of port in front of him, was sitting with the chairman of Blackburn Rovers, who was sipping a large glass of whisky and water. Most of the team were now abed, after a visit to the Holborn Empire where they and the rest of a packed house had been entertained by artistes who included Little Tich, Hetty King and Vesta Tilley. The latter had asked the Blackburn players to 'be upstanding' and to the audience's prolonged applause had introduced them as 'the incomparable football players of Blackburn Rovers'.

Bradshaw raised his glass and said, 'Here's to you, Bob. I just hope we play well tomorrow and give the crowd a treat. The papers say there should be as many at the Crystal Palace as there were at the United ground.'

'Over seventy thousand, they say, Mister Chairman, and I hope this time we can show 'em Rovers football at its best.'

'I've heard, Bob, that you weren't happy with the way we played last week. Is that right?'

'Aye. Some of the lads didn't pull their weight, Mister Bradshaw, and in my view it showed. I'm not taking any credit away from the Corinthians, they're fine footballers, but I'll want a better showing from some of our lot tomorrow, or I'll know the reason why.'

Bradshaw drained his glass and said, 'I'll leave it to you, Bob, you're the captain and you know your business. Now, I'm for bed.'

Crompton stood. 'Me, too. I'm looking forward to a good night's sleep and a grand game tomorrow.'

* * *

Never a man who believed in denying himself or those around him the pleasures of life, Arthur Dickson, the Corinthians' chairman, had arranged an early lunch before the game for the team and several members of the club's committee at the Hyde Park Hotel.

Once again James was the recipient of many congratulations, as well as being the butt of several jokes about his and Richard's joint misfortune at becoming brothers-in-law.

At the end of a sustaining meal of tomato soup, steak, apple Charlotte pudding with custard and cream, and cheese, Dickson said a few words about the importance of the forthcoming game and the pride that he and the rest of the club had taken in their performance on the previous Saturday. 'Play with determination, gentlemen, and also with wit and intelligence. Above all, uphold the great sporting traditions of our club. That's all I need to say and now I suggest that while we committee men have some vintage port, you players maintain your sobriety with some cups of coffee. Thank you.'

Soon afterwards, the players collected their belongings from the porters and set off in a fleet of taxis for the Crystal Palace.

Wavell joined James and Richard in one of the taxis and listened, a rather sardonic smile on his lips, as they discussed the imminent marriage. 'Just to let you know, Emily and Mama went off this morning to arrange a special marriage licence,' Richard said. 'So, James, there's no turning back now. You will be a married man within a few days.'

James grinned. 'I didn't realise such things could be arranged on a Saturday,'

'Apparently so. It's another consequence of the war. The usual formalities go by the board, I suppose.'

'I don't suppose either of you has seen *The Mail* today, have you?' Wavell interrupted.

'I glanced at the preview of our game,' James replied. 'We are tipped to win by at least two clear goals.'

'That won't please Bottomley, I fear,' Richard said.

, Wavell did not join in the laughter, but folded the paper carefully in two and pointed to a report on one of the inside pages. 'Take a look at that.'

The headline read: SCOTLAND YARD DETECTIVE FOUND DEAD.

The report was as follows: 'The body of Inspector David Parker of the Metropolitan Police's Criminal Investigation Department was found yesterday at his home in London's Pimlico district. A source at New Scotland Yard revealed that, when Parker did not report for work, a constable was sent to his home to establish if he was indisposed. He was found on the floor of his kitchen and his neck was broken.

'Inspector Parker had risen through the ranks of the Metropolitan Police to become one of Scotland Yard's most experienced detectives. His dedication and formidable investigative techniques made him a feared opponent among wrong-doers throughout London. There were signs of a forced entry through a rear window, but since nothing appeared to have been stolen, it is suggested that he may well have been the victim of a revenge attack by one of the criminal classes.

'In a tribute to the Inspector, Assistant Commissioner Basil Thomson said, "David Parker was one of the most resolute and effective detectives the Metropolitan Police has ever had. We've lost a fine officer and a man with whom I was proud to serve".'

'Heavens above,' Richard said, 'a broken neck. That would take some doing.'

'More power to the killer's elbow,' Wavell said drily.

'I wouldn't have fancied taking on Parker in a fight to the death,' said James.

'No, but he'd have been easy meat for a certain Staff Corporal,' Richard said.

'Yes,' James replied, 'I'd back him against anybody.'

* * *

The taxis bore the Corinthians through the suburbs of south-east London towards the Crystal Palace, where the Cup Final had been staged since 1895. The most recent final had been played in April in the presence of King George V and had resulted in a victory for Burnley over Liverpool by the only goal of the match. *The Sunday Times* had over-excitedly reported how London had been 'invaded' by the hordes of northern supporters and that there were 'scenes in the streets'.

Over 70,000 people had watched that final and *The Sunday Times* correspondent might well have alluded to such scenes again since, as the players neared the stadium, the roads were packed with eager fans. The game seemed likely to attract nearly as many spectators as had the Cup Final.

The newspaper vendors were shouting their sombre tidings about the Allies' casualties in the battle of the Marne, even though the German army had been temporarily repulsed during the previous two days; to reinforce the news there were dozens of recruiting tents around the perimeter of the ground. They were doing a brisk business as men, both young and more mature, took the King's shilling and vowed to do their duty for their country. There even seemed to be a festive spirit among the spectators; they were there to enjoy what promised to be an exciting game between two renowned football teams. The brooding overtones of a country at war were not going to spoil the fun.

As the Corinthians strolled towards the entrance to their changing room, they were cheered and clapped by many of the crowd. One elderly man, in a smart suit and with the upright bearing of an old soldier, proclaimed, 'Play up, Corinth, show the Rovers how the game is really played.' An immediate retort came from a Blackburn supporter in his broad Lancastrian tones: 'Aye, they'll need to bloody play up, for they'll likely get a proper 'iding from our lads today.'

There was just under an hour to kill before the kick-off and the players dealt with their nerves in their different ways. Max Woosnam took a couple of the others to look at the pitch and later reported that it was bare in parts and rather bumpy; Guy Willett, lolling in a corner of the spartan changing room, was engrossed in a new Sherlock Holmes story which had just been published in the *Strand Magazine*; Wavell was playing a hand of whist with Henry Corbett; and the rest were chatting quietly as they tried to make themselves comfortable on the hard and narrow benches.

Archie Ludlow made the obvious point that the Corinthians couldn't expect the Rovers players to make as many mistakes as in the previous match. 'I've never seen Sedgemore look so fallible,' he said. 'He's normally as reliable as sunset and sunrise.'

'One or two of the others didn't seem too interested, did they?' said Anthony Loxley, 'and I wondered why.'

'You're not suggesting any bad business, are you?' Ludlow replied. 'Any, er, inducements to lose the match?'

Guy Willett looked up from his magazine and said, 'Oddly enough, there were some rumours going round the Turf Club that some heavy bets had been placed on us to win. You don't think that any of the Rovers players were in on it, do you?'

James gave both Richard and Wavell a warning look. 'This all sounds rather far-fetched to me. The Rovers men are solid professionals, maybe a couple of them had off-days. It happens, as we all know.'

Richard laughed and said, 'You chaps have been reading too many Raffles stories. Look, there's a big crowd out there and it's up to us to entertain them and, if we play to our usual standard, we'll do exactly that. We'll also stand a good chance of beating the Rovers again.'

'Well said, Richard,' Guy Willett replied. 'Let's give the spectators a game to remember.'

* * *

In the adjoining changing room, the Blackburn players had donned their famous blue and white shirts and, with a few minutes to go before they were summoned to the pitch, Bob Crompton stood up and the room fell silent. 'Right, lads, I don't usually go in for speechifying before a game. It's what we do out there that counts and fine words can't affect that. However, I wasn't happy with the way we played last week, in fact I was bloody disgusted with some of you.'

Crompton looked sternly at his team-mates and some of them hung their heads to avoid meeting his eye. He continued. 'This is an important game for the Rovers. If any of you don't think the same as me, you can see where the door is. Get back into your ordinary clothes and bugger off out of it. I'll ask for a volunteer from the crowd and he'll probably be more use than some of you lot were last week. One or two of you didn't pull your weight. Anyone can have an off-day, but. . .'

He looked hard at Dodds. 'You, Billy, you might become a decent player, but you looked like a bloody schoolgirl last Saturday. Today I expect you to show me and our supporters what you can do.' Next Crompton pointed at his fellow-defender, Albert Sedgemore. 'You, Albert, you didn't seem very interested last week either, did you? You'd bloody well better be interested today or you can forget about playing in any team I'm captain of. As for you, Wiggins, you were a disgrace. You'd better go out there and show us all what you can do, or it's the last time you'll ever pull on a Rovers shirt.'

Crompton gestured to Wiggins to follow him out of the door and into the corridor; he then shut the door and spoke very quietly. 'And one other thing, if I ever hear that you're treating that wife of yours badly, I'll be over to sort you out myself.'

He led the way back into the changing room. 'OK, lads, let's get out there and show 'em how to play football.'

33

The huge crowd gave the players a resounding welcome as they lined up in the centre circle to be presented to a number of dignitaries, who included, as at the United Ground, the Lords Northcliffe and Kinnaird; also present were the Lord Mayor of London, Colonel Sir Charles Johnston, and the Chancellor, David Lloyd George. In their midst was the dimunitive figure of Marie Lloyd. Lord Northcliffe explained to the two captains that she would toss the coin for choice of ends and would also kick off the game.

Guy Willett looked at Northcliffe for a few moments and then said mischievously, 'Miss Lloyd will kick off, you said, sir? But don't you think that she might get in the way in that lovely long skirt?'

'It's just so that we can get a nice photograph, Mister Willett,' Northcliffe said, unused to being teased but managing a smile. 'Miss Lloyd will then return to her seat and you can start the game in earnest.'

Willett grinned at Crompton and Marie Lloyd chipped in. 'It's nice of you boys to worry about my welfare, but I don't mind being tackled by a few fine upstanding young men, if you get my meaning. Right, Bob Crompton, it's your call.' She spun a gold sovereign and the Blackburn captain called, correctly, tails.

'We'll take the kick-off,' Crompton said, with a smile in Willett's direction.

'Will you indeed. Fine, we'll defend the goal to my right in that case,' Willett replied, wondering whether Blackburn would steal the Corinthian tactic of booting the ball upfield towards their goal, thus seizing an immediate initiative.

However, when the game finally got under way after the photographs had been taken, Blackburn's opening was conventional enough, with the ball being moved left to their winger, Barnett. A tentative diagonal cross towards the Corinthian goal was taken on by Dodds, whose aggressive surge was only stopped by Anthony Loxley's strong tackle. In their turn, the Corinthians moved the ball swiftly along the ground, from Ludlow to Willett and then to May, who sent it crisply towards Wavell. But the Blackburn full-back, Moss, arrived at the same time as the ball and his tackle sent Wavell spinning to the ground.

Horatio Bottomley had been hoping that he would be one of the dignitaries who would be presented to the teams before the kick-off, but had to settle for a front seat in the South Stand. In his usual jovial mood when at large among the public, he turned to Smithson and said, 'Now that's what I like to see at a football match, fast running, good passing and strong tackling, eh, John.' He reached into his coat pocket, found his flask and took a hefty swallow of the twenty-year-old Armagnac which it contained.

In the row behind and ten seats to Bottomley's right, Henry Clifton also had a flask in his pocket. He unscrewed the top and took a nip of malt whisky and then, sighing with pleasure, he lit a Turkish cigarette.

So the contest continued, with each team in turn making determined forays into the opposition's half and being rebuffed just as one of the players seemed on the brink of finding space for a strike on goal. Time after time the Corinthians' incisive passing took them near the Rovers' penalty area, only to founder on the rocks of Crompton's and Sedgemore's covering and tackling. James, Archie Ludlow and Edwin May tried again and again to release Wavell on one of his rapid, jinking runs, but were foiled by the close attentions of the Rovers' full-back, Arthur Moss, whose anticipation was at its keenest.

At the other end of the field, Barnett and Simpson stayed wide on their respective wings in an effort to stretch the Corinthian defence and create the space into which Dodds and Wiggins might run. But the amateurs held fast with Loxley and Pryce-

Morgan fleet-footed, and formidable in the tackle; and Max Woosnam was always on hand to plug any gaps which appeared.

Despite the absence of goals, the crowd was completely absorbed in the thrust and parry of the game and rewarded each team with cheers and applause, and then with murmurs of disappointment when an attack was snuffed out.

The first crack in the Corinthians' resistance came a few minutes before half-time and this is how it was described in Monday's edition of *The Daily Mail.*

'This was British football at its peak, as Europe's two finest teams showed the full range of their skills, both muscular and sophisticated, to an enraptured audience at the Crystal Palace. The game was the brain-child of Lord Northcliffe, the proprietor of *The Daily Mail*, and one of his many guests was our distinguished Chancellor of the Exchequer, Mr David Lloyd George.

'It seemed to your correspondent that a dozen goals could have been scored, such was the speed and adroitness of the attacking play of Blackburn Rovers and the Corinthians; but those skills were met in equal measure by two resolute defences. If Bob Crompton and Albert Sedgemore were the pillars of Hercules for Rovers, Hugh Pryce-Morgan and Max Woosnam were the Colossi guarding the Corinthian citadel.

'Just as the spectators were settling for a goalless first half and anticipating even more excitement in the second term, Crompton struck a long pass to Barnett on the left. His cross into the penalty area appeared aimless, as if he too had settled for equality at the break, but Billy Dodds had other ideas. He trapped the ball efficiently, rolled away from Woosnam's tackle and hit a speculative shot along the turf towards the Corinthian goal. Hildreth, the Corinthians' steadfast goalkeeper, seemed to have it covered, but as he bent to retrieve it, the ball went past his left hand and into the net. For a moment the crowd was silent, as if amazed by this lapse by one of England's finest, and then the cheers rang out.'

As he turned, after picking the ball from the back of the net, Richard could hardly bear to look at his team-mates. James at once ran back ten yards towards him and said, 'Bad luck, Richard, it hit a bump, eh.' Max Woosnam shrugged, then grinned at his goalkeeper and gave him the thumbs-up.

In his seat on the halfway line, Bottomley smiled broadly, clapped Smithson on the back, swigged some more Armagnac and said, 'Who said that the Corinthians were incorruptible? I think young Hildreth is interested in the little present I promised him, don't you?'

* * *

On Guy Willett's instructions an urn of tea had been provided in the Corinthians' changing room and the players, running with sweat, sipped gratefully at the dark-brown brew. Team talks were not the fashion with the Corinthians, but Willett made a point of commiserating with Richard and congratulating the team on their play. With a couple of minutes to go before they resumed the match, Willett delved in his bag and produced a bottle of whisky. 'Come on, chaps, take a little tot in your tea before we play on. It'll put a spring in your step.'

* * *

The whisky certainly had the desired effect. Straight from the kick-off the Corinthians worked the ball down the left side of the field and forced a corner, after an uncharacteristically clumsy lunge by Bob Crompton. Herbert Grosvenor was a strong kicker of a dead ball and he swung it into the Rovers' goal area where Woosnam and Sedgemore collided in mid-air in their efforts to make a decisive header. The ball ricocheted off the side of Woosnam's head and dropped into the path of Edwin May, who volleyed the ball into the Rovers' net.

It was far from a classic strike, but the crowd didn't care and they roared their approval. One goal all and the professionals on their mettle to regain the iniative. Even the dyed-in-the-wool Rovers supporter who before the game had forecast 'a proper 'iding' for the Corinthians turned to one of his neighbours in the crowd and said, 'Not a thing of beauty, yon goal, but the lads in white deserve to be level.'

But they weren't level for long, since within a few minutes Crompton, Parry and Simpson exchanged passes before sending Wiggins clear down the right touchline. Despite Archie Ludlow's despairing tackle, Wiggins cut the ball back into Dodds's stride and he sent a low shot beyond Richard's right hand into the net.

As the correspondent of *The Manchester Guardian* wrote: 'After the light but sprightly Mozartian cadences of the first half, when both teams expressed themselves with sure-footed wit, the tempo changed in the second period to the more compelling rhythm of a Beethoven symphony. The climax, as in all Ludwig's works, was to be well worth the anticipation.'

In the warmth of an early autumn afternoon, many of the players were beginning to feel rather less than sprightly. James, for example, was left leaden-footed as Parry feinted one way and swayed past him on his other side; James grimaced with irritation and thanked Archie Ludlow who, with a solid shoulder charge, saved the situation.

As the game entered its final ten minutes, many of the players were floundering as the fatigue of an exacting game took its toll. Willett, however, was full of energy as he bounded about the field and called for one final effort from his team. His exhortations were not in vain, as *The Times* later reported: 'At last, with some five minutes remaining to the final whistle, R Wavell contrived to release himself from the shackles imposed upon him by Blackburn's admirable full-back, Moss. The elusive winger darted into the opposing penalty area, deftly hurdled Segdemore's challenge and thrashed his shot into the roof of the Rovers' net.'

* * *

As the crowd roared its applause, Bottomley screwed up his face angrily, drained the remnants of Armagnac from his flask and said to Smithson, 'How many more minutes to go, John?'

'A couple. No more.'

'We didn't put any money on the draw, as a hedge, I suppose.'
'No, 'fraid not.'

* * *

The drama had yet more twists in its telling. Bob Crompton, a captain who was never willing to accept a draw, threw all his men into one final assault on the Corinthian position. Again and again the Rovers players tried to thread the ball into positions for a shot; Dodds and then Barnett attempted to insinuate themselves close enough for a decisive strike on Richard's goal; and Crompton used his formidable strength to try to bludgeon his way into a scoring position. All to no avail, until an innocuous-looking punt into the Corinthian penalty area caught Woosnam out of position and both Loxley and Willett in a moment of indecision. As they hesitated, Wiggins darted through the gap, seized the ball and advanced on goal. Pryce-Morgan hurtled back to try to snuff out the danger and in his haste took the legs from under Wiggins. The referee's whistle blew and he pointed, albeit with some reluctance, at the penalty spot.

Pryce-Morgan scrambled upright and helped Wiggins to his feet. 'Sorry, Wiggins,' he said, 'a terrible tackle.' He nodded to the referee and apologised to him.

As the crowd hushed and the players meandered towards the Corinthians' penalty area, the referee said, 'That's nearly it, gentlemen. There is time only to take the penalty and then I shall blow for full-time.' He placed the ball on the penalty spot.

Richard knew what he had to do. Since the Corinthians did not agree with the imposition of penalty kicks, they would neither benefit from them nor try to prevent their conversion by the opposing team. He stationed himself beyond the right-hand goalpost and left an open net for the Blackburn penalty-taker.

* * *

Bottomley, a manic grin on his broad and rubicund face, slung his arm around Smithson's shoulders, and bellowed into his ear,

'We're home and dry, John. It's an open goal and a win for Rovers. And a very big win for us.'

* * *

On the pitch, Barnett, who had a cool head and a strong shot, was preparing to score the easiest goal of his career. He had wagered a modest five pounds on a Blackburn win with his local bookmaker and was looking forward to spending his winnings on an outing with his wife and children when he returned home.

His captain appeared at his side and Crompton said, 'I'll take this one, George.'

Barnett looked at him questioningly. 'It's a tap-in, skipper, what's tha' mean?'

'Don't fret, lad, just leave it to me.'

Some of the crowd knew about the Corinthian attitude to penalties and tried to pass on their knowledge to those who were wondering 'what the bloody 'ell' Hildreth was up to.

The correspondent of *The Manchester Guardian* described the scene as follows: 'Alas, we had to arrive at the final moments of this sumptuously entertaining game of football. All the arts had been displayed: tortuous running, crisp and inventive passing, thunderous tackling, and the whole drama was enriched by the piquant spirit of true sportsmanship. The teams lay locked together at two goals each, like two great warriors "calm of mind, all passion spent". A tragic mishap then overtook the Corinthians, as H B Pryce-Morgan completely mistimed a tackle and felled Blackburn's Wiggins in the penalty area. Even the crowd sensed that something untoward had happened and were hushed; and the referee, Mister Biffen, as he pointed to the penalty spot, assumed a desperate mien, as if he were playing the part of Banquo's ghost and woke up to find himself in the midst of a performance of *The Importance of Being Earnest*.

'But, to state the obvious, the rules are the rules and up strode the commanding, straight-backed figure of Bob Crompton, Blackburn's *nonpareil* and Britain's most accomplished footballer, to take the kick.

'Since R J S Hildreth, the Corinthian custodian, had vacated his goal (the men of Corinth do not approve of penalties and will neither deny them nor profit from them), Crompton was presented with an easy task; or so it appeared to most of the crowd.

'To Crompton, however, there is no honour in a hollow victory; to him, there is a greater cause and this exemplar of all that is finest in our sporting traditions stayed true to his principles by lofting his penalty kick ten feet over the bar, thus ensuring that the most pulsating match which your correspondent has ever had the good fortune to witness ended, appropriately, in a draw.'

* * *

For a few moments James was conscious of an unnatural stillness all around the packed ground. Then the applause began and sustained itself for several minutes; every time it began to flag the spectators renewed their efforts. The exhausted players let it engulf them and then Guy Willett strode up to Crompton and shook him by the hand.

'That was a grand gesture, Bob.'

'Aye, and you'd've done the same.'

They grinned at each other and strolled towards the changing rooms as the Corinthians and the Blackburn players exchanged their own handshakes.

* * *

As the crowd rose to its feet around him, Henry Clifton looked in Horatio Bottomley's direction and tried to imagine what was going through his mind. Someone had once called him 'a damned clever outsider' and Clifton, although a staunchly moral man, had a sneaking regard for the way in which the great fraudster was able to treat a severe setback as just another minor difficulty.

Bottomley had at last risen from his seat and stood motionless with his head bowed for several minutes. Even if Clifton had been closer, he would not have been able to understand what

Bottomley was saying, since a mixture of wonder and extreme bitterness made his words barely comprehensible: 'Please tell me that I am dreaming, John. Britain's best footballer merely needed to roll the ball into an empty net from twelve yards and we would, I think, have relieved the bookmakers of over half a million pounds. Have I got that right, John?'

'Yes, sir, you have.'

'But Crompton chose to hoof the ball over the bar, is that right, John?'

'I'm afraid so, yes.'

'I ought to sue the stupid bastard,' Bottomley growled.

* * *

A few yards away, Lord Kinnaird turned to David Lloyd George and said, 'A capital game, eh? Both sides were a credit to the sport. I hope you enjoyed it, Chancellor.'

'I did indeed. Sport has an unique power to lift one's spirits in times of travail. And I think the game's had its desired effect.'

'Desired effect?'

'The recruiting sergeants have been busy.'

'Ah yes, the harsh realities of a nation at war.' Kinnaird said sadly. 'We must rally our young men to the colours.'

'Alas, yes,' Lloyd George replied.

34

'Have you seen what that damned charlatan, Northcliffe, has put in his rag of a newspaper?' David Lloyd George slammed a copy of *The Daily Mail* on to the Cabinet Room table with such vigour that his teacup rattled in its saucer.

It was the morning of Monday, 14 September, and the first of several meetings of ministers and their colleagues was about to commence. The Prime Minister, Herbert Asquith, was already in his seat at the head of the table, with Lord Kitchener on his left and Lloyd George to his right. Winston Churchill, as restless as ever, was prowling around the room while puffing on a cigar.

'What nonsense is he purveying to his gullible public?' Churchill asked.

Lloyd George snorted and waved the newspaper in the air. 'Look at the headline. "The Mail recruits thousands to the colours" is what it says. Then it goes on to say that the football match he organised at the Crystal Palace – that he organised, mark you, with no credit given to anyone else – resulted in the largest number of volunteers ever to sign up on a single day.'

Asquith turned to his Secretary of State for War. 'Is that correct, Kitchener?'

'It could be so, Prime Minister.'

'And what are the numbers of recruits in total? Are we meeting our targets?'

In his habitually measured tone, Kitchener replied that the number of volunteers had almost reached half a million. 'In fact, Prime Minister, about three hundred thousand men enlisted in August.

'So, September is already looking better than the previous month,' Lloyd George interrupted. 'The campaign is gathering pace.'

'That's correct,' Kitchener agreed, 'but we need more than two million men by the end of the year. That must be our immediate objective.'

Churchill's cigar glowed brightly as he puffed energetically on it. 'And I hear that our administrative abilities do not match the enthusiasm of our brave young men,' he said. 'I have seen reports that these men are being shoe-horned into camps that are inadequately equipped, that they're having to send home for their own blankets and towels and soap. This is surely unacceptable, Lord Kitchener.'

'I agree and the War Office is doing all in its power to rectify these shortcomings.'

'Let's hope that there are enough rifles and bullets for them when they reach the battlefields,' Lloyd George said drily.

'I am sorry to make this point yet again, Prime Minister,' Churchill said, 'but why do we, the British, always neglect our army in times of comparative peace? Why don't we have available, at all times, a professional army equipped with the most modern equipment that we can procure?' His voice grew more sonorous as he warmed to his theme. 'Why do we never realise that a shilling spent in peacetime is worth several pounds when we have to confront the ugly face of war? And confront it we must, since it should be obvious to us all that wars between nations will be the determining factor shaping the present century.'

There was silence for some moments as the others contemplated such an uncompromising idea. Then Lloyd George said, 'I'm sure you're right, Winston, but it's in the nature of man to close his mind to thoughts of war, and that's probably why we are rarely prepared for it.'

'Quite,' Asquith said, 'but we're here to discuss practical rather than philosophical matters. I'm happy to hear that the two football matches have greatly helped to our cause, have they not?'

'Particularly in London and the North,' Kitchener replied.

'That's admirable,' Asquith said.

'And it has also helped to lend impetus to the concept of Pals Battalions,' Kitchener said.

'Ah,' Churchill said, 'General Rawlinson's idea. Wasn't he behind the Stockbrokers' Battalion?'

'Yes,' Kitchener replied, 'and Lord Derby has seized upon it and we are having encouraging results all over the country. Football clubs are volunteering *en masse*, and the Middlesex Regiment, for example, has benefited greatly from that. And cricket clubs and rugby clubs are following suit. Men who went to the same school are banding together, towns and villages are raising battalions, and men from the same trades are volunteering.'

'This is all excellent news,' Asquith said judiciously. He smiled at Lloyd George and Churchill in turn. 'May I go back to the football match on Saturday? I seem to remember that there was some debate between the two of you about the desirability of a win for one side or the other. I think, David, that you were keen for Blackburn to win, is that right?'

'Yes, that was so.'

'You saw the Blackburn players as being representative of the working man, whom we need above all to recruit in great numbers. Is that right?' Lloyd George nodded and Asquith continued. 'And you, Winston, were in favour of a win for the Corinthians, in order to reinforce the rank and file's confidence in its officers. Have I got that right?'

In his turn, Churchill nodded his agreement, but added, 'And, just as important, to ensure also that the British people has confidence in its officers, indeed in all its leaders.'

Asquith ignored Churchill's point and merely smiled mischievously. 'And I see that the game was drawn. So, did that help us or hinder us?'

Lloyd George smiled back at Asquith. 'It didn't matter. It was an enthralling game with a memorable ending. No one could have engineered anything quite so perfect.'

* * *

Two days later, James was married to Emily by special licence at the Chelsea Town Hall. Afterwards, a celebratory lunch took place at the Hyde Park Hotel; the party numbered about a dozen, including the immediate families of the bride and groom, Guy Willett and Rupert Wavell, and two close friends of Emily.

All who were present did their utmost to make it a joyous occasion, but the imminent departure of the four young men to their various military units could not be ignored. Once or twice James caught his mother looking at him with an unspoken appeal on her face. As a pacifist she found it that much harder to contemplate his going off to war.

In the late afternoon the party broke up and, while the families and their guests went their separate ways, James and Emily Clifton went to the top floor of the hotel, where their suite overlooked the park. They were to spend two precious days and nights there before James went off to do his training with the Royal Fusiliers.

Luckily for him the training camps were in Surrey and he took every opportunity to rush back to London to join his wife, even if only for a few hours, in the small house she had rented in a quiet road just to the south of Kensington High Street.

* * *

The date was finally set for James's battalion to leave for Flanders and Emily, determined to spend every possible second with him, joined hundreds of other wives, many of them with babies and small children, mothers, sisters and brothers, and sweethearts in the pandemonium of Charing Cross Station.

Railway stations can be mournful places; even if an arrival can be joyful, many a departure is a cause for sorrow. But, despite the sombre news of the desperate fighting at the first battle of Ypres, the departing troops managed to impose their own indomitably optimistic spirit on the scene. After all, they were with their pals, and they were crossing the Channel to give the Boche what they deserved, a bloody good kicking.

As James prepared to board the train, Emily clutched him to her, 'You will come back to me, safe and sound, won't you, my darling?'

'I'll be back, that I promise you,' James replied.

∗ ∗ ∗

It is estimated that around nine million men were killed during the course of 'the war to end all wars'. But James Clifton did return, together with his great friend, Richard. They both played for the Corinthians again, though James was never to realise his ambition of playing football for his country.